THE LOST COMPASS

THE LOST COMPASS

JOEL ROSS

HARPER

An Imprint of HarperCollins*Publishers*

Library of Congress Cataloging-in-Publication Data

Names: Ross, Joel N., date, author.

Title: The lost Compass / Joel Ross.

Description: First edition. | Broadway, New York, NY : Harper, an Imprint of HarperCollinsPublishers, [2016] | Sequel to: The Fog diver. | Summary: "Thirteen-year-old tetherboy Chess and his crew may have escaped the slums, but they cannot escape the Fog. When they retreat to the mountaintop sanctuary of Port Oro, they discover that the deadly white mist will soon swallow the entire city. Will the slumkids be able to save Port Oro, or will they run out of time?"— Provided by publisher.

Identifiers: LCCN 2015029171 | ISBN 9780062352972 (hardback)

Subjects: | CYAC: Adventure and adventurers—Fiction. | Survival—Fiction. | Recycling (Waste)—Fiction. | Environmental degradation—Fiction. | Orphans—Fiction. | Science fiction. | BISAC: JUVENILE FICTION / Action & Adventure / Pirates. | JUVENILE FICTION / Action & Adventure / Survival Stories. | JUVENILE FICTION / Fantasy & Magic.

Classification: LCC PZ7.1.R677 Lo 2016 | DDC [Fic]—dc23 LC record available at http://lccn.loc.gov/2015029171

Typography by Joel Tippie

16 17 18 19 20   CG/RRDH   10 9 8 7 6 5 4 3 2 1

❖

First Edition

For Karen Schwabach and Kevin Morrissey

MY NAME IS Chess, and I was raised in a junkyard.

Imagine a slum floating on rickety platforms above the deadly Fog that covers the Earth. Now picture a kid shivering in an alley, terrified of the same Fog swirling inside his right eye.

That was me, before Mrs. E gave me a home.

Then Lord Kodoc found us. He ruled the Rooftop, the mountaintop empire that loomed over the junkyard, and he was obsessed with an ancient machine lost in the ruins. Kodoc needed a tetherkid with a misty eye to get this "Compass," so he hunted my crew across the sky until he captured me.

There's only one way off a warship in flight—I leaped overboard in midair.

My crew caught me before I splattered on the ground, and we headed toward the safety of a distant mountaintop called Port Oro. All we want is to heal Mrs. E's fogsickness and start a new life, but Kodoc isn't finished with us yet. And neither is the Fog.

1

LORD KODOC'S WARSHIP swooped through the sky like a falcon. Her propellers spun, and her long-range guns swiveled to target us . . . but she didn't fire.

"We're out of range," Hazel said from beside me on the cargo raft. "And Kodoc is out of luck."

As she spoke, the warship veered away, and I gripped the rigging harder, dizzy with relief and aching from harpoon wounds.

A few minutes earlier, I'd kicked Kodoc in the shin and jumped off the *Predator*'s main deck. I'd plummeted toward the ground, toward certain death. But a few seconds before impact, I'd caught a tether fired from our cargo raft. Safe at last—except that two of Kodoc's harpoons had slashed me before the crew towed me away.

"After all that," I said, "we're still standing."

Then my injured leg buckled, and I sprawled across the deck.

"Spoke too soon." Hazel knelt beside me and frowned at my wound. "Look at that cut."

I looked at her face instead, watching her braids sway like a beaded curtain. She was a couple of years older than me, and pretty enough that people noticed. But more important, she was the captain: she thought faster, and farther, than anyone I'd ever met.

She pressed a cloth to the harpoon slash on my leg, and a sharp edge of pain clawed at me.

I hissed. "You're making it worse!"

"It's not that bad," she said, wincing.

"It's a wound," I told her. "I'm wounded. Like a warrior."

"That's you," she said, tying the bandage tight. "A strong, silent warrior."

"Ow!" I yelped. "Hazel, ow-ow-ow!"

The clatter of clockwork engines grew louder as two mutineer warships roared closer to our little cargo raft. I almost smiled at the sight of them. The mutineers flew airships from the mountaintop settlement called Port Oro: our goal, our hope, our haven. And their convoy—led by the kind Captain Nisha and her brother, the kind-of-scary Captain Vidious—was the only reason that Kodoc wasn't chasing us down.

Our raft swayed in the warships' wake as they sped

4

past. "Why aren't they stopping for us?" I asked.

"Captain Nisha must've told them to chase off Kodoc first." Hazel's voice grew softer. "We—we did it, Chess. We reached Port Oro."

"Of course we did," I said, like we hadn't almost died a hundred times. "You're too stubborn to give up. Now we just need to get Mrs. E healed."

"That's first," she said, her eyes dancing.

"What's second?"

"Brand-new lives! Not in a slum, working for the junk-yard bosses. Not rummaging for trash in the Fog. Real lives. Good lives. Working for ourselves." She raised her voice. "Swedish! Head for the *Anvil Rose*!"

"Why?" At the wheel, our pilot, Swedish, jerked his thumb in the other direction. "Port Oro is that way."

"We need to return the cargo raft to Captain Nisha," Hazel told him.

"We *stole* the cargo raft from Nisha." Swedish gave a lopsided grin. "We should definitely head in the other direction."

He had a point. Captain Nisha had flown us most of the way to Port Oro, pursued by a murderous Lord Kodoc—until we'd realized that we couldn't outrun him. That's when we'd stolen the cargo raft, to buy the *Anvil Rose* enough time to arrive.

Which had been a terrible idea, except for one thing: it worked.

"We don't have any time to waste." Hazel peered at Nisha's ship, the *Anvil Rose*. "We need to get Mrs. E and bring her to the Subassembly. They're the only ones able to heal her."

Swedish grunted and pulled a lever with one big hand. He was burly and shaggy and, at about sixteen, the oldest member of the crew. "You really think the fogheads will heal her?"

"Not if you keep calling them 'fogheads,'" Hazel told him as the cargo raft spun in the air. "From now on, they're 'Assemblers.'"

"I still say we ought to stay away from them," Swedish muttered.

I knew what he meant. I'd never trusted the Subassembly either. No slumkid trusted the so-called fogheads. They were *different*, and when you spent every moment scrambling for survival, *different* meant "dangerous." But then we'd met a Subassembly leader and realized that sometimes *different* just meant "not the same."

"They got us here in one piece, didn't they?" Hazel asked.

"Not really," Loretta said, squatting beside me. "Chess is in three pieces."

"I'm okay," I told her.

She squinted at Hazel. "You call that a bandage?"

"What?" Hazel asked her. "The bleeding stopped."

"Barely. I'll sew him up proper."

6

Hazel eyed her. "*You* know how to sew?"

"Not dresses and shirts," Loretta said, wrinkling her nose in disgust. "Only knife wounds and ax slashes—you know, the good stuff."

"The good stuff," I repeated faintly.

"Hey, I ran with a junkyard gang till last week, remember? Plenty of practice sewing up wounds."

"More practice making them," Swedish said.

Loretta's eyes gleamed. "More fun, too."

"Let's wait until we get to the Assemblers—" Hazel started.

"Nah," Loretta said, and ripped the bandage off my leg.

I howled, swiping at her. "Loretta!"

"You missed the cut on his hip," she told Hazel, batting away my hand. "You know what we need?"

"Painkillers," I moaned.

"A parade." Loretta gave a gap-toothed smile. "We got from the Rooftop to Port Oro with evil Kodoc nipping at our butts. We deserve a parade."

"I'd settle for a nap," I muttered.

"You sleep and I'll sew." She started patting her pockets. "I've got a needle and thread somewhere."

I closed my eyes. I couldn't stand to watch Loretta stitching me up. To distract myself, I started thinking about my father's scrapbook, pages of historical facts from the time before the Fog rose.

"In the old days," I said into the darkness, "they threw

a parade every year for a festival called Thanksgiving, where they stuffed turkeys and ate cramberry sauce."

From beside me, Loretta's voice said, "What'd they stuff turkeys with?"

"Stuffing."

"If you don't know, that's okay," she said, sounding cross. "You don't have to make something up."

"I *do* know!" I said. "They stuffed them with stuffing."

"Sure, and instead of knives, they stabbed people with stabbing."

"Was cramberry sauce made from actual cramberries?" Swedish asked. "Or was it a bunch of different berries all crammed together?"

"It was a kind of berry, but . . ." I paused, knowing that they weren't going to believe me. "Uh, they were too sour to eat."

"That's the opposite of 'berry,'" Swedish said.

"You can open your eyes now, you liar," Loretta told me, tapping my shoulder. "I don't have a needle. Also, the *Anvil Rose* is about to run us over."

My eyes sprang open, and I saw the *Rose* swooping toward us, propellers whirling and rigging snapping beneath the sleek balloon. Captain Nisha stood at the prow, her yellow hair flying all over the place. Not running us over exactly, but speeding in our general direction.

"Where's she going?" Loretta asked.

"To help her brother." Hazel looked across the sky

8

toward the half-broken *Night Tide*, still smoking from Lord Kodoc's attack. "So he doesn't crash before he reaches the Port."

A hatch clanged open in the center of the cargo raft, and Bea's head popped through, her leather helmet askew. "The *Tide* won't crash!"

"Are you sure?" Hazel asked.

Bea squinted at the *Night Tide*. She was the youngest member of the crew, and a brilliant gearslinger who spent half her time chatting to machinery. She wrinkled her nose, listening to the distant grind of the *Tide*'s engines.

"Oh, look at your poor hull," she muttered to the far-off ship. "And your mizzenmast is all cattywampus."

"Is that bad?" Loretta asked me. "Cattybombom?"

"Cattywampus," I corrected her. "It's only a *little* bad."

Bea chewed on her lower lip. "She says her gearwork is strong, though. She'll be okay for a few hours."

Bea didn't only talk *to* engines; she insisted that they answer.

The *Anvil Rose* swerved to a halt nearby, her fans blowing hard enough to tilt the cargo raft's deck. Loretta swore, Swedish goosed the engine to keep us in place, and Captain Nisha swung from the *Rose*'s crow's nest to the deck nearest us.

"I need your geargirl!" she yelled to Hazel.

"She says the *Night Tide* is okay," Hazel called back. "For a few hours."

Nisha eyed Bea. "Are you sure?"

"Yes, ma'am, Cap'n!" Bea sang out. "As long as she doesn't get hit again."

Captain Nisha slumped in relief. She knew Bea was never wrong about mechanical things.

"Come on board, then," Nisha said, tugging at her beaded necklace. "And give me back my cargo raft!"

THE SURGEON ON the *Anvil Rose* stitched my wounds
while Mrs. E slept in the wheeled chair beside me. I hated
watching a needle tugging thread through my skin, so I
watched Mrs. E instead.

Her wrinkled face was paler than ever. She looked frail
and shrunken and weak. I didn't mind the pain of the
stitching so much, but the sight of Mrs. E brought tears to
my eyes. When she'd found me in a junkyard alley years
earlier, she'd seemed invincible. Tall and straight and
sharp, like a spear with gray-streaked hair.

For a long time, I'd thought that the most important
thing she'd given me, aside from the crew, was a roof over
my head and food in my belly. And sure, you didn't live
long without those. But she'd given me something even

more important. When you were scraping for a living in the junkyard, you couldn't lower your defenses; you couldn't catch your breath. When Mrs. E adopted me, she'd given me someone to trust, and nothing was more important than *that*.

Except now, if the Subassembly on Port Oro didn't know how to cure fogsickness, she wouldn't last a week. She might not last a day.

After the surgeon finished with my stitches, Swedish tucked a blanket around Mrs. E and we brought her to the quarterdeck. We wanted to share the moment with her, even if she slept through the whole thing. It didn't make sense, but that didn't matter.

"Mrs. E, look!" Bea bounded toward the railing. "We're here; there it is! That's Port Oro!"

I peered into the distance at the jagged green-and-gold mountain range rising through the Fog. Port Oro. Freedom. Safety. A new start, far from Lord Kodoc and the junkyard bosses of the Rooftop, and the awful slums we'd escaped. We could find a new home and new jobs, and still be the same crew—the same family.

As we flew closer, Port Oro reminded me of the lower slopes of the Rooftop, except with long hills that spread outward, fanning above Fog-filled valleys. Bridges and walkways spanned the ravines, linking neighborhoods, shipyards, and markets. I don't know what I expected, but everything looked normal . . . except that unlike the Rooftop, there was no junkyard. No floating slum of patched-together platforms where life was cheap and food was scarce.

Bea noticed the same thing and frowned. "Where's the slum?"

"I guess there isn't one," Hazel told her.

"Then where do all the slumkids live?"

"There aren't any."

Bea gasped in horror. "What did they *do* to them?"

As Hazel reassured Bea that they hadn't done anything to the slumkids—there just wasn't a slum—the *Anvil Rose* turned slightly. We were heading toward a skeletal building rising from the Fog, with a long rope bridge connecting it to the mountain.

"What's that?" I asked.

"Probably a prison," Swedish groused.

"But a Port Oro prison," Loretta said. "With blankets and one meal every day!"

I borrowed Hazel's spyglass for a closer look at the skeletal building. Then I fiddled with the focus, hardly able to believe my eyes.

"It—it's a *skyscraper*!" I stammered. A building from the time before the Fog, rising above the whiteness into the clear sky. "A real skyscraper."

"No way!" Bea said. "That is so purple!"

"Down near the Fog it's just empty girders and beams," I told her. "Higher up, they built floors and walls and—and

I see people! There are people living in a skyscraper."

"But why are we heading there?" Hazel asked.

I cocked my head. She was right—we weren't just look-ing at the skyscraper skeleton, we were flying directly toward it.

"Because that's where the Assemblers live," Captain Nisha called from the deck above. "And Mrs. E can't wait."

A flock of black birds scattered as the *Anvil Rose* swooped toward the skyscraper. The ship's fans tilted, her rudders creaked, and she angled toward a landing pad on the roof.

Keeping my weight off my injured leg, I watched through a vent in the cargo bay. A hundred yards away, a crowd stared back at us from the skyscraper, their hair whipping in the wind of the warship, their hands shield-ing their eyes.

Beside me, Loretta scratched her burn-scarred arm. "That's not a parade."

"Yeah, what's the deal, Hazel?" Swedish asked, putting one hand on Mrs. E's wheeled chair. "You said that every day on Port Oro is a holiday."

"And every band is a marching band," I added.

"And instead of rain," Bea chimed in, "there's confetti!"

"Just wait," Hazel said, peering at the skyscraper. "When you've got a diamond in your pocket, the whole world is stuffed with stuffing!"

The day before our panicked flight from the junkyard,

I'd salvaged the most precious thing we'd ever seen, a diamond, from deep inside the Fog. And unlike "cash" and "credit cards" and "golden arches," diamonds were still valuable. Only Kodoc and the Five Families were even allowed to own them. Hazel had hatched a plan for us: we'd use the diamond to pay smugglers to sneak us to Port Oro.

That hadn't worked out the way we'd planned, but here we were anyway. In Port Oro, with the diamond safely tucked in Loretta's belt. We'd decided that was the best place for it, both because nobody would expect that we'd trust *Loretta* with a diamond and because she'd fight like a deranged monkey if anyone tried to take it away.

"The Assemblers will heal Mrs. E," Hazel continued, "we'll buy a house, and—and everything's going to turn out okay."

Swedish and I exchanged a glance. Every slumkid knew that you never, ever expected things to turn out okay. That was just begging for disaster.

So to cover my nervousness I said, "That reminds me of an old saying: 'The world is our oyster.'"

"I don't care what your scrapbook says," Hazel told me. "That was *never* a saying."

"It was, too!" I insisted. "It means that great things are possible."

"What's an oyster?" Loretta asked.

"A shellfish," Swedish told her.

"So the world is our shellfish?" Loretta scratched her arm. "How about 'The world is our pigeon pie?' That makes more sense."

"Yeah," I said, "but it's not the saying."

"It is now," she said. "The world is our pigeon pie, and I can't wait to take a bite out of Port Oro. What're we going to do after they heal Mrs. E?"

"Start a shipbuilding workshop," Bea said.

"Join Captain Nisha and the mutineers." Hazel braced herself as the *Anvil Rose* jerked, then hovered in place over the skyscraper. "With our own warship."

"We should lie low," Swedish said. "So *they* can't find us."

Hazel shot me an amused look. Swedish was convinced that a shadowy conspiracy of enemies—which he called "them"—was plotting against us. Even after he'd learned that we had *real* enemies, he still suspected that *they* were out to get us.

"We could start a gang," Loretta said.

I gaped at her. Hazel gaped at her. Bea and Swedish gaped at her. I'm pretty sure that if Mrs. E had been awake, she would've gaped at her, too.

"What?" Loretta asked, spreading her hands. "There aren't any on Port Oro, right? We'd corner the market!"

"Y-you, you—" Bea sputtered. "*You're* a corner market!"

Loretta made a face. "You have to work on your comebacks if you want to be part of my gang."

16

"Who says it'll be *your* gang? Hazel asked, one hand on her hip.

"We're not starting a gang!" I said. "That's the worst idea ever."

"And I am *not* a corner market," Loretta said. "Oh! Maybe that's what you should do with the diamond! Start a market."

"What *we* should do," I corrected her.

"Well, I wasn't with you when you found it."

"You're with us now," Swedish said in a goopy voice, like he wanted to kiss her.

"No lovey-dovey stuff in my gang," I muttered.

"There's no rush," Hazel told Loretta. "For the first time ever, we're free. No rent, no bosses. No Kodoc. Nothing except . . ." Propellers thrummed, and she peered through the vent. "We're here!"

Something about her tone rang warning bells in my mind. "Nothing except what?"

The cargo bay doors creaked and started to open. "Nothing," Hazel said. "Not important."

"Except *what*, Hazy?" Bea asked. She must've heard the same bells.

Hazel ran her fingers through her braids. "The Subassembly sent mutineers to find us on the Rooftop, right? To find Chess and bring him here. That means they want something from him."

"So they can ask," Swedish said. "And we can say no."

"We owe them for helping us, Swede. I'm not sure we *can* say no. And we don't even know what they want."

Airsailors shouted in the distance. The deck trembled beneath my boots; then the gangplank slammed down from the cargo bay, and the light of Port Oro poured inside.

3

HAZEL TOOK BEA'S hand and headed down the gangplank into Subassembly territory. Loretta slunk along beside them, her fingers two inches from her knife. Swedish wheeled a still-sleeping Mrs. E along behind Loretta, and I ducked my head and followed.

After I stepped onto the skyscraper roof, the gangplank slid away, and the *Anvil Rose* veered into the sky above us with a blast of wind.

The dust settled, and a crowd surrounded us. These Assemblers didn't look like Cog Turning, the Subassembly leader who'd helped us escape the Rooftop. They looked fiercer and better armed, with swords on the hips and cannons in the corners of the roof.

Hazel cleared her throat. "Um—hi? We're looking for the Subassembly."

A deep voice called from the crowd. "And you came in a warship!"

"We needed a ride," Loretta explained.

"It's a long story." Hazel smiled into the crowd. "I wonder if we might—"

A woman's voice said, "*You* wonder? Well, you're not the only one! I am *full* of wonder!"

Hazel glanced at me, and I shrugged. I had no idea what was going on.

The crowd parted for an older man and woman with gray dreadlocks, pointy noses, and flowing robes. They must've been "cogs," which was what the Subassembly called their leaders. They looked like twins, each with one blue eye and one cloudy white eye—a filmy, unseeing blankness. Just like mine.

My throat turned to sandpaper, and I tried not to stare. Were they freaks, too? Were those glimmering white eyes real? Or had they plucked out their own eyes and replaced them with glass?

"Hey, check that out, Chess!" Loretta said. "They've got white eyes li—"

Swedish stepped on her foot. "Shht!"

The woman with the dreadlocks didn't seem to notice. She leaned on her cane and asked Hazel, "What do you wonder, *bonita*?"

Hazel took a breath. "If your healers would—"

"I'll tell you what *I* wonder," the dreadlocked man

20

interrupted, with a curious, one-eyed squint. "I wonder if this is the package we ordered."

"Don't say 'ordered,'" the woman told him. "That's rude." She peered at Hazel. "He means the package we 'requested.'"

"We, uh, well . . ." Hazel paused, like she had no idea what to make of these two. "We came with the mutineers, and we need your help." Hazel gestured to Mrs. E. "Our . . . our friend is fogsick. She's sleeping twenty-three hours a day."

A murmur spread through the crowd, and the woman peered closer. "The poor dear!"

"A cog told us that the Subassembly can treat fogsickness," Hazel told her. "He said that you're the only ones who can."

"Indeed, we are unique," the woman declared. "One of a—"

"—kind," the man jumped in. "Inimitable. That means 'without imitators.'"

"However, we are not the only unique people present." The woman looked from Hazel to Bea to Swedish. She considered Loretta, then pointed her cane at me. "Tetherboy."

My breath caught, and I wanted to disappear . . . but I didn't slip behind Swedish. Because I also wanted a closer look at her white eye, even though I didn't know what I was hoping to see. Maybe that she was like me. Maybe that she wasn't.

After a long moment, the woman looked away from me and asked Hazel, "And what's your name, *bonita*?"

"I'm Hazel."

"I am Cog Isandra," the woman said.

"And I am Cog Isander," the man said.

"I'm glad *that's* not confusing," Swedish muttered.

"We're pleased to meet you." Hazel gestured to Mrs. E, who was still slumped in her chair. "This is Mrs. E or, um, Ekaterina. She adopted us in the junkyard, the slums of the Rooftop. She—"

"The Rooftop!" the man blurted. "It *is* them!"

Isandra rapped her cane on the floor, then asked Hazel, "Which cog told you about us, my dear?"

"Cog Turning."

"Today is the day!" Isander announced. "This is the day we've been waiting for!"

Whispers and gasps spread through the crowd: "The Rooftop?" and "Nobody gets here from there!" and "That's the tetherkid!" Dozens of eager eyes focused on me, and a few claps sounded—then the roof echoed with applause and cheering. My cheeks burned, and I hunched my shoulders.

Loretta stepped in front of me, and I felt a spark of gratitude. Then she waved to the crowd. "Thank youuuu!" she called. "Too kind, too kind. No need for a parade! A feast and a marching band are all we ask."

"Please, ma'am," Hazel said to Isandra, setting a hand

on Mrs. E's wheeled chair. "We need your help."

"We'll give you more than our help," Isandra announced. "We'll give you our—"

"—hope," Isander continued. "We are in your hands."

"Um," Hazel said, confused again. "Okay?"

"Now, then!" Isander said. "Let's get your friend to the medics."

"*Both* friends," Isandra said, peering at me. "The tetherboy is hurt, too. Look at his pants."

Great. Now everyone was looking at my pants. Better and better.

"Look at your own pants," I muttered, but nobody heard me.

Isandra and Isander led us across the roof, and I hunched my shoulders, peeking at their foggy eyes. They looked like mine, except they didn't shimmer and flow with Fog. They weren't real. But why were the Assemblers trying to copy my freak-eye? Why were they trying to look like *me*?

I didn't have a clue, but I kept stealing glances as the cogs brought us to a booth where a heavy basket dangled from a steel rope attached to a purring engine.

"That's an automatic winch," Bea said, her eyes wide as the cogs stepped into the basket. "It heaves them up and down inside the skyscraper like a well bucket! It's a . . . an up-and-downer!"

"It's called an 'elevator,'" I told her.

"Don't be silly." Bea sniffed. "It doesn't just *elevate*. It goes down, too."

The cogs told Swedish to carry Mrs. E into the basket with them. There wasn't enough room for the rest of us, so Isander said, "Jada and Mochi, why don't you bring our guests to the infirmary."

Two girls stepped from the crowd. One must've been about twelve, with frizzy hair and crooked teeth, while the other seemed tougher and older even though she was shorter, with a wary slouch and an old-fashioned nosering. They looked scruffy and watchful, like foxes after a hard winter.

"You're tetherkids?" Hazel asked.

"How'd you guess?" Loretta said with a snort. Because they looked pretty much exactly like me.

"I'm Jada," the older one said curtly. "That's Mochi."

"Ohmyfog!" Mochi chirped, falling into step with Bea. "Are you really from the Rooftop? No way. Really? Really-really? No way! That's, like, a hundred days' flight away!"

"I know!" Bea beamed at Mochi. "Except, more like five or six days, if the wind is right."

"If the wind is a *hurricane*," Mochi said brightly, "and blows you in the wrong direction, it could take a *hundred* days."

"It could take *forever*!" Bea said, just as brightly.

Hoo, boy. That's all we needed: someone as bubbly as Bea.

24

"This way," Jada told us with zero effervescence, and stepped onto a wide ramp leading down into the skyscraper.

I limped along as the rest of the Assemblers . . . watched us. Watched me mostly, which was weird. Usually people watched Swedish, because he was so big and tough looking, or Hazel, because she was so pretty and in-charge looking.

"I've never met someone from anywhere else," Mochi told Bea. "I barely even thought there *was* anywhere else."

"I never totally believed in Port Oro," Bea admitted. "I wonder how many *anywhere elses* there are."

"You mean other mountaintops across the Fog?" Mochi asked. "Could be hundreds and hundreds. Or . . ."

". . . none at all," Bea finished, and I knew without looking she was wrinkling her nose. "I bet there's a bunch, though."

"That's what I think, too!" Mochi exclaimed. "Jada's sure we're the only ones, but she's a grouch."

"She'll like Swedish, then. He's a grump."

"She's crabby."

"He's gloomy."

Mochi giggled, then lowered her voice. "Is your tether-boy's name Chess? Is he really . . . *y'know*?"

She was asking if I was a freak-eye, but Bea pretended not to understand. "Nah, he's not cranky," she said. "He's more quiet."

"And ferocious," I told her over my shoulder.

"Plus, he thinks he's funny," Bea added.

I was about to say something hilarious when I noticed Mochi staring at me. So I turned back around. The cogs might show off their freak-eyes, but I'd spent my whole life hiding mine.

"Hey!" Bea said behind me. "Do you want to see my twistys?"

She made figurines out of wire, miniature people and airship and animals, and called them "twistys." As she chattered, I scuffed along, keeping the weight off my aching leg and trying not to think about the look on Mochi's face . . . or the white in the cogs' eyes. Trying not to think about what they'd said: "We are in your hands." I didn't want to be anyone's hope; all I cared about was our crew and Mrs. E.

But Hazel was right. We already owed the Subassembly for helping us escape to Port Oro—and if they saved Mrs. E's life, we'd owe them forever.

4

THE HALLWAYS INSIDE the skeletal skyscraper reminded me of the Rooftop, with rusted tin walls and wood-and-pipe floors. A slow ticking echoed as we followed stairways and ladders lower in the building, and the smell of roasting fish and well-oiled machinery filled the air.

Four floors down, the tethergirls ushered us into the infirmary, a bright room high above the fogline. A breeze wafted through open windows, flimsy curtains fluttered, and two doctors stood at Mrs. E's bed. Medical scopes waited in racks, and complex gearwork devices lined one wall.

Loretta whistled. "This ain't the surgery on the airship."

"Look at this one." Bea touched a device with a gas mask and clockwork pump. "I think it's for helping people breathe."

"You think correctly," Cog Isandra said from where she stood with Isander. "Chess—we had some clothes brought for you." She nodded toward a box on the floor. "There should be a pair of pants that fits."

"Any boots?" Loretta asked. "I could use new boots. Plus Swedish needs a kilt."

"A what?" Swedish asked.

"A kilt," she said. "So you'll look like a *real* thug."

"Hush," Isander said, "and let the doctors work."

I pulled on a new pair of pants, then sprawled onto a chair in the corner with the others. We watched the doctors check Mrs. E's pupils, draw her blood, and inspect her breath with a click-whirring machine. She slept through the whole thing, and her chest barely moved when she breathed.

The doctors murmured and fiddled. The warmth of the room and the rhythmic *hiss-click* of the medical equipment made me sleepy. Bea yawned, then Swedish snored. I smiled when I saw that Loretta was sleeping with her head on his shoulder.

"Loretta's sweet when she sleeps," Bea said, yawning again.

"Don't tell her that," I said. "She'll never sleep again."

"Curl up on the couch, honeybee," Hazel said.

After Bea snuggled into the cushions, I covered her with my jacket. Her eyes closed. A drowsy silence fell. I rubbed my aching leg and looked at Hazel. She was sitting cross-legged on the floor, her bare feet peeking from under her skirt. With her arms raised to fix her braids, she looked like a statue of a dancer at rest. The setting sun filtered through the curtains and brushed her dark-brown skin with yellow highlights.

She paused for a second and tilted her head; she knew I was watching her. She didn't say anything, and she didn't stop fiddling with her braids.

I didn't say anything, either, and I didn't stop watching her. We connected like that sometimes. Without words, without reason—bound together like a fog diver and his raft.

When Swedish gave a yawn that sounded like a yipping baboon, Bea and Loretta woke and rubbed their eyes. We watched the doctors for a while; then Isander dragged us away for a meal.

We followed him to a long room jammed with tables and echoing with conversation. A hush fell as we stepped inside, and for a second I felt like everyone was staring at me. Then a few kids ran toward a legless guy in a steam-chair who showed them a tiny clockwork device, and a couple started bickering in the corner, and everything felt normal again.

We sat on benches as the food came in on carts, fish chowder and potato mash. I dragged a bowl of chowder into the crook of my arm. That's how slumkids ate in public—quick and defensive, so nobody stole your food.

Swedish dug into his bowl, but the Subassembly members didn't even reach for the carts. They bowed their heads, and Isander led them in a prayer.

Hazel kicked Swede under the table. "Wait till he's done!"

When Isander finished, everyone started eating. For twenty minutes, the clink of dishes and the slurp of chowder filled the room. None of us said a word. We'd been hungry our whole lives: we ate until we ached.

Finally, Hazel pushed away her bowl. "If anyone touches me, I'll pop."

"I'm an overinflated balloon," Bea moaned.

Loretta rubbed her stomach. "I'm stuffed like a rat in a rattlesnake."

We griped and groaned, pretty pleased with ourselves. We were actually *full*. That had never happened before.

Bea licked her chopstick. "The only thing that would make this better is you telling the story, Chess."

"Not now," I groaned. "I'm too full."

"Pleeeease?" she begged. "It'll help you die."

"*What?*" I said.

"You know. After you eat, you have to die."

Swedish stopped picking his teeth and said, "What're you talking about, you little lug nut?"

"That's what Mrs. E says!" Bea insisted. "First you eat, then you die, just."

"You don't 'die, just,'" Hazel told her. "You digest."

"That's not a real word." Bea pointed her chopstick at me. "Tell the story! Tell it—tell it!"

"Fine." I leaned back in my seat. "Before the Fog rose, a deadly Smog covered the whole world. The Fog only kills people, but the Smog was killing every single living thing."

"That's why the gearheads built the— Oh!" Bea waved across the room. "Mochi! Come sit with us!"

Mochi waved back and started to stand. Then everyone at her table looked at me, and she paused, like she wasn't sure if it was okay to come over. After a second, Jada nudged her, and Mochi smiled and slipped around the tables and flopped onto the bench beside Bea.

"We're telling the story about how the Fog rose," Bea told her. "I guess you know all about that?"

"Which part?" Mochi asked.

"That hundreds of years ago, nanotech gearheads—"

"Engineers," Hazel corrected.

"Same thing!" Bea said. "They made the Fog, which is zillions of teeny-tiny airborne machines called nanites, built to scrub pollution from the world."

"Yeah, except the Fog thinks that *people* are pollution." Mochi grabbed a potato rind from the table. "And chased us to the mountaintops, and here we are."

"What I don't understand," Hazel said, "is where the Compass comes in."

31

Mochi crunched her rind. "The Compass is an ancient machine, I guess."

"That controls the Fog," Loretta said. "Yeah, we heard that much."

"It still doesn't make sense." Swedish rubbed his nose. "If they had a machine to lower the Fog back then, they would've used it."

"Maybe they couldn't," Jada said, appearing behind Mochi.

"Why not?" Swedish asked.

Jada shrugged.

"So you think the Compass is real?" Hazel asked her.

"Kodoc does," Swedish muttered when Jada just shrugged again. "And he'll kill to get his hands on it."

"The cogs do, too," Mochi said. "They're the ones who discovered it. A long time ago, they found an old scientific journal. Uh, do you know what that is?"

Bea nodded. "A kind of book."

"*Books*," Loretta muttered, scraping her bowl with her spoon. "What's the point? You can't wear 'em, you can't eat 'em, and you can't even stab someone with 'em."

"What did it say?" Hazel asked.

Jada sat beside Mochi. "The engineers predicted that a machine called a 'Compass' would eventually self-assemble in the Fog—and trigger the Fog to lower."

"Eventually?" Hazel asked. "When?"

"When the time is right."

"Self-assemble?" Bea chewed her lower lip. "Like, build itself?"

"The cogs aren't sure," Mochi told her. "They think so, but most of the old books were written on ear eaters, so we can't read them anymore."

I peered at her. "Written on *what*?"

"Ear eaters. You know, books on screens."

"I think those were 'e-readers,' not 'ear eaters.' They're why we know more about the old days, back when they used paper and plastic."

"Yeah," Bea said. "Everything they wrote on e-readers is lost."

"'E-readers' can't be right," Mochi said, tugging at her frizzy hair. "I mean, who'd want to read just the *e*'s? You need the rest of the letters, too."

"That's true." Bea giggled. "Otherwise you'd just sound like *eeeeee!*"

"*Eeeee!*" Mochi said. "*Ee!*"

I glanced at Hazel and caught her covering her mouth to hide a smile. Her brown eyes shone.

"Mochi!" Jada said sternly.

Mochi flushed. "Sorry."

"So they found a journal that predicted a Compass?" Hazel asked, trying to keep a straight face. "Then what?"

"Then nothing," Jada told her.

"Not for years and years," Mochi said. "I mean, what could the cogs do? Nothing but wait. So they kept looking until finally, *finally* they found something. . . ."

She paused, and I leaned forward eagerly. Had they really found a way to control the nanites? To lower the Fog?

"Some of the cogs think the Fog is different in different places," Jada said. "Like the nanites programmed themselves to adapt to different regions. So there could be a thousand Compasses, no two exactly alike, spread out from here to—"

"What did they find?" Bea interrupted. "Tell us, tell us!"

"Yeah," Loretta said. "You're as bad as a *book*."

"They found a map," Mochi said.

"Not a map," Jada corrected. "Just a clue about a map."

Mochi nodded, her eyes bright. "Some lady wrote in her diary about a map she'd seen in the Station. A map with pictures and directions and—"

"—a Compass," Jada said.

"A *huge* Compass," Mochi said. "We'd found the Station a long time ago, so then the cogs knew where to find the map. Now we just need to get to the map, find the Compass, and *shabazz!* We're all set."

Hazel tucked a braid behind her ear. "Something tells me it's not that easy. What's a 'Station'?"

"A place in the Fog," Mochi told her.

"So getting the map and finding the Compass will take at least two dives."

"Surrounded by driftsharks and polar bears," Loretta

said grimly. "And . . . and haze rays!"

"What're haze rays?" Bea asked me.

I shrugged. "Never heard of them."

"I made those up," Loretta said. "I mean, who knows what's in the Fog after all this time? *I* wouldn't go diving for all the Compasses in the world."

"She's right," Jada said. "There's worse than polar bears in the Fog. There are ticktocks."

Swedish grunted. "Clockwork monsters."

"Nobody's ever seen a ticktock!" Bea said.

"Not for a hundred years," Mochi told her. "But a long time ago, a girl was born with Fog in her eye." She glanced at me and then away. "She spent more time in the white than anyone. And she saw ticktocks. Just once, but—"

"Crawling in the Fog," Jada cut in grimly. "Chewing through everything in their path."

"Horrors from the deep," Swedish added. "Lurching toward higher ground."

Jada nodded at Swedish. "Lurching and creeping and killing."

"You're such a chuzzlewit," Mochi scoffed at Jada. "They can't still be around after a hundred years!"

I had no idea what "chuzzlewit" meant, but Bea pointed a finger at Swedish and said, "That's *exactly* what you are! You're a chuzzlewit!"

"If ticktocks existed," Hazel said, "Chess would've seen them."

I shrugged a dubious shoulder. After three years of diving, I'd seen plenty—but I hadn't seen *everything*. The world inside the Fog below was still full of surprises, not all of them pleasant.

"They're out there somewhere," Jada said.

"Hiding," Swedish said. "Waiting."

"Stop it!" Bea muffled her ears with her hands. "Tell a story from the scrapbook or I'll get nightmares!"

"What's a scrapbook?" Mochi asked.

"A book of facts from before the Fog." Bea peered around the room, then asked me, "Do you know anything about the food back then?"

I thought for a second. "They used to eat 'fast food,' which came with something called 'catchup.'"

"'Catchup'?" Loretta scratched the tattoo on her cheek. "Like a race?"

"I don't know. Tomato catchup."

"How do you race tomatoes?" Mochi asked.

"How hard is it to catch them?" Bea asked.

"The ancients were totally peanuts," Loretta said.

"Yeah," Hazel said, and I nodded. Even Swedish and Jada couldn't argue with *that*.

5

WHEN WE RETURNED to the infirmary, we found a doctor talking with Isandra at the foot of Mrs. E's bed.

"Ekaterina is very sick," the doctor told us. "While we can't cure her—"

Bea gasped and grabbed Hazel's hand.

"—we *can* help her," the doctor finished.

"She'll never recover completely," Isandra told Bea. "But she'll live. She's not going anywhere for a long time."

A knot in my heart loosened. Hazel plopped down on a chair and closed her eyes, Bea hugged herself, and Loretta squeezed Swede's arm.

From the doorway, Isander said, "Unless . . ."

The knot in my heart tightened again.

Hazel opened her eyes. "Unless what?"

"Unless, *bonita*," Isandra said, "the entire Port is doomed."

"If Lord Kodoc kills us all," Isander said, "he will not spare Ekaterina."

I frowned at the cogs. What were they talking about? Port Oro wasn't doomed. Port Oro was *safe*. That was the whole reason we'd come. To find treatment for Mrs. E and safety for the crew.

"Kodoc's not going to kill anyone," Loretta told them. "His ships can't get us while we're here. Hazel says he attacked like a dozen times, and the Port's still here."

"He's never tried to conquer us," Isandra said. "Only to weaken us. Which was painful enough. However, an invasion isn't our primary—"

"—concern," Isander finished, his blue eye grave. "We're facing something worse."

"Far worse," Isandra said, leaning on her cane.

"If Kodoc finds the Compass before we do," Isandra said, "he'll kill us without firing a shot. Or he'll take everything we have—including our freedom."

"If the Compass exists," Hazel said. "And actually works."

"We can't take that chance. We need to stop him."

Swedish cracked his knuckles. "Next you're going to say that we owe you."

"We'll say what?" Isandra asked, brushing a dreadlock from her face.

"You'll tell us the reason you bothered helping us in the first place," Swedish told her.

"We always help when we can," Isandra told him.

"We don't always succeed," Isander added gently. "But we do try."

"Nobody helps for free," Loretta said.

I nodded. That was a lesson that every slumkid learned young—and learned over and over again. "Just tell us what you need, and we'll—"

"—talk it over," Swedish interrupted. "We owe you, but that doesn't mean we'll pay *any* price. You want Chess to dive? We'll see. There are risks we won't take."

"There are risks," Hazel said, "we won't let him take."

A silence fell, and the medical machines rattle-clicked. I wanted to tell Swedish and Hazel that *I'd* decide which risks to take . . . except I wouldn't. We'd decide this as a crew, just like we decided everything.

Isander and Isandra exchanged a glance. "Let's step onto the balcony," Isandra said, and left the room, her cane thumping the floor.

We headed down a corridor with open doorways on both sides. I peeked inside them as I passed, and saw workshops and bedrooms. I paused for a moment outside a big room where dozens of small kids sat on the floor facing a bald guy.

"What're they doing?" Loretta asked beside me.

"Working, I guess." That's what little kids did—they

assembled delicate mechanisms in factories where small hands were worth more than brute strength.

"But they're not," Loretta said.

I looked closer. She was right. They were just sitting there, listening to the bald guy talk. "Maybe they're on break?" I guessed.

"That's a classroom," Isander told us.

"So they're . . . learning?" I asked him.

Isander nodded. "Math and gearwork and reading."

"How do you sell any of that?" Loretta asked, rubbing her spiky hair. "I mean, where's the money in it?"

"We—we don't—" Isander sputtered to a halt. "There isn't any money in it, Loretta. We teach them because they're children."

"So you don't get anything?"

"Other than educated children? No."

Loretta shot him a scornful look. "You wouldn't last a week in the junkyard."

The balcony was a corner of the skyscraper with a low ceiling and a chain-link fence instead of exterior walls. The fence faced the Port mountains, and the sight took my breath away. The high spires of buildings caught the sunset above a cliff where a stream of people climbed steps carved into the rock. Farther down, Port Oro looked more normal, with buildings made of rusted car bodies, shiny plasteel, and mud bricks. Smokestacks dotted the hillsides alongside bustling squares and marketplaces, and I heard a few faint shouts and the distant grind of engines.

Dozens of bridges arched from one neighborhood to the next, and below them, in the valleys between the ridges of the mountain, the Fog billowed and swirled.

"Whoa," Loretta said.

"Check the mutineer docks," Hazel said, pointing.

A high platform rose on the nearest mountain peak, held up by massive struts. A dozen mutineer airships lined the edge of the platform, hunched over the city like gargoyles, with the last rays of sunset glowing behind them.

"Ooh," Bea said, "and those repair bays are the purplest!"

"Instead of gawking," Swedish said, "maybe we ought to ask the cogs what they want from us."

"Oh! Right." Hazel took a breath, turning toward the cogs. "You helped us for a reason."

"Perhaps we did," Isandra said. "Perhaps we—"

"Well, of course we did!" Isander said. "What's the alternative? That we helped for no reason?"

"You know what she means," Isandra scolded him. "That we helped because we want something." She nodded to Hazel. "I suppose we helped for a variety of reasons, some more selfish than others."

"And now we're in your debt," Hazel said. "Exactly where you wanted us."

"That's a . . . harsh way of looking at it."

"But it's true," Hazel said.

Isandra's eyes narrowed. "We're not going to *make* you do anything."

"We'll pay our debts," Hazel told her. "If we can. And after that, we won't owe anything to anyone. Not the bosses, not the mutineers—not you. We'll start over, free and clear. So tell us what you want."

"You're quite blunt," Isandra said, leaning on her cane.

"She's honest," Isander said.

"We need to get the Compass before Kodoc does," Isandra told Hazel. "You know this already. Which means we need a crew—and a diver."

"You have your own tetherkids," Hazel said.

"A special diver." Isandra turned toward me. "Do you think you know the Fog?"

"Yeah," I said. "I guess."

"We need more than a guess," she said.

"Chess survived three years diving down into the Fog for salvage," Hazel told the cogs. "Moving through the ruins like a shadow. Does he know the Fog? He *lives* the Fog. Nobody alive knows the Fog like Chess."

Isander *hmmmm*ed and Isandra inspected me, her gaze narrow and intent. "Show me your eye, Chess."

My breath caught. After a moment, I said, "What—what happened to *your* eyes?"

Isandra touched her cheek. "We tried to fill them with Fog."

"And we failed," Isander told me.

42

I looked at Hazel for guidance, and she silently returned my gaze. Instead of telling me what to do, she was saying that she'd back me up whatever I decided. Still, she was right. We owed them. I needed to do this. For Mrs. E, for Port Oro. And for myself. So I raised my hand to my face to brush away my hair. Isandra and Isander leaned closer, and flickers of lamplight glinted off their white eyes—and all in a rush, I saw that they were glass.

Cold, lifeless marbles.

A shiver ran through me. They'd willingly sacrificed their eyes to the nanites of the Fog and replaced them with glass. Why? Because of an old story about a girl with Fog in her eye? My freak-eye meant something to the Subassembly—something big and meaningful—and I couldn't face that, no matter how nice they seemed. Not yet. Their glass eyes meant that I wasn't just me. I was part of something bigger than my crew—and I didn't want to be.

I lowered my hand. "I don't think so."

"Please," Isandra said.

"Not yet." I stepped back. "Not yet."

"You can't blame him," Isander told her. "Born on the Rooftop, marked by the Fog . . ."

"I don't blame him," Isandra said. "But we must know for certain what he is."

"What're you talking about?" Loretta asked them. "You know what he is. We all know. He's got a Fog-eye. You want me to draw a picture?"

"Actually, that's not a bad id—" Isander started.

"We need to see it," Isandra cut in. "To be sure that the nanites are truly embedded, and this isn't merely an illness or mutation."

Great. Now I might be a sick mutant? I frowned, and Hazel nudged me with her hip. "You're not a mutant," she murmured. "You're a chuzzlewit. There's a difference."

"We'll need to test him, in any case," Isander told Isandra. "To ensure he can survive these dives."

"What kind of test?" Hazel asked.

Swedish shifted uneasily. "The same kind they give lab rats."

"Don't press Chess too hard," Isander told Isandra. "If he's the diver we need, he'll come around."

Isandra huffed. "If he's the diver, then Kodoc knows he's here. And Kodoc won't wait. He's already planning."

"Planning what?" Bea asked in a small voice.

"*Something*," Isandra said ominously.

"Something bad," Isander explained.

"Yeah, we figured it wasn't a parade," Loretta said.

"Let the children explore the mountain," Isander told Isandra. "Let them meet a few people, eat a few meals. Give Chess's leg a little time to heal."

"And then what?" Hazel asked.

"And then," Isander said sadly, "we ask that you pay us what you owe."

6

THE NEXT MORNING, I woke on a comfy rag-stuffed mattress in a bedroom near the infirmary. The cogs lived lower down in the skyscraper, closer to the Fog, while the gearslinger workshops were near the roof. That way, the Fog didn't mess with the engines—and airships could launch directly through wide doors that opened into midair.

Still half asleep, I prodded the bandages on my leg. The harpoon cuts ached, but not too badly. I'd always healed fast. I lay there blearily until a wind buffeted the skyscraper, and the whole building swayed, creaking and squeaking.

"That's better," Bea said from the next mattress, stretching her arms overhead. "It's weird when the floor doesn't move around."

"Yeah," Loretta said, after a huge yawn. "Feels more like the junkyard now."

"Don't get used to it," Hazel told them, lifting her head from painting her toenails in the corner. "We're moving to the Port as soon as . . . y'know."

"As soon as Chess dives for those fogheads." Loretta rolled onto her side and prodded Swedish awake. "I don't see what the big deal is. He's a diver. He dives. If they wanted me to bust heads, they'd just have to ask."

"'Cause you're sweet that way," Swedish told her, crossing to the water pump.

Hazel fanned her hand at her toenails to dry the paint. "The question is, why not use their own tetherkids? Why *Chess*?"

"Because he's a fog-monster," Loretta answered. "You've seen his eye."

Bea whacked her with a pillow. "He is not a monster!"

"He's a fog-goblin!" Loretta giggled, curling into a ball beneath Bea's blows. "He's a mist-monkey!"

I'd never heard Loretta giggle before, and it made me smile. "I'm more of a steam-beast," I said, making claws with my fingers.

"For an ordinary dive," Hazel said, her voice sharp, "they'd use an ordinary diver. Whatever they want Chess for, it's something big. They know what he is, and they're *still* afraid to make him dive before they test him."

Bea lowered her pillow. Loretta stopped giggling. I

unclawed my fingers. Swedish kept working the water pump, though, which creaked and groaned and spewed into a sink.

"So . . ." Loretta scratched her cheek. "What're we going to do?"

"Muddle through," Hazel said, grabbing a ladle from a hook on the wall. "Like always."

"I just want this diving stuff to be over." Bea wrinkled her nose. "I mean, we lost everything. Hazy's clothes and my workshop and our shack—"

"We didn't lose the diamond," I told her.

"Yeah, and now I want to *spend* it." Bea grabbed her leather cap from beside her mattress. "We can afford to buy a whole garageful of tools!"

Hazel dunked the ladle in the water-filled sink, then raised it in a toast. "Here's to turning our sparkly diamond into sparkly new lives."

She drank and passed the ladle to Swedish, who said, "Here's to my own bedroom, so I don't have to sleep in the kitchen."

"Here's to Swede's own bedroom," I said, taking the ladle, "so I don't have to listen to him snore." I gulped the cool water. "And to a comfy shack on the Port, with a woodstove and blankets and so much food that we forget what hunger feels like."

"And to rivets!" Bea said, taking the ladle. "And foggium filters!"

47

She drank and babbled about intake valves until Hazel told her that it was Loretta's turn.

Loretta dipped the ladle, then didn't say anything.

"Retta?" Swedish prompted.

"Here's to . . ." She frowned at the water for a moment. "Here's to making one good choice in my whole entire life. Here's to leaving the Rooftop slums and joining the crew. Everything else is gravy." She wiped her eyes with her shoulder. "And if you ever tell anyone I said that, I'll bite you."

"We won't say a word," I promised. "But Hazel will write it in her logbook, so future generations will know what a garbo you were."

Loretta threw one of her shoes at me. "What's a garbo?"

"Like a lug nut," Swedish told her, "with double the 'lug.'"

"You have a logbook?" Bea asked Hazel.

"Don't look at me," Hazel told her. "I don't know what he's talking about."

"Hazel needs a captain's log," I said. "I read about them in my dad's scrapbook. You begin every entry with 'Start-8' and some numbers. Like, 'Captain's Log. Start-8 nine fifteen point four five. Today Loretta cried like a baby and sang a song thanking Chess for being so awesome that—' Hey, ow!" I fended off Loretta's punches. "Ow—help!"

I dashed behind Swedish, and Loretta chased me around him a few times before we knocked into the sink.

The water sloshed and some spilled onto the floor—which wasn't a big deal in a Subassembly skyscraper, maybe, but water was precious back in the junkyard. So we stopped fooling around, finished drinking, then grabbed our shoes and jackets.

"In the old days," I said, pulling a boot on, "they pooped in fresh water."

Bea giggled, and Loretta scoffed. "They did not."

"They did! Then they'd flush it away into the ground."

Hazel dried her face with a cloth. "They pooped in drinking water?"

"And peed, too," I said.

"In *drinking* water?" Swedish asked.

"Yep."

"Sometimes," Hazel told me, "I think you get your facts wrong."

I tugged on my bootlaces. "Yeah, this one might be fiction."

"Fixin' to what?" Loretta asked.

"*Fiction*," I repeated. "That's another word for *lies*. Like stories about jellyfish and the Olympics."

When we headed into the corridor, nobody was in sight. We were alone in a Subassembly skyscraper on the edge of Port Oro. Far away from the Rooftop and the slum. Hazel caught my eye, and I saw that she was thinking the same thing: not too shabby for a bunch of kids from the junkyard.

She gave a lopsided grin, and I said, "Ha!"

Bea giggled. "I know, right?"

"Free food, too," Swedish muttered—and we all started laughing.

Loretta tossed Swedish the bootball that she'd swiped from somewhere, and he juggled it on his knees, then kicked it to me. I whacked it toward Hazel with my head, but Bea jumped up and caught it.

"No hands!" Hazel scolded.

"I'm the goalie!" Bea told her, and tossed the ball to Loretta.

Loretta punched it down the corridor. "What?" she asked innocently. "I'm the *other* goalie."

We swaggered the rest of the way to the infirmary, but our smiles faded a bit after we stepped inside. Mrs. E still hadn't woken. The doctor told us she'd slept well, though, and that her condition was stable.

"What does that mean?" Bea asked.

"That she's not getting worse," I told her.

"Which is the first step," the doctor said, "of getting better. Give her time. And a reason to recover."

Hazel sat with Mrs. E for ten minutes, holding her hand and murmuring in a low voice. Mrs. E didn't move a muscle and didn't hear a word. The whole thing seemed sort of pointless . . . but then Swedish and Bea did the same.

When it was my turn, I looked at Mrs. E's wrinkly face

and watched her eyelids flicker. She looked so small and weak, but I knew the truth. She'd been the biggest thing in my life, and the strongest. I owed her everything—even though she'd never accept payment.

"Well, this time," I told her sleeping face, "it's my turn to take care of you."

7

WE FOUND ISANDER and Isandra in an observatory on the roof, peering at the Fog through big scopes on tripods.

"What're you looking for?" Bea asked.

"Patterns," Isander told her.

"Like Norse code?" I asked.

"What's that?" Bea said.

"An old tapping code," I told her. "That Vikings used."

Isander coughed into his hand. "Not exactly. The nanites that make up the Fog are machines. Their behavior is complex, but we believe that if we watch how the Fog acts, we might understand why it acts that way."

"We're ready," Hazel announced. "Chess is ready. For the test."

Isandra turned toward me, her white eye flashing.

"Not a moment too soon."

"Are you sure?" Isander asked me.

I fiddled with my jacket.

"Of course he's sure!" Isandra said, her dreadlocks bobbing. "Look at him! He's the very picture of certainty!"

"You must be looking at a different picture," Isander said, with a laugh in his voice. "Are you ready, Chess?"

Sometimes I liked speaking for myself, but sometimes I didn't. So I shrugged and kept my mouth shut.

"That depends," Hazel said. "What's the test?"

"The Fog ebbs and flows around this skyscraper, *bonita*," Isandra told her. "Sometimes covering one floor, sometimes another. Rising and falling."

"Ebbing and flowing," Isander said.

"I just said that," Isandra told him.

"Did you?" He tugged at the collar of his robe. "Well, I couldn't agree more."

Isandra clunked her cane against the floor. "The Fog covers the lower half of the skyscraper," she told Hazel. "The floors where nobody lives. And that is where we—

"—test ourselves," Isander continued. "On the highest floor that's completely covered by the Fog."

"You test yourselves?" Hazel asked. "So you've done this?"

"We have," Isandra said. "Though Chess's test will be far more challenging."

"Your tetherboy will climb into Fog on one side of the

53

building," Isander told Hazel. "He'll walk across a slippery beam, with nothing below him, until he reaches the other side."

"He must balance high above the ground," Isandra said, gesturing with her cane, "inside the Fog, with his senses dulled and the wind whipping past. One false step and he'll fall."

"Chess is a salvage diver," Hazel said, "not an acrobat."

"He once lost a fight to a *goose*," Swedish muttered.

"I crossed the beam," a voice from the observatory crowd called. "We all did."

"On our hands and knees," Isander said. "And with a rope to guide us."

"If he's so special," the voice said, "make him walk the girder *twice*!"

"Three times!" a woman shouted.

Isandra lifted her cane until the crowd quieted, then asked Hazel, "Do you agree to the test?"

A warm wind swirled past. The ribbons in Hazel's braids fluttered, and she chewed her lower lip. She trusted me in the woods and ruins, but she didn't know about a slippery beam.

"I don't see what walking across a skyscraper proves," Hazel said. "When Chess dives, he has a tether."

Isandra spoke more gently, her expression softening. "Because if he can't pass even this simple test, *bonita*, he'll never survive the real dive. We must know what Chess can do before we send him to the Station."

I met Hazel's gaze. We didn't need words. A glance, a stillness, the twitch of her lips or shrug of my shoulder, and we understood.

"Then let's do this," Hazel said.

Isander and Isandra took the elevator and invited Bea to join them. She squirmed with eagerness to try the "up-and-downer," but in the end she took my hand and led me into the building. She told me that everything would be okay. She said that I'd pass the test easy-peasy, and there was nothing to worry about. Nothing at all. Not even a smidge of a sliver of a shiver of something.

The more she reassured me, the more nervous I felt.

After we followed the crowd down five or six flights, Swedish said, "Bea? Bea! Stop helping."

She stuck her tongue out at him, then stopped short when a pipe *whoosh*ed nearby. "Whoa! Purple!"

"What is it?" I asked.

"Pneumatic tubes! Can you hear that?"

"Hear what? Are those pipes chatting at you? I bet they know all the gossip."

She wrinkled her nose. "This entire building is geared like an airship."

"Like an airship?" I blinked in surprise. "Can it fly?"

"Not a *real* ship, silly! The Subassembly's tech is completely loco."

She babbled about gears until we reached the lowest livable story of the building. Then we descended into the exposed skyscraper skeleton, where there weren't any walls or floors, just a framework of beams with ladders and walkways around the edges. We followed the crowd of Assemblers down three flights of jury-rigged stairs to the lowest Fog-free floor. The basket from the elevator had already arrived, and the cogs watched the rest of us spread out on the narrow walkway.

Isandra thumped her cane for attention. "Are we testing this tetherboy today?"

"Yes!" someone shouted. "Make him cross ten times!"

"No," Isandra said. "*We* are not testing him. The Fog tests him, the Fog judges him, the Fog saves him or swallows him whole. . . ."

Hazel leaned closer to me. "Are you okay?"

"Yeah."

"Good," she said, "because if you fall off a skyscraper, I'll be so mad at you."

"Um, do you want me to pass the test?" I asked, keeping my voice down.

Hazel understood immediately, of course. "Because if you fail on purpose, maybe they'll think you're useless and leave us alone. . . ."

I nodded, then shoved my hands into my pockets and watched her think. Maybe some kids wouldn't lie, but we'd been raised in the junkyard. We knew that the truth could be dangerous.

A thousand options flashed behind Hazel's eyes. "No," she said. "We owe them for helping Mrs. E. Show them what you've got."

I nodded again, and we listened to the cogs for a few minutes before Isander turned to me, his dreadlocks bobbing.

"Go and face the Fog, young Chess!" he called from his place in front of the crowd. "Climb down the ladder and cross the beam—" He turned to Isandra. "How many times?"

"The tetherboy knows the Fog," Isandra said, her glass eye shining. "He knows the swirl and the flow and—"

"—the swirl," Isander said.

Isandra cleared her throat. "Let's let *Chess* decide what will satisfy us. The ladder awaits."

I crossed to a ladder that disappeared into the Fog. The crowd rumbled in anticipation, but instead of climbing down, I turned my back on the Fog and stood with my heels on the edge of the walkway. I felt the emptiness behind me, the endless sea of Fog five feet below.

The crowd hushed. I swallowed a lump in my throat and almost smiled, hearing Hazel's words—*Show them what you've got*—and feeling the thrill that came before a dive.

"You want me to cross that beam?" I called to the crowd. "Three times? Five times?"

"Ten times!" someone shouted.

"You think I'm afraid of falling?" Sudden excitement bubbled in my chest. "You want to know what happens when *I* fall?"

Everything went quiet, except for the muffled grinding of gearwork and the cry of a distant bird.

"When I fall," I said a little softer, "the Fog catches me."

I spread my arms and fell backward off the walkway. Bea screamed, the Assemblers gasped, and the Fog surrounded me.

8

A COOLNESS TOUCHED my face, and the silent white world slowed. I was diving with my back to the skyscraper, but that didn't bother me. In a split second, I completed the flip, my reflexes faster and my mind quicker than in the world above, until I was facing the building as I dropped through the mist.

I flexed my fingers. No sound except my ragged breathing, no smells this high above the ground. White on white. So peaceful that I almost wanted to stay forever.

Then a beam *whoosh*ed at me from below. With a grunt, I grabbed for it. In the clear light above the Fog, I would've missed, and splattered on the ground.

Good thing I wasn't in the clear light above the Fog.

My palms slapped the beam. I was falling too fast to

stop short, so instead I swung toward the interior of the skeletal skyscraper. I flew through the center of the building with nothing in sight except whiteness.

Then . . . *there*!

Another beam, one story below. I grunted in triumph and landed hard, smacking the metal on all fours. Pain flared in my injured leg, but nothing I couldn't handle. The world was my pigeon pie.

Then a whirl of dense Fog caught my eye, and my feeling of triumph shriveled. I'd heard that driftsharks liked cities, especially skyscrapers. I couldn't smell their sulfuric stench, but I scrambled away just in case.

I ran across the beam, found a ladder, and climbed. I expected to pop out of the Fog on the next floor but didn't. I frowned in confusion. Where was I? What went wrong?

Oh! I must've fallen two stories!

I climbed another ladder, and when I emerged from the Fog, I saw the crowd on the walkway opposite, staring into the white where I'd disappeared. The Assemblers muttered, Bea gazed down with wide eyes, and even Loretta seemed a bit uneasy, scratching nervously at her scarred arm.

Hazel, however, wasn't looking over the edge. She was standing at the rear of the crowd, facing away from them. Facing me. Waiting for me. She'd known exactly where I'd reappear.

She mouthed, "Took you long enough."

I grinned, tugged my hair lower, and called, "Are you looking for *me*?"

The crowd turned toward me, gasping in amazement. I felt a familiar flush of self-consciousness—but also a tingle of pride. For the first time in my life, a bunch of strangers knew about my freak-eye and didn't want to beat me for it. Instead, they gathered around me and looked like they wanted to applaud.

Still, I was pretty relieved when Swedish shoved through the Assemblers and stood beside me, with Hazel and the others trailing in his wake.

Isandra banged her cane for silence. "This is the fog diver," she called. "The one we've spent so long—"

"—searching for," Isander continued. "This is the tether-boy who will dive into the Station and find the Compass."

"The path ahead is dangerous," Isandra said, "and we may not succeed. *He* may not succeed. First, we must—"

"*First*," Isander interrupted, shooting her a look, "we must let Chess explore his new home. While we prepare."

"Prepare for what?" Swedish asked, but the cogs didn't seem to hear him.

"Who cares about prepare?" Bea piped up. "He said '*explore*'! And we're in a *skyscraper*!"

"Bea's right." Hazel tugged me through the crowd. "Let's poke around."

"I bet there are tools I've never even seen before!" Bea

gushed. "And valves and—"

"Ribbons and bows?" Swedish interrupted. "For Hazel?"

Unlike most slumkids, Hazel liked wearing bright colors, with veils and bangles and sparkles. And we liked teasing her about it, though sometimes I wondered if she did it as camouflage. Because her clothes were gauzy and decorative, but her mind was a scalpel.

I started to say something about fancy dances, then noticed the Assemblers eyeing me like I was an upper-slopes lordling. The adults peered at me quickly, while the kids giggled and nudged one another.

Isandra and Isander even offered me a ride in the elevator. I said no, but Bea hopped around, squealing, "Me! Oh, me, I'll go!"

"You don't want to see the gearslingers' shops instead?" Hazel asked Bea offhandedly.

I scratched my cheek to hide a smile. I knew that Hazel just wanted Bea to stay close to the rest of us so we could keep an eye on her.

Bea immediately forgot about the "up-and-downer" and dragged us to the garages on the second floor. When we stepped inside, she gasped in awe, then called a friendly greeting to a machine near the door. Foggium compressors hissed, and tools drilled and whirred.

Swedish and Hazel wandered off, while Bea tugged me and Loretta past deflated dirigible skins toward some Subassembly gearslingers in a spark-welder workshop.

"And look at *you!*" Bea said to a wall of transparent nanofiber. "Such a pretty, flitty glide-wing."

"That's a glide-wing?" I asked.

"Of course! What'd you think it was?"

"Um. A wall."

She slugged me in the arm. "It's leaning *against* the wall!"

"Oh." I rubbed my arm and looked closer. The fiber glide-wing wasn't quite as long as the wall, but it was close. "Right."

"What good is gliding?" Loretta asked.

"The idea is to save fuel." Bea trailed her fingers across the nanofiber. "You turn off your engine and glide. But it takes more fuel to carry a wing than you save by—" She spun toward a worktable. "Look at that gyroscope! Look at the gimbals!"

"I would," I told her, "if I knew what a gimbal was."

"It's a ball of gim," Loretta said. "Obviously."

Bea slugged me in the arm again, giggling. "Silly!"

"Hey! What'd you hit *me* for?"

"But that poor tes-array." Bea frowned at some disassembled gear. "See how unbalanced he is?"

"The balance is fine," a leathery-looking gearslinger said from the worktable.

Bea wrinkled her nose. "The spindle arms are cattywampus."

"What's 'cattywampus'?" the gearslinger asked.

"'Cattywampus' is bad," I told the gearslinger.

"And 'purple' is good," Loretta explained.

"You're the kid!" the woman gasped, shocked and thrilled.

I lowered my head in embarrassment. "Yeah, I guess."

"She's not talking about you, lug nut," Loretta said, elbowing me.

She was right. The leathery lady was staring at Bea. "You're the girl who fixed the warships! Captain Nisha told us all about you." She raised her voice. "Hey, everyone! It's the geargirl from the *Anvil Rose*!"

9

GREASE-SPECKLED GEARSLINGERS CROWDED around Bea and started pelting her with technical questions. Loretta and I hung around until I was sure that Bea was okay, then slunk away. The air smelled of oil and iron shavings as we pushed through one of the heavy curtains that divided the garage.

We found Hazel sitting with the legless guy from the mess hall at a desk cluttered with brass and springwork devices. "This is Captain Osho," she told us. "He's been farther across the Fog than anyone. He flew for months—and used this gear to get back."

"What's that one?" Loretta asked, pointing at a boxlike thing.

"A chronometer," the captain told her. "You need a

fixed time standard to calculate your airship's longitude."

"I do?" she asked.

When Captain Osho laughed, his beard shifted like an animal's pelt. "I mean, a captain does," he said.

"Oh." Loretta pointed to a brass disk with hinged arms. "How about that one?"

"It's an astrolabe!" Hazel said.

"That's right," the captain said, reaching for another device. "And this is a crossbow quadrant. . . ."

"Wow," Loretta said as we slipped away. "That's a hundred new kinds of boring."

"Yeah," I said. "Where's Swede?"

"Playing bootball on the first floor."

"You don't play?" I asked her.

"Not anymore. I kept getting penalties for . . . y'know."

"Stabbing the other team?" I guessed.

"No." She sighed. "Stabbing is against the stupid rules. I just kicked too hard."

"There's no penalty for kicking the ball too hard!"

"Not the ball," she said. "The players."

So Bea tested Subassembly technology, Hazel researched navigational techniques, Swedish made friends with bootball players, and Loretta and I focused on the important stuff: complaining about how bored we were.

The two of us spent the day together, getting lost in the hallways, swiping food from the kitchen, and trying not to worry about Mrs. E. Well, at least *I* was trying not to worry. Loretta never worried much. She just figured that if any problem arose, she'd punch it in the earlobe.

When we met the rest of the crew in the mess hall for dinner, Bea chattered about the new gear, but I heard an undercurrent of nervousness in her voice. And Swedish, Hazel, and I kept exchanging silent glances. None of us could relax until we checked on Mrs. E.

When we crowded into the infirmary, we found Mrs. E sitting up in her bed, a tired smile on her face. A kimono pooled around her frail body, and her eyes looked like *her* eyes again. Pale, but not white.

Bea bounded forward for a hug. Before she could ram Mrs. E, Swedish caught her and swooped her into the air with a sudden laugh. He lowered Bea to kiss Mrs. E's cheek. Then everyone starting talking at once. Telling her everything that she'd missed from before we left the junkyard.

"—then we stole a thopper," Bea babbled, her voice rising above the hubbub. "Such a *purple* mayfly! But militia ships came after us, with flamethrowers and cannons, and Swedish crash-landed and—"

"That wasn't a crash," Swedish said. "That was as soft as a kitten's purr."

"—and the engine exploded!" Bea continued. "I think because the seals melted? Or maybe the—"

"I'm so glad." Hazel pressed Mrs. E's hand. "I'm so glad."

I didn't know what to say, so I just stood there watching Mrs. E's face. Every flicker of humor in her eyes was a miracle.

"Don't tire her out," the doctor told us from the corner.

After quieting for a moment, Bea couldn't contain herself: she bounced on a nearby cot and told Mrs. E about hitching a ride on the *Anvil Rose* and fleeing from Kodoc, and how I'd dived off the *Predator.* Except according to Bea, all the really exciting stuff centered around engines and propellers. So the rest of us chimed in, until Hazel wrapped up with a description of my Fog test, and Swedish added a list of all the food we'd eaten since we arrived.

Mrs. E smiled faintly. "Roasted eel sounds grand. Now where's Loretta? Come here, child, let me see you."

Loretta slunk from behind Swedish. "I don't look like much."

"Nonsense," Mrs. E said, peering at her. "You look like a girl of rare sense and strength."

"I do?"

"You do. Perfect for my Swedish."

"That's what I keep telling him!" Loretta said, her eyes bold again. "You know what he's like, though, the big lug nut."

Swedish muttered, "What I'm like is 'standing right here.'"

Mrs. E caught me making mocking kissy faces at Bea and said, "When you're done with that, Chess, why don't

68

you tell why they tested you?"

I unpuckered my lips. "They want me to dive for them. To find some map that leads to the Compass."

"Before Kodoc does," Bea added.

Mrs. E frowned, then looked at Hazel, a silent question in her gaze.

"I don't know what to think," Hazel admitted. "The cogs aren't telling us everything. They're keeping secrets."

"You don't trust them?"

"I trust them to protect Port Oro."

"That's an important job."

"I guess." Hazel tucked a braid behind her ear. "But it's not mine. My job is protecting *us*."

"But is that enough?" Mrs. E asked, her voice fading slightly.

"She got us here, didn't she?" Swedish demanded. "Nobody else could've done that."

"Nobody else could've come close," I added.

"That's why Hazy's the cap'n," Bea said.

"She's way more than enough," Loretta agreed. "Sometimes she's too much."

"I didn't mean to criticize Hazel," Mrs. E said, a weak smile on her wrinkled face. "She is the best example I know of the saying 'Fall down seven times, stand up eight.'"

"Chess is better," Hazel told her. "He's fallen down a thousand times."

"What I mean is . . . if Kodoc gets the Compass, he'll be a danger to everyone. Defending Port Oro might be the only way to defend ourselves."

I scratched at the bandage on my leg. All I cared about was the crew, but maybe Mrs. E was right. Maybe the best way to protect us was to protect everyone.

"So what should we do?" Hazel asked, taking one of Mrs. E's hands in both of hers.

"I don't . . ." Mrs. E's voice trailed off. "I'm not sure."

"Well, what do you *think*?" Bea asked.

"I think . . ." Mrs. E closed her eyes briefly. "I think you should spend a day on the Port. Listen to what the cogs tell you. And then . . ." She opened her eyes and looked at Hazel. "Do your job."

10

AFTER BREAKFAST THE next morning, we headed to the sixth floor, where the skyscraper connected to the mountain.

A sort of airlock opened onto a wide cable bridge that stretched a hundred yards before reaching a square building on the mountain. The alumina planking swayed underfoot, and Loretta groaned when she saw the drop.

"I don't know why you're scared of heights," Swedish said. "You're not scared of anything else."

"Because I can't *stab* heights," she told him.

We crossed through the square building, where heavy posts anchored the bridge to the ground, then stepped onto the mountain.

"Port Oro," Hazel announced, with a spin that made her skirt twirl.

Bea hopped up and down like she was testing the firmness of the ground under her feet. "Not too bad," she decided.

I laughed at her—then I started jumping up and down, too. Enjoying the solid earth of Port Oro underfoot for the first time. Swedish grabbed Loretta and spun her in a circle. She gave a happy shriek, and Hazel kept twirling and twirling.

Finally, breathless, we stopped—and everyone looked faintly embarrassed. Swedish cracked his knuckles. Loretta checked her knife. Hazel smoothed her skirt, I tugged my hair over my freak-eye, and Bea skipped uphill along a path of crushed asphalt, singing, "Port Oro, Port Oro, we're on Port Oro!"

We followed her past cramped huts and neat two-story houses that lined the road. Carts rattled on the bustling street, and shrieking kids chased a pigeon behind a woven-plastic tent.

A lady in a straw hat watched us from a doorway. When we got closer, she called out, "Hey there, kids."

My hands clenched into loose fists. What did she want? Why was she talking to us? My junkyard survival instincts kicked in, and I stepped in front of Bea, while Loretta started drifting in a wide circle to flank the woman.

I swept the street with my gaze and didn't spot any threats, . . . but I didn't know what threats looked like in Port Oro, and my ignorance scared me.

As Swedish edged toward the doorway, Hazel cautiously said, "Hello."

"Headed to the market?" the lady asked.

"Maybe," Hazel said.

"Nice day for it," the lady said.

"Okay," Hazel said, and tilted her head a half inch.

The head-tilt meant "keep moving," so I slunk past, keeping Bea close behind me. A minute later, Loretta fell into step beside me with the sharp alertness of a hunting cat, and Swedish and Hazel brought up the rear.

At the end of the block, I exhaled in relief. "What did she want?"

"I think," Hazel said, tucking a braid behind her ear, "I think she wanted to say hello."

"Why?" Loretta asked.

"Maybe that's what they do here," Hazel said.

Loretta squinted at her. "But . . . *why*?"

"Just to be friendly!" Bea said.

We teased her for being such a baby—nobody would say hello to a bunch of slumkids just to be nice—and followed the road into a neighborhood where smokestacks rose above stone cottages. Higher on the mountain, pinwheel-blimps spun overhead, powering machines below . . . and two more people said hello.

"Next time, you try it," I told Loretta. "Say hello to someone."

"I'm not trying it. You try it."

"I don't even like saying hello to people I *know*."

"Hi, there!" Bea called to an old guy wheeling a chick-pea cart. "I'm Bea!"

The old guy peered at her. "Well, hello, Bea."

"Hello!"

"Are you . . . lost?"

"Not really," she told him. "We just don't know where we're going."

I almost groaned, and I swear I heard Loretta gritting her teeth. The first rule of the junkyard was Always pretend you know what you're doing. Well, maybe that was the second rule, after Don't talk to strangers!

"You should head to the market." The old man pointed uphill. "There's a bridge not three blocks from here."

"Thank you, sir," Hazel said, and dragged Bea away.

"What?" Bea said, squirming free. "This isn't the junk-yard!"

"We don't know *what* this is!" Hazel scolded. "All we know is that we're somewhere in Port Oro, and . . ." She paused. "And you're right."

"She is?" I asked.

"I am?" Bea asked.

"Yeah," Hazel said. "It's silly to act like we're still in the junkyard."

"Ha-ha!" Bea crowed. "Who's the baby *now*?"

"You're still the baby," Swedish told her. "Now let's see what this marketplace is all about."

We followed the old guy's directions and crossed a footbridge toward a bustling marketplace where drummers beat rhythms on plastic buckets and cracked data pads. Most people ignored us, but a few said hello. The first few times that happened, we all said hello back and they eyed us strangely. That was apparently too many hellos, even for Port Oro.

We gaped at barrels of pickled eggs, cages of lizards, and tables with ostrich jerky. One stall sold camel-tail stew and goat's-foot jelly, and the next offered tamales and sticky rice balls.

So much food, and so few guards. Way too few to keep a gang from grabbing everything. Maybe there really *weren't* gangs here—but then, what did alley kids do for food? I was still trying to figure that out when Bea and Swedish stopped at a table with springs and bolts and corroded batteries.

Apparently I wasn't the only one wondering about stealing, because while Bea chatted with a radiator, Loretta swiped a cucumber at a veggie stall.

"Put that back!" Hazel hissed. "We can't afford any trouble."

"He's got more'n he needs," Loretta said.

"Now!" Hazel snapped.

"I just want to know what it tastes like," Loretta grumbled, and started slipping the cucumber back into the pile.

The vendor spotted her and slammed his hand on the table. "Hey!" He scowled at Loretta. "You've never tasted a cucumber?"

"Nah," she said warily. "I hear they taste like pigeon."

"Pigeon?!" The vendor pulled a cleaver from his smock and slashed at Loretta.

She said, "Eep!"

Hazel said, "Hey!"

I said, "Wha!"

Then Loretta was standing there with half a cucumber in her hand. She looked at the vendor. She looked at the cucumber chunk. She looked back at the vendor.

"Share that with your friends," he growled at her.

We didn't wait around. Hazel grabbed Bea's hand, and we scurried across the marketplace. We slunk behind a crate of rock salt where nobody could see us and ate the cucumber. It didn't taste anything like pigeon.

When we finished, we licked our fingers and wandered the market. The scent of hog maw made me dizzy, and my stomach rumbled. The whole cucumber theft had gone so well that Loretta wanted to steal a sugar beet for Swedish, but he stopped her: "*They* might be watching."

"I thought *they* were only on the Rooftop," Hazel teased.

He eyed the crowd warily. "That's what I thought—but now I'm not so sure."

"You're such a needle-nose!" Bea told him. "This is the

purplest place on Earth! "

"It's too good to be true."

Hazel smacked his arm. "Bea's right. You *are* a needle-nose."

"That doesn't even mean anything."

"Now you know how the rest of us feel when you talk." Hazel suddenly stared across the market. "Ooooh! Look at *that*."

She squirmed through the crowd toward a stall overflowing with colorful dresses, military regalia, and gauzy scarves. While she fingered every ribbon and bandolier, Loretta tugged a cap onto her spiky hair, and Bea bought a bundle of wires and started making a twisty.

When nobody was looking, I rummaged in my pocket for the fancy see-through plastic fork I'd been saving and traded it for a blank notebook. Then I tucked the notebook into my jacket, feeling pretty pleased with myself.

After we dragged Hazel away from the clothing, we strolled past stalls that sold fishing nets and pigeon-feather blankets toward a display of tools.

"Check it out!" I said, eyeing a hacksaw on a cluttered table. When I scavenged in the Fog, I needed a saw to cut metal free from the ruins, and I'd lost my old one on the Rooftop.

Loretta made a face. "You can't fight with that."

"It's not a weapon," I told her.

"Exactly," she said, like I was being stupid. "That's why

you can't fight with it."

"It reminds me of your old one," Bea told me, touching the blade with her thumb. "Ow! But sharper."

She sucked her thumb as Loretta swung a pipe wrench experimentally and I rummaged through a box of corroded plastic squares until I found one with writing.

"What's it say?" Loretta asked.

"Uh . . ." I peered at the words. "'We make no claims that the AngelSoft Life Support System will support life.'"

"Ta-da!" Hazel sang out, and offered me the hacksaw. "For you."

"You bought it?" I felt myself smiling. "You didn't have to do that!"

"That's true," Loretta muttered. "I could've just stolen it."

Bea giggled, and I pulled the notebook from inside my jacket. "In that case," I told Hazel, "here."

"A notebook!" She flipped the pages. "This is great, Chess."

"It's not a notebook. It's your captain's log."

"But I'm not a captain anymore!" she said. "I don't have an airship."

"You have a crew."

"Yeah, and another ship is just a matter of time," Swedish said, glancing toward Loretta's belt, where the diamond was hidden.

I nodded, then told Hazel, "Just promise me one thing."

"What's that?" she asked.

"That you'll start every entry the way I told you."

"You mean, like, 'Captain's Log. Start-8 three two seven point eleven'?"

"Perfect!"

"Why start at 'eight?'" she asked. "Why not 'Start-1'?"

"I don't know," I told her. "Tradition."

"You're weird," she said, tucking away the notebook.

"Here, Swede." Bea handed Swedish a twisty. "This is for you."

He frowned at the little wire sculpture. "Scissors?"

"Pliers," she said. "*Needle-nose* pliers."

11

FOR THE NEXT hour, we crossed walkways and bridges, wandering through shabby neighborhoods with patches of corn and cassava, and fancier ones where street vendors sold monkey fur and toothwash.

Two naked toddlers bolted from a roadside tent, racing toward a pile of scrap metal, and Swedish scooped them up before they hurt themselves.

"Thank you!" their father called, adjusting his turban as he trotted closer. "Sorry. Thanks. They're small, but they're quick!"

After Swedish set the kids down, the man chatted with us for a minute. Hazel mentioned that we were a crew looking for work, and he said, "Have you ever heard of email?"

"No," Hazel told him. "What's that?"

"The quickest way to send a package."

"Like a messenger service?"

The man nodded. "Crews make deliveries across the Port, flying lightweight craft."

"What does the *e* stand for?" Bea asked.

"Envelope," he told her. "*Email* is short for 'envelope mail.'"

"Sounds perfect," Hazel said. "Where do we find an email shop?"

"They're actually called 'email addresses,'" he told her, then gave directions.

When we found the place, Swedish and Hazel went inside to ask about work, but Bea refused to leave a strip of grass alongside the building. She'd never seen a real lawn before, and she pulled off her boots and walked barefoot through the soft, thick grass.

Loretta and I lazed on a bench, bickering about my new hacksaw and enjoying the midday sun . . . until I saw something that turned the world to ice.

Three toughs were standing over Bea. Two girls wearing the "neckties" that only thugs wore and a boy with his hair in a topknot.

No time to call Swedish and Hazel, so I stood and said, "Get behind them."

Loretta didn't say a word. She didn't waste a second. She slipped from the bench and disappeared into the shadows of a building.

I pulled out my hacksaw and headed for the thugs. If they focused on me, they wouldn't noticed Loretta until she stabbed them in the back. In the junkyard, you only fought fair if you didn't have a choice.

"Hey!" I called, strolling closer, giving Loretta time.

When the toughs straightened, they looked about two years older than me, and about twice as big. The older girl eyed my hacksaw warily. "Hey," she said. "What're you doing with the saw?"

"Cutting things," I told her.

"Guess what, Chess?" Bea sang out, sitting cross-legged in the grass. "Antwan makes twistys, too!"

I blinked at her. "What?"

"Well, wire sculptures," the boy with the topknot said. "I don't call them 'twistys.'"

I said, "Well, yeah, no—I, um . . . what?"

"He saw me making one," Bea explained, "and introduced himself. He uses thicker wire, but it's the same idea." She tilted her head to look up at the boy. "Show Chess your runner!"

The boy showed me a twisty. "I'm not as good as Bea."

"No, that's nice," I said faintly.

Loretta slid from the shadows behind them, and she looked like I felt: ashamed. If someone was polite, we were suspicious. If they offered friendship, we planned violence. We thought we'd left the junkyard behind, but instead we'd brought it with us. All the anger and lies, all the fighting and stealing was inside us.

"So what're you cutting?" the older girl asked me.

"Oh, nothing. Maybe I will later if . . ." I trailed off. "Can I ask a question? Do your neckties, um, mean anything?"

"They're our bootball colors," the older girl told me. "We play for the best team on the Port!"

"Well, the *third* best," the younger girl said.

"One bad day doesn't mean we're not the best!" the older girl insisted. "Our winger was sick, and their goalie is the size of King Gong."

"Did someone say goalie?" Swedish asked, shambling closer.

"You play bootball?" the younger girl asked him.

"What's up?" Hazel asked me as Swedish and the younger girl chatted.

I exchanged a glance with Loretta. "Nothing. We just met some bootball players."

"Best team on the Port," Loretta said.

The older girl laughed. "You know it!"

"How'd the email thing go?" I asked Hazel.

"They're not hiring." She eyed me suspiciously. "What aren't you telling me?"

"Um," I said. "Antwan makes twistys!"

"You should see his runner," Loretta told her.

"C'mon!" Swedish said. "They're going to show us around!"

The bootball players spent the next few hours showing us the highlights of Port Oro. They showed us their favorite bootball patch. Their second-favorite bootball patch. And then? Their *third*-favorite bootball patch.

Finally, we followed the music of a brass band toward a mountainside park and saw the biggest flowering tree in the world. Streams of purple blossoms draped the branches and shimmered in the sunlight. Hummingbirds darted and swooped and vanished. The breeze smelled like honey, and a wave of warmth rose in my heart. I'd never seen a flowering tree this clearly in the misty Fog, and the others had barely even seen *normal* trees.

"Look, Bea," Hazel said in an awed whisper. "Look."

"Now that," Swedish said, "is purple."

The brass band played in the shade of the tree, on the bank of a wide, burbling stream. Flower petals bobbed and darted in the current, spinning around little kids playing in the water and older kids washing clothes.

We didn't take our boots off and splash in the water. Swedish didn't stomp around chasing Loretta, and Hazel didn't dunk her head in the water, then emerge sputtering and laughing, with rivulets running down her face. Bea and I didn't race purple petals down the current.

We were way too old for that. And far too mature.

After we dried off, Hazel asked the bootball kids how to find the fishing docks. They told us to use the "steam trolley," reminded Swedish about bootball practice, and waved good-bye.

"Probably good that we didn't stab them," Loretta muttered to me.

"On the other hand," I said, "they're only the third-best team."

We crossed bridges over terraced hills of rice paddies. We watched camel-drawn plows dig furrows in farmland. We dragged Bea away from a glassblower's shop, and we were following a path along a high plaster-and-Styrofoam fence when we heard the chatter of kids' voices.

I looked at the smokestacks rising above the fence. "I wonder what's in there."

"Probably a playground," Bea said.

"There's no such thing as playgrounds," Loretta told her. "Not even on Port Oro. There never was. I don't care what Chess says."

"There was, too," I told her as we approached a gate in the fence.

We looked through and saw stubby furnaces roaring in a factory. Dozens of grimy kids shoveled gravel onto conveyor belts, and dozens more stirred vats of melted asphalt and pulled the guts from busted iSlates.

"What're they making?" Loretta asked.

"I don't know," Hazel said.

"Let's ask," Bea said, and headed toward four kids squatting around a patch of earth outside the fence.

They were playing a pebble game. Flicking big pebbles at a smaller one, and if they missed, they spread their fingers on the ground and gave the other kids a chance to drop a pebble on their fingertips.

We watched for a while. Then I asked, "What is this place?"

"It's the Home," one of them said, flicking his pebble.

"What home?"

"The Noza Home for Orphan Kids."

"The *Espinoza* Home for Wayward Wanderers," another kid corrected.

"You work here?" Hazel asked.

"Ten-hour shifts!" the first kid said, puffing out his skinny chest proudly. "We live here, too. A hundred of us. Two meals a day, and it stays warm in winter."

"Plus new shoes every year," the second kid bragged. "Whether we need 'em or not!"

"Sounds good," I said.

The first kid squinted at me warily. "You're *way* too old."

"Yeah, there's no way they'll hire you," the second kid said. "Sorry."

"That's right, gramps," Loretta told me. "Don't get any ideas."

Bea giggled and told the kids, "He's not trying to move in!"

"*You're* not too old," the first kid assured her. "Are

86

you any good at shoveling?"

"I'm not," I said, "but I'm deadly with a pebble."

"Oh, yeah?" a third kid asked, giving me a dubious glance.

I grabbed a pebble. "You know it."

"Me, too," Loretta said.

We played for ten minutes, while Hazel, Swedish, and Bea explored the neighborhood. Then Loretta and I surrendered, blowing on our aching fingertips, much to the Noza kids' delight.

"Next time," Loretta threatened them, "we'll take you down."

"Oooh, do you hear that?" One of the kids cupped his ear. "That's the sound of me not shivering in my boots."

Loretta mock-scowled. "Why, you little pebble-pincher!"

"Least I'm not a goat's granny," he said with a grin.

"What you are is a chuzzlewit!"

They happily traded insults until Bea called, "Come see the trolley!"

Loretta tossed the kids a strip of ostrich jerky that she'd snagged in the market, and then we followed Bea uphill for three blocks. The trolleys dangled on cables that stretched between the peaks and ridges of the Port, then clamped onto tracks and rumbled like trains through the neighborhoods.

Bea chatted with a foggium generator until the trolley

arrived. Inside, the trolley was pretty small. It tilted when we boarded, and a curly-haired passenger snarled at us, "What're you doing? Stupid kids! Sit down or I'll crack your heads!"

"*Finally*, someone normal," Loretta muttered with a sigh of relief.

Hazel and I exchanged a quick glance, then looked out the window at the ground slipping away. The trolley swayed through the air, and the roofs of Port Oro looked like a patchwork quilt beneath us.

A smile tugged at Hazel's mouth, so I said, "Good to be in the sky again?"

"Where we belong," she said.

"Speak for yourself," Loretta grumbled, her knuckles white on the railing.

"The gearwork says that the cable can hold ten times this much weight," Bea told her.

"Well, you can tell gearwork that I said it's full of rust."

Bea made a face. "I would *never*!"

We rode across the mountain to the docks on the lakeside of Port Oro, then wandered among the smokehouses, net makers, and land docks on the hillside above the floating piers. In the distance, airships dotted the sky, trawling for fish with nets that dropped hundreds of yards into the lake hidden below.

"Fish smell fishy," Bea said, wrinkling her nose.

"They taste tasty, though," Swedish said.

"You really want a fishing ship?" Loretta asked him.

"Sure. We're a salvage crew. We're good at pulling stuff from the Fog."

"I guess I could learn to gut them," she said as a shadow flickered past us.

A huge crane swiveled over the nearby wall of a ship-building dock, carrying a load of foambelts scavenged from pod-cars.

"We could buy a gunship," Hazel said, watching the crane disappear back into the yard. "And join the mutineers."

"Or we could buy a workshop," Bea said as a rivet gun sounded with a *thwp-thwp-thwp*. "And *upgrade* the mutineers."

"How about you, Chess?" Swedish asked. "What do you want?"

"Me?" I hunched my shoulder. "All I want is *this*. Hanging around without anyone chasing us. Without getting dragged into trouble."

"Trouble isn't so bad," Loretta said.

"If it's not bad," Swedish told her, "it's not trouble."

"Chess is talking about diving into this Station," Bea told Loretta. "That's the trouble he means."

"Once we pay back the Assemblers," Hazel promised me, "we'll spend years just hanging around. With nobody hurt, nobody sick, nobody hungry."

"And a really big harpoon," Loretta added.

"What are you going to do with a harpoon?" I asked.

"Spear things," she said, then listed everything she thought needed spearing.

It was a pretty long list.

After we finished poking around the warehouses and wharfs, we hopped onto a trolley going back. Bea chattered with the cable assembly while the rest of us peered through the windows, watching farmers wade through a rice paddy setting eel nets. We left the trolley near the marketplace and continued on foot. When we reached the street of crushed asphalt that led to the Subassembly skyscraper, I realized that Hazel hadn't said anything for a while.

"Why are you so quiet?" I asked.

"I don't know," she said. "I guess I'm thinking about those kids at the Noza Home."

"Two meals a day and a warm patch in the winter," Swedish said. "Imagine if the junkyard bosses on the Rooftop gave slumkids half that much."

"At least the slum's safe from the Fog." Hazel brushed a braid from her face. "If Kodoc gets the Compass, this is all gone. The marketplace and that brass band, all the kids in that stream."

"The bootball players," Swedish said.

"The Noza kids," Loretta added.

"If Kodoc controls the Fog," Hazel said, "the Port won't have a choice. They'll surrender or die."

"What—" Bea swallowed. "What will he do with all this?"

"He'll suck it dry," I told her. "He'll turn the Port into the junkyard."

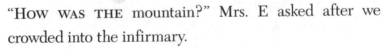

12

"HOW WAS THE mountain?" Mrs. E asked after we crowded into the infirmary.

"There was a triple-hulled thopper!" Bea blurted. "With three hulls! But the exhaust hoses were too flopsy, so I spliced 'em together with an accordion valve!"

Hazel eyed me. "When did that happen?"

"No idea," I said.

"You were right there!" Bea told us. "Maybe you were busy *shopping*."

"Speaking of shopping . . ." Hazel twirled for Mrs. E. "I bought this."

"It's gorgeous," Mrs. E said, her eyes sparkling.

I looked at Hazel. Was she wearing something new? I couldn't tell, so I just nodded and said, "Mm."

We told Mrs. E about the marketplace and food stalls,

the rice paddies and flowering trees and email address. Bea explained how the steam trolley worked, then Swedish described the fishing piers, and I described the taste of cucumber, feeling a glow of pleasure in my chest. Not just because of the cucumber, either, because with Mrs. E feeling better, we were *complete* again.

"Tell me about this Home for Children," Mrs. E told Loretta.

"Chess tried to join up," Loretta said with a gap-toothed smile, "but they just chased him off with shovels."

Mrs. E laughed. "Is that so?"

Loretta launched into an elaborate tall tale about our flight from the kids; then we chatted until the doctor told us that Mrs. E needed rest.

When we stepped into the hall, I told Loretta, "I can't believe you said that *I* lost the pebble game."

"You did," she said.

"Like you did any better," I started—then stopped at the sight of Isandra and Isander.

They were sitting at a laptop-case table just outside the infirmary door, playing what looked like a three-person game called Beat the Bosses. And sure enough, there was an empty third chair at the table, behind a pile of facedown cards.

Isandra swept us with her one-eyed gaze. "So what did you think of Por—"

"Thank you!" Bea scampered across the hallway. "Thank you, thank you!"

"Wait, child, I—" Isandra started.

Bea hugged her tight. "*Thank* you!"

"Oh!" Isandra flushed, in what looked like both pleasure and embarrassment. She wasn't used to random hugs from overeager geargirls. "You're very welcome."

Bea buried her face in the cog's shoulder. "Mrs. E's been so sick for so long, and now she's so much better!"

"I—I'm pleased to hear that," Isandra said, trying to disentangle herself.

Bea clung tight. "I never thought she'd talk to us again! Not like that! Not like *herself*!"

Isandra shot Isander a desperate look, but he just laughed. "We're happy to help, Bea. Ekaterina is a remarkable woman."

"Sure is," Swedish said.

"Chess?" Hazel's dark eyes shifted toward me. "What do you think?"

She meant what did I think about diving for the Subassembly. And with Mrs. E's laughter still echoing in my mind, I said, "I think, yes."

"Okay," she told the cogs. "Let's hear about this Station."

Isandra's shoulders sagged in relief. "He'll do it, *bonita*? He'll dive?"

"We'll listen," Hazel said. "That's all we're saying."

"No promises," Swedish said.

"Fair enough." Isandra tapped the tabletop a few times.

"We need to find the Compass before Kodoc does, or—"

"We know that part," Loretta interrupted. "But how come Kodoc hasn't already grabbed this thing?"

"He doesn't know where it is," Isander told her. "When he destroyed the Subassembly on the Rooftop, he stole all our records—"

"—all our knowledge," Isandra continued. "But we kept studying, here on Port Oro. We found a map to the Compass. Or at least—"

"—we think we did." Isander shuffled the playing cards in front of him. "We believe the map is on the bottom floor of the Station, deep inside the Fog. And that—"

"—is why we need *you*," Isandra finished, looking at me.

"We'll do anything," Swedish muttered, "if you'll stop finishing each other's sentences."

"What's the catch?" Loretta asked, squinting at them.

"The 'catch,'" Isandra said, "is that the Station is dangerous. The top floors aren't always so risky, but the bottom floor . . . is."

"That's why you don't send your own tetherkids," Hazel said, an edge to her voice.

"Yes," Isander replied. "At least—not anymore."

Hazel frowned. "You used to? What happened?"

"In the past five years" —Isandra took a quavering breath— "we sent nine tetherkids to the bottom floor of the Station."

"And?"

95

"And," Isander said, bowing his head in grief, "nine of our finest young people now rest with the Fog."

For a second, I didn't understand—then a chill touched my heart.

"Are you out of your ever-fogging minds?" Loretta snarled. "You sent nine kids to *die* for this map?"

"If Kodoc reaches the Compass first," Isandra said, her blue eye glinting with unshed tears, "many more will die."

"Chess is different," Isander added, raising his head. "He can do this."

"None of our tetherkids had his"—Isandra looked at the hair covering my freak-eye—"background."

"His *background* isn't armor," Swedish snapped, stepping closer to the cogs like he might hit them. "You want to see his scars?"

Hazel put her hand on his arm. "So you want Chess to search the ground floor of this Station. Is that right?"

"Not the ground floor," Isandra said. "The bottom floor."

"Huh?" Loretta said.

"The Station is *under*ground," Isander told us, shifting in his chair. "In what was once called a 'subway.' We want Chess to dive three floors below the ground, past stairways and platforms and train tracks. And then, yes, he must find the map."

A sick feeling twisted in my stomach as I imagined a thousand Fog-blurred dangers and nowhere to run.

Swedish clenched his jaw. "If he's underground, he's trapped. He's stuck. We can't drag him out of trouble with his tether."

I frowned at my boots. There was something else, too, something they weren't telling us. No way had nine kids died in regular dives—even underground dives—if they'd just needed to get to the bottom floor.

"There's something else," Hazel said, sharp enough to cut glass. "Something you're not telling us."

"You're right, *bonita*," Isandra told Hazel.

"The truth is"—Isander took a breath—"the Station attracts driftsharks."

13

"ARE YOU *loco*?" Swedish gaped at them. "You want Chess to dive with driftsharks?"

"What are driftsharks?" Isandra asked. "Merely dense ropes of Fog. And what is Fog? Clouds of tiny machines called nanites that—"

"I don't care!" Swedish slammed the table with his palm, which made the playing cards jump. "We're not feeding Chess to the sharks! That's final."

For a moment, the only sound was the whir of medical equipment from inside the infirmary.

"Very well," Isander said.

"We respect your decision," Isandra told Swedish.

"What?" Swedish looked baffled. "You what?"

Isandra grabbed her cane and pushed to her feet. "You're welcome to stay with us for as long as you need."

"For as long as any of us survive," Isander said, pinching the bridge of his nose. "Until we lose Port Oro."

A snake of worry coiled around my heart . . . but Swedish just snorted. "What's the rush? Kodoc's been looking for this thing forever."

"Yeah." Loretta rubbed the tattoo on her face. "No way he's going to find it *now*."

"They want us to think this is urgent," Swedish said. "But nothing's changed."

"One thing has," Hazel told him.

Before she could explain, a shadow fell across the card table from the end of the hallway. A figure strode toward us, silhouetted in the light of the windows, and a man prowled closer, his cloak rippling.

Then his voice echoed in the corridor. "More than one thing has changed, poppet."

Hazel lifted her chin. "Captain Vidious."

Vidious stepped into the light, a tall man with a scarred face, a cutlass on his belt, and rings on his fingers. He was Nisha's brother, the captain of the ship called the *Night Tide*. He'd once threatened to toss our crew into the Fog—and he'd once saved us all.

"How's the *Tide*?" Bea blurted, her eyes wide. "Is her hull okay? She was feeling all tilty and embarrassed."

"The *Tide* is fine," Vidious assured Bea, sprawling onto the empty chair at the card table. "Which is more than I can say for the Port."

Bea blinked. "What's wrong?"

"Ask your captain." Vidious gathered the cards in front of him. "What one thing has changed?"

"Kodoc saw Chess," Hazel told him. "He knows Chess is alive, and in Port Oro."

"Which means what?"

"That Kodoc can't wait any longer. He has to strike, or the Subassembly might get the Compass before him."

"Yes. And the question is, what are you going to do about it?"

"Captain Vidious," Isandra said sharply. "I'm not sure if we can ask the children to—"

"I didn't come here to play games." Vidious threw his cards onto the table. "I came to talk to the girl." His cold gaze flicked to Hazel. "More than one thing has changed. The entire *world* is changing. Kodoc is—"

"They don't need to hear this," Isander cut in. "We never agreed to tell them—"

"They're slumkids," Vidious said. "Not idiots."

Isandra rapped her cane on the floor. "They're children."

"Do you think Kodoc will spare children?" Vidious demanded. "You sent me and Nisha to bring you a salvage crew. We brought them. Now use them, or watch them die."

The cogs exchanged a glance and fell silent.

"What's happening?" Hazel asked Vidious. "Kodoc is what?"

"He's coming. With an armada."

A prickly silence fell.

"So what?" Swedish said, after a moment. "Every time the Rooftop attacked Port Oro in the past, you mutineers beat them."

"This time it's different. This time he's invading with everything he's got."

"Why?" Bea asked, her eyes shiny with worry.

"Because for the first time," Vidious told her, "we pose a threat to him."

"We do not! We just want to be left alone!" Bea said.

"Chess is the threat," Hazel told her. "Kodoc is coming for Chess."

My throat tightened, and my shoulders hunched. Kodoc was coming for me with an entire armada. The whole Port was in danger because of my freak-eye.

"If we reach the Compass first," Isander explained, "we'll control the Fog. We'll clear new mountaintops, where people can live free."

"And we'll use the Fog to stop Kodoc," Isandra said.

"So either you find the Compass and life gets better," Vidious said, pinning me with his gaze, "or you don't, and Port Oro dies."

"Maybe I don't care about the Port," I told him.

I knew that I sounded like the worst kind of slumkid, a junkyard thug who didn't give a fog about innocent people. I sounded exactly like a kid who'd attack a couple of friendly bootball players for talking to Bea. I still felt ashamed about that, but . . . I *was* a slumkid. If you pushed me, I pushed back. Plus, I wasn't about to let Vidious order me around; that was Hazel's job.

"You care about your crew," Vidious told me, unruffled. "And your crew doesn't have anywhere else to go."

"We'll talk it over," Hazel told Vidious before I could say anything, "and we'll tell you tomorrow."

Vidious glared at her. "There's nothing to talk about."

"Then don't say anything."

Vidious leaned toward her again, his expression darkening. "I didn't drag my crew to the Rooftop to save you for nothing."

"I didn't drag my crew to Port Oro," she told him, "to lose one of them in a suicide dive."

He started yelling at her, and I quaked in my boots. Vidious was scary when he got mad. Hazel looked scared, too, but she refused to back down. Swedish cracked his neck, I stepped in front of Bea, and Hazel tilted her chin higher and higher until she finally said, "We'll talk it over," and stalked away.

As I followed along, I caught Vidious watching her, a faint smile on his scarred face.

WHEN WE GOT back to our room, Hazel said, "You know what?"

"What?" I asked.

"Let's *not* talk it over."

Instead, we dug into the baked yams that Loretta had swiped from the kitchen. Swedish flopped onto his pallet and groused about *them* while Bea worked on a twisty. Hazel and I sat against a beam and watched the sunset through an opening in the tarp that covered one window.

We talked about the junkyard and the Port, about our best salvage dives and our scariest one. We talked about nothing, falling into the aimless chatter of an airship crew drifting high above the Fog. We'd spent years searching for new places to scavenge, new places for me to dive into the mist—because diving was what I was trained for. It's what I was *born* for.

So after we climbed into our beds, I said, "I'll need a new rig. Not a regular tether, something special."

Hazel's breath caught. "For diving inside the Station?"

I nodded. "Yeah."

Bea peered at me. "Three stories underground? You'll need a tether that never snags. I wonder what the Assemblers use."

"They lost nine kids," I told her. "I need something better."

"I've got a bad feeling about this," Swedish grumbled.

"I'm not exactly thrilled myself," I said.

Swedish ran his fingers through his shaggy hair. "We could sneak back into the junkyard."

"Really?" Loretta asked, brightening. "Could we?"

"No," Hazel said.

"Oh."

"What about driftsharks?" Swedish tossed a bootball at me. "You think you're faster than a shark?"

"No." I caught the ball. "But I'm close."

"Would you *tell* him, Hazel? Diving underground is loco."

"It's loco," Hazel agreed. "But Chess can handle it."

Swedish scowled. "Unless he can't."

"Swede," I said, "what if it was you? Would you dive? To save Port Oro, to stop Kodoc?"

"No," he muttered, but we all knew he meant *yes*.

"I would, too," Hazel said. "How about you, Bea?"

"You wouldn't *let* me!" she said.

"No, but would you?"

Bea nodded. "This is important."

"*I* wouldn't jump into the Fog in a million years," Loretta said. "But stop acting like garbos. Of course Chess is going to dive. What else is he good for?"

14

Two mornings later, I climbed up a ladder to the lowest Fog-free floor of the skyscraper after my tether practice. I'd been messing around in the white so I wouldn't get rusty. The only problem was, every time I emerged, a bunch of kids—and a few adults—stood on the walkway, watching me with wide eyes.

I shot them an embarrassed smile, unhooked my tether, and found Bea on the walkway two flights up. She hopped to her feet when she saw me. "C'mon, Chess! Your harness is done! I've been waiting *forever.*"

She tugged me into the elevator—which she still called an up-and-downer—and we rose through the open shaft. When we reached the garage, Bea yanked me toward her workshop in a well-lit corner of the garage. A few gearslingers worked on metal lathes nearby while Hazel and Captain Osho pored over charts.

"Here." Bea tossed me a harness. "Wiggle into this. Buckle there and there—the belts, too."

"Okay, okay." I tightened the final strap. "It's pretty much like my old harness."

"You only think that because you're a chuzzlewit," Bea explained. "Your old harness connected in one place. This one has three pivot joints—you can turn a backward somersault *sideways*."

I half laughed. "I don't even know what that means."

"Oh, hush!" She showed me a length of tether. "Look—no links, no joints."

"It's five times thicker than my old tether."

"Because there's a torsion cable inside, so you can whip yourself through the Fog like a, um, like a—"

"A whip?"

"Yes!" She beamed. "Exactly! Like a *whip*."

"Good guess," Hazel called over.

"I'm still working on the hand brake," Bea told me. "So you can ring the bell like before, if you want to tell us something."

I never should've doubted Bea. The tether might be heavy and slow, a flexible black hose as thick as my wrist, but it carried me through the white in a blur. With a tether like that, I actually had a chance—even against driftsharks.

When I finished testing the tether, I climbed from the Fog to find Loretta on the walkway, stabbing a cushion beside the tether ratchet that Bea was operating.

"What are you doing?" I asked Loretta.

"Stabbing a cushion," she told me. "How's the harness?"

"Totally harness-y."

Bea giggled as she coiled the line. "And this new tether won't snag on anything." She turned to Loretta. "Help me drag this stuff to the up-and-downer while Chess unbuckles?"

"Sure," Loretta said. "The elevator."

"It's not an elevator!" Bea said. "You might as well call it a *lower*ator."

Loretta shot me a grin, then headed off with Bea while I started on my harness. It might have three pivot joints, but it also had a thousand buckles. I was only halfway done when Mochi and Jada came down the ladder.

"You look like you need a hand," Mochi said.

"I need at least three," I told her, "to get out of this thing."

Jada grabbed my elbow and spun me around. "I've got the ones in back."

"Thanks."

Behind me, Jada started tugging and jerking at the harness straps. I felt like a human-sized puppet.

"I've never seen a tether that thick," Mochi said.

"Yeah, but it's crazy fast," I told her as Jada roughly

turned me back and unwound a strap from a loop. "You want to give it a try?"

Mochi brightened. "Oooh, that sounds—"

"No, thanks," Jada said. "All done."

As I tugged the harness off, Mochi said, "So what's it like?"

"What's what like?"

"You know." She glanced toward my freak-eye. "Diving into the Fog when you're . . . *you.*"

"I don't know. What's it like when you're you?"

"Scary and quiet and . . . scary."

"Like walking blindfolded past a hundred rattlesnakes," Jada said. "Over broken glass."

"Same for me," I told them, and didn't mention the rush of speed and freedom that I felt every time I dove. I was enough of a freak already, my one eye filled with Fog.

Nobody spoke for a minute. A ticking sounded, and the scent of roasting grain surrounded us. Then a flock of birds rose from the Fog nearby, wheeled in the air, and darted back into the mist.

"I still can't believe we're standing in a skyscraper," I said.

"In the old days," Mochi told me, "there were hundreds of them."

"There were pyramids, too. At least, according to my dad's scrapbook."

Jada squinted at me. "What's a pyramid?"

108

"They're where mummies come from."

"Mummies?" Mochi squinched her face. "Mummies come from when a woman has a baby."

"Yeah," I admitted. "I'm not really sure what—"

"Chess, c'mon!" Bea called down the walkway. "Mrs. E wants you."

The doctor stopped me at the infirmary door. "Be careful— she's still weak. She was very ill, and she's not out of the fog yet."

"I won't stay long," I said. "I promise."

A breeze wafted through the windows when I stepped inside, bringing the scent of rain. I crossed toward Mrs. E, who was propped up in bed, flipping through a collection of papers. She looked good. She looked better than I thought I'd ever see her again.

"What're you reading?" I asked.

"An instruction manual." She showed me a page. "For a modular, snap-on construction technique called Lego. Look, it can make a bus station!" She showed me the picture on the front. "If only we had the bricks."

I peered at the illustration. "And the buses."

"Did you hear the news?" she asked, putting the papers aside.

"What news? There's news?"

She took my hand. "Mutineer scouts spotted Kodoc's Rooftop armada. They're closer than we thought."

"How close?" I asked, my stomach souring.

"A few days away."

I closed my eyes, struck by a wave of fear. A few days. In a few days, they'd hit Port Oro. They'd set fire to the trees and blast the neighborhoods into rubble.

"You need to dive now, Chess," Mrs. E continued. "Today."

My breath caught, and my mind whispered, *I'm not ready! I'm not ready to dive into the Station.* I couldn't dive three floors underground, into a dark hole writhing with driftsharks. Not yet.

"Not a problem," I said in a wavering voice.

Mrs. E squeezed my hand. "What did the cogs tell you about the Station?"

"It's underground," I said as sweat beaded on the back of my neck. "Deep underground."

"And there are sharks."

I swallowed. "Yeah."

"But you're still going to dive?"

"Yeah," I said again.

She brushed my hair aside to look me in both my eyes. "There's a saying of the ancient spidermen: 'With great power comes great responsibility.'"

"And way too many legs." I gave a feeble smile. "Don't worry. I'll be okay."

She patted my hair back into place. "I think . . . I believe that new *things* are rising from the deep places, Chess."

110

"What do you mean?"

"They say . . ." She seemed to drift off for a moment. "A teacher of mine once told me that when the Compass is triggered, the ticktocks will follow."

"Ticktocks don't exist." I rubbed the back of my neck. "Clockwork trash-monsters . . . they're just a scary story. Aren't they?"

"There are secrets in the Fog, Chess, that even you don't know."

I swallowed. "No way. I can't even handle driftsharks."

"You listen to me." Mrs. E started trembling, and her grip tightened on my hand. "You can do this. You were born for this. You trained for this. I trained you, Hazel, Swedish, and Bea. You can change the future. Whatever happens—"

The monitor attached to her arm started clattering, a loud, scraping sound that froze my blood.

"I told you not to upset her," the doctor snapped at me, rushing from across the room. "It's time for you to leave!"

"But I—"

"Go!"

When I started to step away, Mrs. E grabbed my wrist. "You think the Fog makes you faster, Chess? You think it makes you lighter? You're wrong. The Fog doesn't change you. *You* change the Fog."

15

I STUMBLED INTO the hallway and found the crew standing around the card table.

"What's wrong?" Swedish asked, turning toward me. "Is she okay?"

"I don't know," I said. "She started to—"

"She's fine," the doctor said from inside the infirmary. "She just needs peace and quiet."

The door slammed, and we stood there for a second until I said, "Okay."

"Okay what?" Hazel asked when I didn't continue.

"Okay," I repeated. "Kodoc's armada is on the way. They'll get here in—"

"A couple of days," Hazel said. "We know. We're on the way to the raft now."

"Now?" I asked. "Like, *now* now?"

"What other kind of now is there?" Loretta asked.

"Now now," Hazel told me with a nod. "Let's go."

"There's something else," I said. "Mrs. E said . . . she said we trained for this."

"Trained for what?" Hazel asked.

"I don't know. For *this*. Diving into the Station, I guess. She said she trained us."

"Trained us?" Swedish said. "What do you mean? I thought she just found us."

Bea wrinkled her nose. "Yeah, that's weird."

"Who cares?" Loretta asked. "She fed you, didn't she?"

"Maybe she did both." Hazel wrapped a braid around her finger. "We always wondered, why did she adopt *us*? Why me? Why Swedish? Sure, he looks like a thug, but he's not." She smiled softly. "Mrs. E once told me that the first time she saw Swedish, some gang had crammed him into a broken wingframe and thrown him off the edge of the slum. But he didn't fall. He *flew* that thing."

Swedish shook his shaggy head and managed to look both proud and embarrassed. "I don't remember."

"That's your gift, Swede—you're a born pilot."

"Flying's easy," he grumbled, but I heard the smile in his voice.

"Mrs. E picked us for a reason. You fly, Bea's a gear genius. And I'm—" Hazel fussed with her necklace. "Y'know, whatever."

"You're what?" Swedish asked.

Hazel chewed on her lip. "Well, Chess says I'm bossy."

"Only 'cause you're the boss," I told her.

"And you kind of are," Bea said.

Swedish nodded. "Like a junkyard knee breaker."

"So bossy," Loretta agreed. "*So* bossy. So, so, so—"

"Okay, okay!" Hazel interrupted.

"Bossy," I added.

"*Fine!* I'm . . . good at being in charge. Anyway, Mrs. E took our strengths and made them stronger. All this time, she's been training us. We're the best salvage crew on the Rooftop. You think there's a better one in Port Oro?"

Swedish gave a derisive laugh.

"Me neither." Hazel tugged at a braid. "After Mrs. E burned down Kodoc's house, she didn't run and hide. She went into the junkyard looking for slumkids with natural gifts—"

"And a freak-eye," I said.

"Yeah." She gazed at me. "Hm."

"'Hm?'" I said. "What does that mean?"

"Well, what if . . ." Hazel frowned. "What if she was putting together a crew for you?"

The idea freaked me out a little. "Well, then she messed up, because she missed Loretta."

"Aw, shut up," Loretta said, scuffing the floor with her boot. "You chucklenugget."

Bea wrinkled her nose at Hazel. "You mean Mrs. E

knew the Assemblers would need a diver?"

"No," Hazel told her. "Maybe. I guess she knew that a kid with mist in his eye was special, and she knew he'd need help. A pilot, a gearslinger. People he could trust. Our whole life, she's been shaping us into a tool."

"A tool?" I said. "I thought she shaped us into a crew."

"She fed us; she taught us; she raised us." Hazel caught me with her clear brown eyes. "She hid us from Kodoc and saved us from the junkyard bosses. And look around."

I looked from her to Loretta to Swedish to Bea, then back to Hazel.

"You know what we are?" she asked. "To the folks back in the slum?"

"Slumkids?" Bea asked.

"Bottom-feeders?" Swedish asked.

"Dead meat," Loretta said.

"*Legends,*" Hazel said, with a sudden, wolfish smile. "We snatched a diamond and got away. Who beats the bosses?"

"Nobody," Loretta said.

"Nobody," Hazel agreed. "But we did. Who outruns the roof-troopers? Nobody. But we did. Who escapes from the Rooftop to Port Oro?"

"Nobody?" Bea said.

"Nobody," Hazel agreed. "But—"

"We did," Bea finished.

The strength in Hazel's voice made something expand

in my chest, something fierce and happy.

"Who got help for Mrs. E?" Hazel asked.

"We did," I said.

Hazel stood a little taller. "And who is going to dive three stories underground—and come back bragging?"

"Chess is." Swedish said.

"Not quite," I told them. "I'm too awesome to brag."

16

WE PASSED ONLY a few Assemblers on our way to the roof, which was strange—usually the skyscraper buzzed with activity.

Loretta frowned at the empty hallways. "Where is everyone?"

"Probably plotting against us," Swedish muttered, kicking his new bootball against the wall.

"They'll meet us at the dive site," Hazel said.

"They're coming to the Station?" I asked. "Like, to watch?"

"Yeah, but I told them we want to be left alone first."

"We do?" Loretta asked.

"Chess does. You know he gets all blushy and nervous when they stare at him."

"I don't *blush*," I said.

Hazel hunched her shoulders and ducked her head, letting her braids fall over her face. "Hey, who am I?"

Bea giggled and slouched along behind her. "I'm a tetherboy!"

Loretta didn't have enough hair to hide her eye, so she clapped a hand over her face and said, "Nobody look at me! I'm horrible."

Swedish laughed and tossed me his bootball. "You haven't been hiding your eye so much in the past few days."

I bounced the ball off the wall. He was right. Spending time with the cogs here had made me care less about my own freak-eye.

"Because he's living with a bunch of other eyeclopses," Loretta said.

"What's an eyeclops?" Bea asked.

"A one-eyed ogre from an old story," Loretta told her.

So I tossed the bootball at her head. Bea intercepted, and we kicked the ball around until we reached the roof. We crossed toward the raft that the Assemblers were lending us: a two-balloon ship with a small deck, a shiny engine, and a hefty winch.

"Not bad," I said.

"Those balloons need painting," Hazel said. "They're boring."

"It's still an airship," Loretta groused, eyeing the edge

118

of the skyscraper unhappily. "Why'd I join a crew that's always flying everywhere?"

"Because you didn't want to die in the junkyard, fighting over a pair of ratskin gloves, remember?" Hazel asked. "Don't blame us if you're afraid of flying."

"I don't mind flying," Loretta said. "I just don't see why it's always got to happen in the *air.*"

"What kind of crew stays on the ground?" Swedish asked her.

"A gang." She sighed fondly. "Ah, the good old days."

"You used to work for *Perry,*" Swede reminded her. "He's a yellow-haired snake."

"Perry's worse than a snake," Loretta said with a faint shiver. "They say he tossed his own parents into the Fog."

"And that squeaky voice of his," I said, with a shiver of my own. "That little-kid voice coming from such a stone-cold thug."

"He's not all bad," Swedish said.

"Are you kidding?" Loretta said. "Name one good thing."

"We'll never see him again."

"Huh," she said. "That *is* good."

Bea hopped aboard the raft for a chat with the starter coils. Swedish tapped the ignition sequence on the keyboard, and Hazel headed for the crow's nest, with her new logbook in one hand and her spyglass in the other.

Loretta and I uncoiled the tie-down straps. Well, I

uncoiled the straps—she tugged and grumbled at the knot.

"Hey, Loretta?" I said.

"I know, I know," she muttered. "Swede keeps telling me to go easy."

"That's not what I was going to say."

"Use a little finesse?"

I shook my head. "Not that either."

"I'm hurting the raft's feelings? Bea says I'm rude."

"Nope."

"What, then?"

I untied the strap with a single tug. "If anything happens to me . . ." I glanced toward the crew. "Take care of them."

"I will," she told me with a nod. Like that settled that. And it did.

As we sailed away from the skyscraper, Bea monkeyed with the engine for a few minutes, then crossed to the winch. "I didn't have time to rig a bell on your new tether," she told me.

She meant the system she'd invented where I squeezed a hand brake on my harness that rang a bell on the raft, hundreds of yards above me. We'd arranged a few codes, for common messages like "I'm okay" and "Get me out of here!" and "Get me out of here NOW!"

"That's okay," I told her. "I won't need one. As long as nothing goes cattywampus."

Bea wrinkled her nose. "If you're in trouble, give three

sharp tugs, and we'll pull you up. Okay?"

"Sure."

She shoved me. "Don't say 'sure' like you weren't even listening!"

"If I get into trouble," I told her, raising my hands in surrender, "I'll tug my tether three times."

"Sharply," Bea said.

"Sharply," I repeated.

She frowned at the tether, and her lower lip started trembling. "You better not get hurt."

"I won't. It's just a hole in a ground with a shark or two."

"Here!" She gave me a twisty. "For good luck."

"Thanks." The burnished copper wire was shaped into a rose in full bloom, and it glowed when I raised it into the sunlight. "It's perfect."

"It's a rose."

"I know it's a rose, you chuzz."

"Because you gave me one after our last dive, so—"

"Bea," I said, "it's totally purple."

She kicked my boot. "You be careful."

"I will."

"Slow her down, Swedish!" Hazel called from the crow's nest. "We're almost there."

"What?" I squinted behind us, and the skyscraper was still in sight. "We've only been flying for five minutes! I could've walked."

"Yeah, but they're sending other tetherkids down with

you," Hazel said. "And these kids don't like leisurely strolls in the Fog."

"Because unlike you, they're not mist-monsters," Loretta informed me.

I spotted movement off the prow. A hundred yards ahead of us, a fleet of Subassembly ships hovered above the Fog: rafts, cargo ships, and fishing trawlers, all packed with people.

"This is a huge day for the Assemblers," Hazel told me. "They've been diving for this map for years."

I rubbed my face. Yeah, they'd been diving long enough to lose nine kids.

Swedish angled the raft toward the Assembler fleet, and a big ship spun toward us, creaking under a silver balloon. Isander and Isandra stood at the prow, dreadlocks and robes whipping in the breeze. The other Subassembly ships formed circles around us, until we were in the center of an amphitheater in the sky.

"Our best divers will guide you to the Station," Isandra called to me. "But remember this, Chess. You *must* reach the lowest level. That's where you'll find the map to the Compass."

"You already told me that," I said. "A hundred times."

They'd also told me that they didn't know exactly what the map looked like. They'd spent years researching this stuff but still didn't know anything for sure.

"What'll happen then?" Hazel asked Isandra.

"First Chess gets past the driftsharks and finds the map."

"Then he memorizes it exactly," Isander said. "And comes back."

"That's the only part of this I like," Hazel told him.

Isandra gestured to the diving platforms behind her. "Mochi and Jada will dive from my ship and lead you into the Station. They've searched the top floor in the past."

"Are you ready?" Isander asked the tethergirls.

Jada nodded briskly. "Yes, Cog Isander."

"And you, Chess?"

"Sure," I told him as I crossed toward the diving plank on my ship.

Hazel swung down from the crow's nest and stood beside me. We looked at each other for a second—then she hugged me. "Don't take any chances. With driftsharks nearby, you can't afford mistakes."

"I know."

"You mess up, they'll kill you."

"Hazel," I said. "I know."

She stepped back. "If you get in trouble, come back. Nobody's going to blame you."

"Okay."

She almost chewed on a braid, then caught herself and said, "Oh! I just made my first entry."

"In your logbook?"

She nodded and showed me:

Captain's Log. Start-8 9532.2

Here we go.

I looked at her. "'Here we go'? That's all you wrote?"

"Well, I was in a rush!"

"You could've mentioned my warrior spirit."

"Or that time you glued your thumb to your face?"

"She's all set," Bea called from the winch.

Hazel fiddled with my harness buckles and caught my eye. A few seconds ticked by. She started to speak, then stopped. And from the look on her face, I saw that whatever she wanted to tell me was something I already knew. Finally, she nodded, and I turned and walked to the end of the plank.

"Goggles down," she said, her voice soft.

I lowered my goggles. "Goggles down."

"Tether free?"

"Tether free."

"Dive at will, Chess." Hazel took a breath. "And come back safe."

"Every time," I promised, and I dove.

17

WISPY WHITENESS SURROUNDED me. My heart pounded, and wind tugged my hair. I spun on the end of my new tether, slicing through the mist until I sensed the ground beneath me.

I landed softly, my boots scraping a hard surface. The dark outlines of ruined buildings loomed around me, and wide cracks zigzagged across the concrete slab underfoot. I squinted into the whiteness but couldn't see the tethergirls. At least I didn't see wild dogs or angry boars, either—or driftsharks.

Saplings grew from the cracks in the ground, and I followed them across the plaza toward the crumbling fountain where we were supposed to meet. A minute later, a shape blurred into sight eight or nine feet away: it was

Mochi, walking alone in the Fog, her tether rising in a thin line above her.

"Over here!" I shouted.

She didn't respond.

"Mochi? Mochi!"

She crept along, scanning the ground through her goggles.

"You can't hear a word I'm saying, can you?" I tested her: "Hey, propeller-head! Mochi, you goose-feathered cockroach-cobbler, over here!"

She paused, and I thought she'd heard me. Oops. I hadn't meant for her to hear that. Then she started moving again, and I exhaled in relief and headed toward her.

Six or seven feet away, I tried again. "Hey! What're you doing?"

Mochi looked at me, but her quizzical expression didn't change. She still couldn't see me at that distance.

I shouted, "Mochi?"

"Chess?" Mochi cocked her head. "Is that you?"

"Right here," I said, stepping closer.

"Oh!" A flash of relief shone in her eyes. "I couldn't find you."

"I . . . just got here," I said. "What were you looking for?"

"What?"

"Were you looking for something?" I shouted. "On the ground?"

"Yeah," she shouted back. "My *feet*!"

For a second, I didn't understand. Then I realized that Mochi couldn't even see five feet beneath her. For all she knew, any step might take her off a cliff—or into a slashing edge of metal. And when I saw Jada slowly inching through the Fog nearby, I got a little annoyed. I mean, *these* were the best tetherkids in the Subassembly? These stumbling slowpokes were supposed to help me?

Except as I watched Jada groping toward Mochi, something else occurred to me. These girls were seriously brave. The Fog scared *me*, and I saw five times farther than they did and moved ten times faster. Yet here they were, trying to help the Subassembly save Port Oro. Trying to help me.

"The Station is over there," Jada said after we huddled together. "Forty or fifty feet away."

"Cool." I turned away. "See you topside."

"Wait!" Mochi called. "We're going with you."

I frowned. "Oh, right. To the top floor. Why?"

"No, all the way to the bottom," Jada said, looking scared but determined. "That way, if something happens to you, maybe Mochi or I can sneak past."

"First," I said, "nothing's going to happen to me."

"We're going," she said. "That's final."

"And second, nothing's going to happen to me."

"But if it does—"

"And third," I interrupted, "the sharks would eat you alive."

"We're going, Chess."

"I've got a special tether, and you can't even tell your feet from a hole in the ground!"

"We're going," Jada snapped at me. "Don't you try to change our minds."

"I'd have better luck changing a monkey's diaper," I muttered, too softly for them to hear in the Fog.

"I have a little brother and sister," Mochi said. "If Kodoc takes Port Oro, what happens to them?"

"We're fighting for our home," Jada told me. "We're fighting for our families."

"Just like you," Mochi said.

"Oh, fine," I said, kicking at the concrete slab. "C'mon, then."

We crossed the plaza to a staircase that disappeared underground. A deerfly buzzed my ear, and I smelled spent matches on the breeze wafting from the Station: the scent of driftsharks.

Okay. Head three floors belowground, find the map, and don't die. How hard could that be?

I led the tethergirls down the stairs to the first floor of the Station. Soggy leaves and broken ceiling tiles crunched underfoot . . . but I couldn't see them. For a second, I panicked: why couldn't I see five feet away?

Then Jada shouted in my ear, "Your light!"

Oh. Right. I couldn't see because it was dark underground. I switched on my headlamp and crossed a tile-floored corridor lined with rusted metal doors.

"So this is a subway, huh?" I bellowed.

"What?" Jada asked.

"I bet they launched submarines from down here!"

"What?"

"A '*sub*way'?"

She shot me an exasperated look, then slunk silently to the end of the hallway. She pointed to a sign on the wall that looked like a tangle of colored snakes.

"The cogs say the map will look like that," Mochi yelled. "But totally different."

"Different how?" I asked into her ear.

"More map-y. And with a compass."

"I guess that's the important part."

"One level deeper," Jada yelled, "the colors and labels are different."

"What do they look like two levels deeper?" I asked.

"Nobody knows," she said.

"Right," I said, hunching my shoulders. Because the tetherkids who went that far never came back.

"Keep moving," Jada yelled. "Before the sharks find us."

"I thought they stayed off this floor," I said.

Mochi shifted uneasily. "Usually."

"Hoo, boy," I muttered, wiping my goggles and peering into the Fog.

I didn't spot any suspicious curls of mist. Yet.

We followed the corridor into a concrete ditch with

three sets of tracks but no trains. In the darkness, the whiteness felt suffocating. We climbed the other side of the ditch and followed the hallway to another stair-case—the one that dropped to the second floor, where driftsharks swam and tetherkids died.

I looked into the gloom and swallowed a sudden lump in my throat.

Mochi plucked at Jada's sleeve, then glanced around, looking for me. When she didn't see me standing five feet away, she shouted, "People die on the second floor, Jada!"

Jada gave her a quick hug. "I know."

"I'm scared!"

"We're all scared," Jada said. "Just . . . trust Chess."

My heart shrank two sizes. Trust *me*? What if I couldn't do this? What if I let them down? What if I let everyone down?

"Okay." Mochi's lips trembled. "Okay."

And that's when I saw them: driftsharks.

18

Two pale wisps slithered through the glow of my head-lamp. One veered out of sight ten feet away, while the other corkscrewed closer.

I lunged for the tethergirls. "Sharks! Move! Go!"

"Which way?" Mochi asked, eyes terrified. "Where?"

The fact that she couldn't see the sharks scared me more than anything. How many sharks were floating beyond *my* sight? Five? Ten? A hundred?

"Run for the exit!" I screamed as the first shark jutted toward us. "Now!"

I leaped into the air, grabbed the girls' tethers, and hit the ground sprinting. The driftshark flashed out of sight, and I yanked Jada and Mochi toward the train tracks, shouting, "Move! *Move!*"

They scrambled across the tracks, and I landed beside them, tugging and shoving until we reached the stairs to the outside world.

I shouted to Jada, "Get out of here!"

"We're staying!" she said.

"Please!" I begged. *"Go!"*

"This is our only chance to save the Port. We didn't just come to show you the way, Chess." Jada swallowed. "The cogs asked for volunteers, and . . ."

"We're numbers ten and eleven," Mochi told me.

For a second, I didn't understand. Then I realized: nine Subassembly tetherkids had already died. They'd volunteered to be the next two.

"We're going all the way," Jada said, her determination clear in her voice. "If you get us close enough, we'll find the map or distract the sharks for you. This is our last shot. We need to try *everything*. We're not turning back."

"You're—" I didn't know what to say. "You're loco."

"We have faith," Mochi said faintly.

"You have courage, too," I told them, stepping closer. "But I have this."

I swept my hair back and revealed my freak-eye behind my goggles.

"It's t-true," Jada stammered, while Mochi whispered, "You're blessed."

"Yeah, lucky me. Now, would you please—"

A driftshark whipped toward us through the Fog, and

for once, my mind didn't blank. For once, I reacted just like Hazel: immediately.

I somersaulted into the air, pulled my new hacksaw from my leg sheath, and sliced through my tether in a single motion. Grease speckled my face, and moving fast with fear and Fog, I knotted the end of my tether to the girls' tethers—theirs weren't half as fast as the one Bea made—and gave three sharp jerks.

As I fell to a crouch on the broken tile floor, my tether yanked the girls into the stairwell. They crashed against the wall, shouting in surprise. I caught a glimpse of Mochi's terrified eyes through the Fog before she disappeared, dragged upstairs and out of sight.

The driftshark twisted into a sinewy curve and looked almost confused at the sudden disappearance of its prey. It didn't seem to notice me, trembling beside the wall, and a moment later it shimmered away.

I exhaled in relief. At least Mochi and Jada were safe.

Then the fear hit me.

What was I doing? I'd just cut my tether to save two girls I barely knew. And this wasn't a normal dive. This was a Station plunging three stories underground, into dark caverns where driftsharks swam.

Sweat broke out on my forehead, and my body screamed at me: *Go, run, leave now or die.* Maybe with the tether I'd stood a chance. But now? Alone and untethered, in a nest of sharks? I'd never get out alive.

I glanced toward the stairs. Nobody would blame me if I left—that's what Hazel had said. I should run. I should flee. Except *I'd* blame me. I'd watch Kodoc invade Port Oro, I'd see white waves of Fog drown the green peaks, and the crew would lose our new home. Our only home.

So I squared my shoulders. "Okay, Chess. Stop moaning."

Forget running—I was born to dive. And the Fog didn't just swirl in my eye, it ran through my veins.

I retraced my steps through the rubble to the second stairway. My boots squelched in puddles as I climbed down into a long corridor with a wide railing in the center. The driftsharks' scent of spent matches grew stronger, and the Fog seemed to darken around me.

"Well, maybe a *little* moaning is okay," I muttered—and a driftshark thickened from the Fog.

Fear spiked in my chest. I yelped and vaulted onto the railing and started to run. My boots skittered, and my heart hammered like a blacksmith throwing a temper tantrum.

The driftshark lashed the air behind me, and halfway down the corridor the railing ended in a jagged hole, a dark pit opening below me like a gaping mouth. But like a mouth leading *away* from the shark—and toward the bottom floor. No time to think. No time to hesitate. I reached for my tether, then remembered I didn't have one anymore. *Great. Perfect. Peachy.*

So instead of swinging down on my tether, I screamed and dove headfirst into the hole.

The dark Fog blurred around me. I grabbed a dangling length of the broken railing and jerked to a stop an instant before the driftshark blasted past my shoulder.

The broken railing swung wildly, and I careened through the air—then I fell. Flailing downward, I couldn't see the walls or floor; but the moist air smelled of rust and decay, and the room felt like a huge, cavernous space.

I smacked the floor hard, curled into a ball, and groaned. Pain throbbed in my leg, and I was scared of turning my headlamp toward the injury. If I'd broken a bone, I'd die here, alone in the dark. I wanted to cry out for Hazel. I wanted to open my eyes and wake up in bed. For a second, I'd have given anything just to feel safe again.

My goggles misted, and my breath sounded harsh. Then I looked down at my leg, and tears sprang to my eyes. Tears of relief: the pain was just from the mostly healed cut where Kodoc's harpoon had slashed me days earlier. I was okay. For now.

I stood and swept the room with my headlamp. Vaulted ceilings. Dozens of alcoves with what Mrs. E called "at 'ems," which is how you pronounced *ATMs*. Plasteel seats lined the walls. Under the highest arch of the ceiling, a massive sail dangled from a scaffolding, frayed and corroded, exposing the circuit boards woven inside.

I'd never seen cloth like that and wondered how much the junkyard bosses would pay for it. Then the squiggles of the circuit boards reminded me of the colorful-snake maps, and I remembered why I was there.

My boots scuffed as I crossed the room, looking for the map. The air smelled like mildew and rotten eggs, and a soggy chill gave me goose bumps. I'd spent years diving into the Fog, but I'd never felt so alone.

Except I wasn't alone. There were driftsharks down here.

I zigzagged across the trash-heaped floor. Instead of a map, I found blotches of spongy mold on big metal cubes surrounding a collapsed kiosk. I found a nest of rusted nano-wires. A trickle of fluid oozed down one of the walls, leaving a wide orange smear behind it.

Then something crackled under my boot. I swiveled my headlamp beam downward and saw a thin plastic sheet poking out from a puddle of goo. A few lines squirmed across the corner of the sheet. A colorful snake?

Was it the map?

"No way," I said. It couldn't be that easy.

I grabbed the sheet, and the goo felt oily and corrosive, like acid. My fingers tingled, and I couldn't get a strong grip on it, so I plunged my hand into the puddle and groped around. Elbow-deep in the burning goo, I finally felt the other edge of the sheet. My goggles fogged as I turned my head and yanked.

With a slurp, the plastic sheet oozed from the puddle, and in the light of my headlamp I saw these words:

—EMPLOYEES MUST WASH HANDS

BEFORE RETURNING TO WORK—

"Oh, boogers," I muttered, and the Fog rippled in the dim light of my headlamp.

The bulky mouth of a driftshark snapped at me through the mist. The Fog muffled my whimper as I shot backward. My vision narrowed in terror, and I stumbled into one of the metal cubes. A sharp edge jammed my leg. A driftshark lashed at me, and I shoved myself sideways, sick with fear. I didn't want to die. I didn't want to die here, lost and alone in the dark.

I scrambled through a pile of trash. My heart thundered and my breath thinned, and the driftshark vanished into the Fog. I stumbled and fell, and almost wept in panic. *Please, please. I don't want to die. Not yet, not here.* I shoved to my feet and sprinted away—

Until my boot snagged on rubble. A *snap* shot through the cavern as my foot tangled in cloth. I sprawled to the ground, my headlamp shining on the rubble I'd tripped over.

Except it wasn't rubble . . .

It was a body. A corpse. A skeleton with a skull for a face—and wearing the gear of a tetherkid. That *snap* had been my boot breaking one of its bones.

My shriek was swallowed by the darkness. I forgot the Fog, I forgot the driftsharks—I forgot everything except the horror of that body, shrunken and still, staring at the ceiling with eye sockets blacker than nightmares.

A tetherkid sent to find the map. A tetherkid who'd never see the sun again. Who'd never laugh or cry or dream again. A tetherkid lying forgotten on the floor with all the other trash. A tetherkid just like me.

After far too long, I tore my gaze away from the body's grotesque stare, and my terror faded to a dull throb. That's when I spotted a scrap of paper in the tetherkid's sagging glove. I swallowed the lump of fear, then wriggled the paper from between the bony fingers.

Most of the paper was rotten and black, but swirls of ink ran across one corner. A map. I even saw a hint of a circle that might've been a compass. But the paper had mostly rotted away into a mess of water stains.

"You found it," I whispered to the body. "You did it— you found the map. . . ."

But it was ruined. Completely torn and illegible and— Driftsharks swirled toward me.

Terror cut through me like a knife. I leaped straight upward as the sharks lashed through the Fog beneath me. I grabbed a fistful of the circuit-board sailcloth and climbed like a monkey with his butt on fire.

A misty jaw slashed at me, and a tail flicked the cloth

inches from my elbow. I jerked away, swinging through the darkness as another shark uncoiled from the Fog.

My mind dizzy with terror, I climbed until I reached the plasteel scaffolding from which the sailcloth hung. I clambered on top, scanned the ceiling for the hole that led to the second floor.

If I stayed down here, I'd die. I'd rot on the floor next to the other tetherkids. Nobody could beat a driftshark, not for long. Not even me. And I couldn't find the map anyway. I trembled on the scaffolding, scanning the ceiling for the hole. Then my neck prickled with sudden fear. My blood froze, and I spun, certain that driftsharks were swarming at me.

Behind me, the Fog glowed quietly in the light of my lamp. No driftsharks, no dangers. Nothing scary except my shaky, panting breath. But when I looked upward again, the fear returned. I twirled and dodged, grabbing a beam and swinging across the scaffolding before scanning for sharks.

I still didn't see any, so I scanned the ceiling for a third time—and gasped.

"No way." My knees turned to jelly. "No way."

In the glow of my lamp, I saw a map painted on the ceiling itself: a tangle of streets and subways, parks and rivers, even a few mountains. The smudged outline of a city loomed to one side of the painting, and farther down, boxy buildings and flowery shapes bled together where the ceiling was peeling from moisture.

I jogged across the scaffolding, memorizing every shape and squiggle—then my gaze fell on a circle in the city.

My breath caught. Not a circle, a *compass*. A fancy compass, with a smiling sun in the center, on the shore of a lake or ocean.

I burned the map into my memory, taking in every detail. My lamp beam sliced through the dark Fog, from the mountains to the Compass to the city and back again.

Then the mist thickened before me, and driftsharks writhed like eels in a bucket: a dozen of them, swarming toward me.

19

TIME SLOWED.

A driftshark sliced forward, and I leaped toward the hole in the ceiling. I caught a jutting bar and hefted myself to the second floor—and one of the sharks smacked my thigh.

At its touch, my leg went numb, and my muscles slackened. That was what happened when a shark touched you: first they drained your strength, then they ate your mind. When I landed on the shattered tile of the second floor, my deadened leg buckled, and I fell to one knee.

The sharks paused, like they were savoring the victory . . . then they shot forward. A blast of terror erupted in my mind and burned away all my hopes, all my dreams, all my strength. I was going to die. And in that instant, I saw my own death as clearly as I'd ever seen anything.

The sharks whipped closer, and images strobed from my memory: *Swedish winning his first thopper race and Bea whispering to an engine. Hazel standing in the crow's nest with her skirt flapping, her spyglass scanning the distance. A bear roaring out of the Fog as I vaulted over a boulder. Mrs. E holding my wrist and saying, "The Fog doesn't change you. You change the Fog."*

What if the Fog didn't make me stronger and quicker? What if I changed the Fog? What if I *made* the Fog lift and spin me? What if I harnessed the currents like a driftshark unfurling through the white? Maybe I even *created* the currents, my mind linked to the tiny invisible machines, forcing the swirls of Fog to carry me. Maybe—

—the sharks whipped closer, inches from my face.

And for the first time, instead of diving *through* the whirls of Fog, I moved the whirls themselves, like a bird controlling the wind. Misty jaws snapped at me, and I darted away. I dodged and spun, powered by my new understanding: I changed the Fog. I moved the Fog with my mind.

Not much—thickening a swirl here, clearing a current there—but enough to save my life. For a few seconds, at least.

"Ha!" I shouted, twirling in the misty air. "You can't touch the tetherboy!"

I almost laughed. I'd found the map. I'd touched the

Fog with my mind. I couldn't fail now. I couldn't—

A white wedge blurred at my face, too close to dodge. And instead of trying to move the Fog, I panicked. I focused on the shark itself . . . and the sledgehammer of a snout smashed into me.

I guess they *could* touch the tetherboy.

The blow felt like being clubbed by a tree trunk. Pain flared in my cheek and chest, and the impact flung me backward. I hit a wall and bent double, gasping for breath. What *was* that? Driftsharks weren't solid. They were mist—they were steam. They numbed you and drained your life; they didn't stomp you to death like a junkyard gang.

Then it hit me. I hadn't moved the Fog, but I'd changed the shark. I'd condensed the driftshark's nanites, so instead of numbing me—and killing me—they'd slammed into me.

A fin sliced toward my face, and my mind flared. I changed it, solidified the fin an instant before it slashed my forehead. Instead of brushing my face with deadly mist and killing my mind, it struck like a knife blade. Hot blood trickled along my goggles, but I was still alive. If I condensed the shark's nanites, they wouldn't deaden my brain—they'd just batter me into cockroach relish.

At least I'd taste delicious with noodles.

Another shark rammed my side, lofting me through the air like one of Swedish's bootballs. My body slammed against the ground; my vision blurred. Through teary eyes, I saw that I was sprawled on the rubble near the stairs leading to the first floor.

A dozen driftsharks looped through the air above me. Gasping and shaky, I screamed at them to stop, to freeze. My mind ached. My nose bled. In a panicky haze, I scrambled for the stairs . . . and didn't even see the shark that suddenly smashed me to the floor.

My head smacked the tile, and I whimpered in pain. Then the Fog turned a pure, blinding white. The driftshark surrounded me. I was enveloped, enclosed—*swallowed* by a shark.

I focused all my fear and hate and love and hope on keeping the driftshark from killing my mind. I sobbed and begged and prayed for a miracle.

And something clicked.

Something clicked.
A flash of fear.
A bolt of light.
A thunderclap.
For the first time, I felt the Fog inside me, not as an interloper, not as a stranger or an invader. It was a part of me. I felt the Fog woven through my brain, touching every neuron and synapse and—

A vise tightened around my chest. The driftshark plucked me from the stairs and hurled me into the ceiling. The impact was heavy and hard, like a giant's boot stomping me. For an instant, I blacked out. The shadowy world shrank to a distant star and—*blink*—disappeared.

Then I was falling through ropy, shark-infested Fog.

Whimpering with fear, I spun sideways. I caught a stair railing with my boot and launched myself up the stairs. I hurtled from the stairwell onto the first floor, my lungs heaving, my goggles speckled with blood. My mind felt numb and dreamy, but my breath sounded harsh in the silence.

A shark clamped misty jaws around my shoulder, shook me until I thought my neck would snap, then whipped me up into the air. I cartwheeled into the concrete ditch with the train tracks and hit the ground hard, breathless and beaten.

I was done. Finished. Too spent to focus, too weak to flee. Unable to tell the difference between my fears and my reality. Barely strong enough to watch the sharks rippling toward my head. *Stop*, I begged them. *Stop, stay away, stop. . . .*

I'd miss the crew. They'd miss me, too . . . but not for long. Because now that I'd failed, Lord Kodoc would finish Port Oro for good.

I closed my eyes . . . and imagined Hazel standing beside me. Even though she was drifting high above the Fog, she was still with me. Even though I'd cut my tether, we were still connected.

Come back safe, she always told me.

Every time, I always said.

Every time.

Opening my eyes, I felt the Fog all around me—and inside me. With every breath I took, Fog filled my lungs and seeped through my body. *Every time.* Driftsharks flickered ten feet away, but I just thought, *Stop, stay away,* and dragged myself from the concrete ditch, my head bowed like a beaten dog.

I crawled toward the stairs. *Every time.* Three drift-sharks writhed and lashed . . . but didn't come closer. When I reached the stairway that led to the plaza, I swayed, light-headed and barely conscious.

"Every time," I said.

Fog billowed and shimmered, and a weightless feeling surrounded me. I felt half asleep and daydreaming. The world swam, my mind spun. I took a breath—

tick tock

—crawled onto the bottom stair—

tick tock

—grabbed the railing and—

tick tock

—pulled myself to my feet.

What *was* that? The autowinding click of my harness? The chattering of my teeth?

I blinked into the Fog, and the noise came again: *Tick. Tock.* Then a spiny plasteel strut slashed through the whiteness, and a mound of rust and blades and scales emerged from the Fog.

For a heartbeat, I stared in disbelief. A ticktock.

Was I seeing that? An actual ticktock, grinding toward me? A junk-monster from the depths? Or was the Fog playing with my mind after the driftsharks had broken me?

The ticktock rumbled closer, and I staggered backward in horror. The spiny plasteel strut was just a foreleg. Other legs—and tentacles and swollen growths—bulged from a central humped shell of rusted scales. Chains clattered; misshapen gears spun. Liquid sloshed in murky tanks, and vapor wafted from jagged slots.

An upwelling of disgust made me dizzy. Stumbling away, I tripped on the stairs. The ticktock shuddered, and something wet splattered my cheek. The world dimmed, and I scrambled up the stairs, listening for the *tick tock* behind me. I heard nothing except the panicked rasp of my breath. My arms trembled, and my leg dragged.

Finally, I crawled from the stairs into the plaza. I looked over my shoulder, and nothing moved in the dim whiteness of the Station.

No gearwork monster. No ticking. Nothing.

With a pained grunt, I rose to my feet and swayed. I was aboveground. I'd survived. A flicker of triumph glowed in my heart . . . until I remembered that I still didn't have a tether. I couldn't get home. I was trapped in the Fog with driftsharks and—and maybe *ticktocks*.

Then I noticed weird lines all around me. Faint, skinny, wobbling lines outlined against the white . . .

Through the Fog, I saw a forest of tethers. Hundreds of them, dangling from every ship in the Subassembly fleet. I grabbed at the nearest one, but my shaking fingers couldn't take hold. I choked back a sob and dropped to my knees, and my vision narrowed into a dark tunnel.

Something brushed my shoulder, and I turned, expecting to see the driftshark that would finally kill me.

Instead, I saw a wiry girl with an old-fashioned nosering.

Jada groped toward my face, and the Fog turned black.

20

AN AIRSHIP'S DECK swayed beneath me. I heard the whir of propellers and the screeching of birds. Pain throbbed in my arms and legs and face.

"Hazel?" I whispered, not bothering to open my eyes.

Her hand curled into mine. "Right here."

"Ow," I said.

"Shhhh," she said. "You're okay now."

I heard muffled voices and felt people tugging at me. Rough hands slit the straps of my harness. Gentler hands washed and bandaged my cuts, and for some reason, the air stank of manure.

After a time, someone lifted me into a seated position, and someone else held a cup of bitter liquid to my lips.

"It'll help the pain," Hazel told me, tilting the cup higher.

I swallowed, then gasped. "Tastes like rat feet."

"Rat feet are delicious," Loretta said. "Barbecued."

"Just drink it," Swedish said from behind me.

"That's what *they* want," I muttered, but I swallowed another mouthful before I drifted off again.

Somewhere belowdecks, rudders shifted and valves whistled. I opened one eye and watched a balloon swaying high above. I didn't recognize the balloon, and the stink of manure hit me again.

I wasn't on any ship that I knew—and a jolt of fear roused me. Where was I? What had happened?

Then Swedish sat beside me and squeezed my shoulder. He didn't say anything, but for once he looked completely happy.

"You stink," I told him.

A smile spread across his face. "Well, Jada hooked you to a tether from a plow ship—what do you expect? We're hitching a ride back to the skyscraper—"

"He's awake!" Bea squealed, hugging me tight.

"Ow!" I yipped. "Ow-ow!"

"Bea!" Hazel half laughed. "You're crushing him!"

"Sorry," she said, not sounding sorry at all. "But he's so purple!"

"He even *looks* purple," Loretta said from beside Swedish. "With all those bruises."

"That bad?" I asked, wincing. My face hurt when I spoke.

"You look like a bootball," Swedish told me. "After a high-scoring game."

Loretta nodded. "With metal boots."

Bea wrinkled her nose. "What happened down there?"

"I got lucky," I said, blinking until she came into focus.

"Because you had my twisty rose!" she said.

I nodded weakly. "Definitely."

"You stayed down too long," Hazel told me, lines appearing on her forehead. "We thought, I thought—"

"She wanted to dive after you," Loretta said.

"Hazel!" I peered at her. "That's the stupidest thing I've ever heard."

"It *was* pretty dumb." She squatted beside me. "So?"

The deck dipped as the ship turned, which set the plows beneath us clinking. Seagulls squawked and flapped, then settled somewhere behind me. Probably on the manure in the cargo bed.

"So?" I repeated, watching Hazel's braids sway.

"So did you find the map?" she asked.

"Of course I found the map," I told her with a half smile that made my face ache.

Hazel's eyes brightened. "No way!"

"Yeah, get me a marker."

A wind rose and blew the stench around as Hazel scrambled for a marker and a square of paperboard. Swedish propped me up, and I scrawled a sloppy version of the map, talking Hazel through everything I'd seen.

"This part here is the city," I said, tapping the paper-board.

"What's that?" She pointed to a wiggly line. "A lake?"

I nodded weakly, feeling dizzy again. "Or an ocean or something."

"And you think this mountain is Port Oro?"

"No, that's a bunch of roads joining together."

"An intersection?"

"Yeah." I prodded the map. "*This* is the mountain that's maybe Port Oro."

"That's not a mountain," she said. "That's a stick figure with a straw hat."

"I thought that was you," Bea told me from behind Hazel.

"I don't wear a straw hat," I said. "I mean, it's *not* a straw hat! It's a mountain, and this is a . . . an intersection. And these bits are parks or fields, I think."

Bea propped her chin on Hazel's shoulder. "I can't believe you found the map!"

"That's not all I found." I rubbed my eyes with a shaky hand. "I think I saw a ticktock."

Hazel looked at my face. "What? No way!"

"Told you so," Swedish said, frowning toward the farmer at the wheel of the plow ship.

"What happened?" Hazel asked me.

"I'm not sure." I took a shuddering breath. "The drift-sharks swarmed and . . . I . . . I don't know. I think one of them ate me."

"You don't look eaten," Loretta said.

"He always looks a bit gnawed on," Swedish said.

"Shut up!" Hazel snapped at them. "Tell us what happened, Chess."

"A shark kind of . . . swallowed me? Things went blurry, like a daydream." I blinked a few times, forcing myself to stay awake. "Except it was more of a nightmare. I heard the clicking and I—I saw a ticktock coming at me. Unless I imagined the whole thing . . ."

"Hazel," Loretta said, after I trailed off, "you'd better tell him before he passes out."

"Tell me what?" I asked.

Hazel hesitated for a moment. "Jada and Mochi saw your eye."

"Yeah." After the cogs and driftsharks and maybe a ticktock, my fog-eye didn't seem so freaky after all. "I showed them."

"They told the cogs and . . ." She gestured past the stern of the raft. "Look."

When I propped myself on my elbow, all my aches flared up. Through teary eyes, I saw the entire Subassembly fleet hovering nearby, watching us. Watching *me*.

Apparently they'd been waiting for me to notice them, because Isandra suddenly boomed from the prow of her airship: "Today we found the map to the Compass! And today we found a true child of the Fog!"

"The Fog marked Chess," Isander shouted, his

dreadlocks whipping in the wind. "And led him to us."

"Long ago," Isandra called, her voice ringing over the Fog, "the engineers predicted that a Compass would emerge when the time was right."

"A nano-machine that controls the Fog!" Isander announced. "Assembled by the Fog itself!"

"Chess will trigger the Compass," Isandra said, gesturing toward me. "And he will save the Port!"

Hundreds of Assemblers turned toward me, and for once, instead of ducking my head, I grabbed Hazel's arm and pulled myself to my feet. The sky tilted, darkness seeped across my vision, and my knees almost buckled. I sagged against Hazel, and she held me upright as I brushed the hair off my face.

Most of the Assemblers were too far away to see, but that didn't matter. I wasn't showing them my freak-eye, not really; I was showing myself that I wasn't scared anymore. Next I'd tell them that I wasn't a "child of the Fog." I was just a regular kid with a weird eye who wanted to live a normal life with his crew.

Hazel took a sharp breath. "Chess!"

"What? What's wrong?"

"The Fog's in *both* your eyes," she told me. "It's in both of them."

The day spun into a dizzy blur. Was that what had happened when I'd felt that *click* in the Station? Had the Fog started blooming in my other eye? Now the nanites

154

swirled in both of them, shifting clouds of tiny machines?

"What does it mean?" Loretta said, sounding awed.

"I don't know," Swedish grumbled. "But I have a—"

"*Good* feeling about it," Hazel interrupted, though she looked scared. "It's probably nothing. It's probably what saved him. It's probably just—"

"Chess," Bea said, taking my hand. "It's just Chess."

"Yeah," Loretta said. "What's one more weird eye around here?"

"For a second there," I told them, "I wasn't scared."

Then I fainted.

21

I **WOKE IN** a warm bed. My leg throbbed, and my arm tingled as I drifted there, watching the shadow of the curtains dance on the infirmary ceiling.

The shapes reminded me of driftsharks. I thought about blunting the sharks with my mind. Had the nanites in my brain spoken to them? Had they seen me not as a stranger, but as a brother? As a fellow fog-monster? And had I really seen a ticktock?

The memories kept slipping away, like a fever dream. But I'd found the map! I remembered that much. Then how come I felt anxious instead of victorious? Something about my eye . . .

A warm grip squeezed my left hand, interrupting the thought. I weakly lifted my head, peered a hundred miles down the bed, and saw skinny fingers wrapped around my palm.

Mrs. E lay in the next bed, holding my hand in her sleep. I felt myself smile as I watched her eyelids flicker with dreams. She looked peaceful and safe, and I enjoyed her silent company for a minute. Then I realized we weren't alone.

Loretta sprawled in a chair beside my bed, her legs up and her boots on the mattress. "Hey, Chess," she said, her voice softer than usual. "Can you hear me?"

"Course I can hear you," I said. But my tongue felt too big for my mouth, and it sounded like "Curzacaneeroo."

"What?" she said. "Who?"

"Course a can eer oo!"

"Oh! Why didn't you say so?" She plopped her feet to the ground. "Hazel told me to stay by your bed till she's done inspecting her ship."

"Erzip?" I asked.

"Yeah, Captain Vidious gave her a ship. She's helping the mutineer fleet hold off Kodoc, to buy you time to find the Compass."

I worked my tongue around in my mouth. "When we leave?"

"As soon as you get your skinny butt out of bed."

"Sushagarbo," I said, which meant "You're such a garbo." "The map 'sokay?"

She nodded. "The map is good. Well, the fogheads

figured the general area. You'll still need to find the exact spot."

"Wazlooklie?"

"'Wazalooklie?' That sounds like one of Bea's names for an airship."

I spoke more carefully: "Wha duz it look like?"

The *clomp-clomp* of a cane sounded, and Isandra appeared at my bedside. "You want to know what the Compass looks like?" she asked.

I nodded. "Yuh."

"We're not sure."

"Guess," I told her.

"It's probably a machine powered by Fog, or perhaps a building or an ancient workshop." She lifted a wash-cloth from a steamer. "Maybe trillions of nanites, joined together into some sort of construct."

I grunted, which meant, "How'm I supposed to find it if I don't even know what it looks like?"

"We hope that when you see it, you'll know." Isandra showed me the still-steaming cloth, then nodded at my eyes. "May I?"

In a sickening flash, I remembered Hazel saying, "The Fog's in *both* your eyes." My stomach soured, and fear and disgust clogged my throat.

Still, I swallowed a few times, then managed to nod. "'Kay."

Isandra brushed my hair off my forehead. She took a

sharp, amazed breath. A smile tugged at her lips, and she made a noise that was half gasp and half laugh.

"Is . . ." I swallowed again. "Are they *both* foggy?"

"Not anymore. Just the one you keep hidden."

Relief swelled in my chest. "Why? Why'd the other one change?"

"It was jealous," Loretta said. "It never got any attention."

"We don't know," Isandra told me. "Perhaps the concentration of nanites in the Station drew more into your other eye—or activated ones already there. And then, after a few hours topside, the nanites dissipated from your left eye."

"She means they faded," Loretta explained. "That's what *dissipated* means. They talked like this for hours while you were sleeping."

"The doctors say you're not getting fogsick." Isandra focused on my freak-eye. "It's like floating pearls of Fog. Do you know what Hazel told me?"

"What?" I asked.

"That your eye is the *least* special thing about you."

I felt myself flush.

"I don't know," Loretta said. "I can think of plenty of things that aren't special about him. His feet, his cooking. His sense of humor."

Isandra wiped sweat from my forehead. "You must find the Compass, Chess. This is our last chance, our only chance."

"Whazzat mean?"

"His clothes," Loretta continued, "his hair . . ."

"While you were diving," Isandra said, her blue eye intent, "the Fog rippled. Like dropping a rock in a puddle."

"The Fog doesn't ripple."

"It never has before," she agreed.

"His face," Loretta suggested, still listing the things that weren't special about me. "His personality."

"But—" I shook my head and asked Isandra, "Why?"

"We don't know. Either Kodoc learned how to interfere with the Fog . . ." Isandra's white eye glinted. "Or something changed, and the Compass is ready. Maybe it's waiting. Waiting for you."

Captain's Log. Start-8 312.93

Two days have passed since Chess dove into the Station and found the map. He still tosses and turns in a fog-fever in the Subassembly infirmary, though the doctors assure me that he will soon recover.

Upon the recommendation of Captains Nisha and Vidious, I've been given the command of a gunship. More of a gun raft, a six-person vehicle, the smallest combat ship in the mutineer navy.

Bea wanted to name her the Purple Piston. *Swedish voted for "nothing." As in, a ship called the* Nothing. *He thought that might confuse them.*

Loretta suggested the Bloodcutter. *In the end, we settled on the* Bottom-Feeder, *because she's an ugly little thing, patched together with castoffs and stubbornness—just like us.*

I adore her.

Swedish is learning how she flies; Bea is furiously upgrading her engine; and before I sent Loretta to sit with Chess, she struck a pose beside our new, undersized harpoon and declared herself "chief harpoonist."

We may need a fighter on deck, so I asked one of Nisha's marines to teach Loretta how to repel enemy boarders. After a few hours, he bandaged the bites on his arm and said, "That girl fights like a wild animal."

"That's my Retta," Swedish said proudly.

We're not a crew without Chess, though. We're a sail without wind, a bow without an arrow. Especially me. I need Chess. I check in with him a hundred times a day, with a word or a glance. Swedish judges a ship by the feel of the controls, Bea checks an engine by the sound of the exhaust, and I measure the crew by the hunch of Chess's shoulders.

Thinking of him lying on his cot, limp and flushed, makes my stomach ache. He didn't even get beaten up that badly. Not for him. After three years in the Fog, there isn't a square inch on Chess that hasn't been broken or slashed or stabbed. He's usually a fast healer, uncommonly fast, but not this time. This time, a driftshark touched his mind. That's worse than any injury.

I refuse to worry, though. Chess will come through. He always does.

22

THE NEXT TIME I woke, Hazel was curled into a chair beside my bed, writing in her logbook, her tongue peeking between her teeth.

I watched her for a while. She finished a paragraph. She wrote another few words. Then she glanced at me and her brown eyes sparked. "Welcome back."

"How long have I been asleep?"

"Three days, on and off."

"Three days! No way."

"We had this same conversation this morning. You don't remember?"

"Not really." I yawned. "No wonder I'm so hungry."

"You ate this morning, too," she said, but she brought me a tray of rice balls and eel jerky, along with a jug of goat's milk.

"Where is everyone?" I asked around a mouthful of jerky.

"Swede's playing bootball. Bea's in the dry dock, rebuilding the engine from scratch." She grabbed a rice ball. "You'll never guess where Loretta is."

"Knocking someone down?"

She laughed. "In the kitchen."

"She's knocking someone down *in the kitchen*?"

"Helping the cooks. She decided she likes cooking."

"Nah," I said, licking my fingers. "She just likes cutting things."

Hazel smiled. "And Mrs. E is out there."

"What do you mean, 'out there'?"

"In the hallway, with the doctors, exercising." She looked toward the door. "She's still sleeping most of the time, but she's getting better."

"Not bad for a bunch of slumkids."

Hazel nodded, her braids clattering with new beads. "Could've been worse."

"So . . . what's next?"

She brushed my hair from my face to check my eye. "After the Station, the Fog was in both your eyes."

"Yeah." I felt myself frown. "They still don't know why?"

"No."

"How come you're not freaked?"

"I was," she admitted. "But the cogs say you looked okay, and your eye returned to normal, and—you're okay. At least for now."

"Thank you, Little Miss Cheerful."

"Well, the good news is that Loretta hasn't decided if you're a 'biclops' or a 'binoculon' yet. And you'll never guess what Swede thinks."

"That *they* turned my other eye white?"

"Well . . . yeah."

"What did Bea do? Try chatting with it?"

"No, she said . . ." Hazel paused, remembering. "Uh, she said maybe your eyes matched the Fog like a synchronous magnetic field?"

"I don't even know what *language* that is."

"Me neither," she admitted. "But Bea thinks it's pretty purple."

I grabbed a rice ball. "What do *you* think?"

"I think we're good to go." She patted my hair back into place. "Thanks to you, the cogs now know where to find the city with the Compass."

"And they gave you a ship?"

"The *Bottom-Feeder*," Hazel said with a proud glint in her eyes. "She's just a harassment raft. We were going to annoy the roof-troopers, to keep them busy while the muties took them down."

"It was going to be our *job* to annoy someone?"

"I know—it's a dream come true!" She laughed. "But that was only if you didn't wake up."

"So what're we waiting for now?"

"Nothing. If you're awake for real this time, we'll leave in the morning."

"I'm awake for real." I wiped my mouth. "How close is Kodoc?"

"A few of his ships are already here."

I frowned. "They're *here*?"

"They've tested our defenses a few times." Hazel tucked a braid behind her ear. "The bulk of his fleet is farther out, but I don't see how he can take the Port without heavy losses."

"Maybe he doesn't care about losses." A chill touched me. "Wait. So Kodoc is almost here, and we haven't even started looking for the Compass? Aren't we supposed to use the Compass to beat him?"

"Yeah. The muties will have to hold him off till we get back."

My stomach twisted. "They'll fight him for *days*?" An alarm shrilled in the distance. "What's that?"

"Probably just a few more Rooftop scout ships," Hazel told me, crossing to the window. "I guess Kodoc's trying to find weak spots in the Port's defenses."

"Are there any?"

"We're outnumbered and outgunned," she said. "But Kodoc is five days from home. If he runs low on supplies before—"

A cannon roared outside, and Hazel pushed the curtain aside and squinted into the day. The sunlight painted stripes on her face, and her squint turned into a scowl. "Oh, no," she cried.

Another cannon roared. "What?" I asked, suddenly edgy. "Hazel, tell me!"

"This isn't just a few scout ships," she said, her voice strained.

I half raised myself from the bed. "How many?"

"Three warships. Also three gunships and six or seven clippers." Cannons boomed, and faint voices shouted. "This is it. This is the invasion."

"What—what do we do?"

She kept staring outside. "They're never going to break through. What's Kodoc doing?"

"I don't know; I can't see!"

She described the chain shot and broadsides as the battle crackled and roared outside. "Now the Rooftop ship's taking aim at— Oh! That's the *Night Tide* and the *Anvil Rose*! They're swooping into battle— Ha! Take that, Kodoc!"

I threw off my blanket. "I've got to see this."

"You stay there!" Hazel snapped at me.

"I'm okay—I can stand up."

"That's what you said two days ago. *Stay!*"

"Fine," I grumbled, staying on the bed despite the air battle in the distance and the footsteps pounding in the hallway outside.

Hazel turned back to the window. "What's Nisha doing? She's flying too high. No, wait. Vidious is drawing them into a trap and—"

The infirmary door crashed open. Medical gear rattled and boots scuffed, and I turned, expecting to see Swedish and Loretta and Bea.

Instead, three strangers burst in, wearing goggles and camel-leather helmets, carrying clubs and knives—and one was wearing a necktie. They looked like junkyard thugs, but that was impossible. There were no junkyard thugs on Port Oro.

The tall one was holding a little girl's upper arm like he'd dragged her through the skyscraper. When he spotted me, he shoved her into the corner and said, "Looks like I don't have to slit your throat after all."

"She led us straight here," another thug said. "Just like she promised."

The little girl pulled her knees to her chest and started sobbing.

"Just like I *made* her promise," the tall thug said.

I barely heard them. Because when the tall one spoke, I recognized his high-pitched voice. And as he pulled off his helmet and stepped toward me, yellow hair fell around his shoulders.

"P-Perry?" Hazel stammered.

Fear clawed at my chest. Perry was one of the Rooftop bosses' scariest hitters. But—but we'd left him behind. We'd left all that behind forever.

"Happy to see me?" Perry squeaked, a mean smile on his face.

Hazel's eyes narrowed. "What are you doing here?!"

"Lord Kodoc needed someone who could recognize Chess. All *that*?" Perry nodded toward the window. "That's a distraction so nobody would see us tethering onto foghead territory and grabbing *him*. He's the only thing Lord Kodoc cares about."

"Over my dead body," Hazel said, stepping closer to him.

"Sure," Perry squeaked, and swung his club at Hazel's head.

She threw a punch at his face, but she was a captain, not a brawler. Perry's club blurred past her fist and I heard a dull *thup*, and Hazel collapsed onto the floor. Still breathing, but barely.

A red haze of anger filled the room, and I threw myself at Perry. Except I was still weak—and I wasn't a brawler, either. I staggered toward Perry, and he punched me in the stomach and grabbed my neck.

"I always thought you were worthless," he sneered, "but his lordship's paying a heapload for you. You're going to make me rich."

From the hallway, Bea's voice shouted, "—telling you, I finished the engine and came to get Hazel and saw *Perry* heading this way!"

The door slammed open again, and Swedish and Loretta shoved inside.

Swedish paused in the doorway, looking big and angry and surprised—but Loretta didn't pause at all. She *was* a brawler. She struck fast like a snake, dropping a shoulder and ramming the nearest thug. He sprawled backward, and she sprang at the second thug, a girl with stained teeth. The girl punched Loretta once, then Swedish body-checked her into a cabinet so hard that she broke the door and fell moaning to the ground.

Perry dragged me closer to the window while Loretta stalked him, wiping blood from her mouth.

"You can't beat me," Perry told her. "You never could."

"Not by myself," she said.

Swedish stepped beside her, cracking his knuckles. "She ain't by herself. Not anymore."

"Neither am I." Perry whistled a piercing note. "You think you can mess with Lord Kodoc? He'll stomp you into paste."

"I don't see Kodoc," Swedish said. "All I see is you. And if you hurt Chess, I'll rip your spine out."

A figure swooped through the open window, a skinny boy wearing goggles and a tether. He landed just inside, then caught his balance and scuttled toward Perry, unfastening a spare tether from his belt.

Ice gripped my heart. I knew that a spare tether meant Perry hadn't come to kill me—he'd come to kidnap me.

"Keep him away from Chess!" Loretta snapped.

I took a shaky breath and was about to throw an elbow into Perry's gut when I felt the edge of a blade on my neck. My knees wobbled, and my breath caught. Forget throwing any elbows. Even without a knife at my throat, I was too weak after three days in bed.

"Take one more step!" Perry squeaked. "And I'll cut him."

Swedish stopped were he stood, his fists clenched and an angry flush staining his cheeks. The little girl in the corner kept sobbing softly. The ice from my heart flowed through my veins as the skinny boy hooked the spare tether to a harness beneath Perry's jacket.

"Next time I see you," Loretta told Perry, her eyes murderous.

"You'll never see either of us again," Perry said.

Swedish didn't even glance at him. "We're coming," he told me, his voice shaking with emotion. "We're already on the way."

Perry grabbed me in a bear hug and jumped backward through the window. We flung into the air. Tears stung my eyes, and the night sky blurred overhead. Swedish shouted my name from the infirmary window. We dropped twenty feet; then the tether swung us away from the skyscraper.

In the distance, Rooftop warships blasted at the Nisha and Vidious and mutineer navy. Cannons roared, and harpoons hissed. And high above, a small, stealthy airship towed me away from the Port, away from my crew.

23

"I HEARD ALL about you," Perry said in my ear, his arms like leather straps around my chest. "You and your eye."

The cold wind whipped past and numbed my cheeks. My stomach throbbed from his punch, and my mind reeled with fear and failure.

"Maybe Kodoc'll take it from you." Perry's grip tightened, squeezing me painfully. "Maybe he'll scoop that eye out with a spoon."

Bitterness rose in my throat, and I barely heard the roar of cannons over my gasping breaths. The night sky was a blur of dread.

"Maybe he'll s-s-set the rats on you," Perry whispered.

His slight stammer stopped me cold. My mind cleared, and the night sky was just the night sky. Because that stutter told me that *Perry* was scared. Swinging high above the Fog on a tether, he was more than scared. The height and motion were nothing for me, but for him, they must've been a clawing terror.

My fear turned to anger. We'd left the junkyard, we'd fled from Perry and the bosses—and now they'd come after us. They'd plucked me from Port Oro like I couldn't ever escape them, like I'd never break free of my past.

"Or maybe," I said, squirming in his arms, "I'll drop us into the Fog."

"What're you doing?" he squeaked.

My fingertips scrabbled at a buckle on his harness. "This."

"Stop!" He held me with one arm and punched me with the other. "No, you crudnugget!"

I tugged the strap free, and the cold wind suddenly felt wild and exhilarating. "You're going down, Perry. You're going to fall. You're going *splat.*"

"Stop it!" he shrieked, flailing at me. "Stopstopstop!"

I hunched against his smacks and popped another buckle.

"You'll die, too!" he squealed. "You'll die, too!"

"You heard all about me," I said, throwing his words back at him. "Me and my eye. Maybe I drift through the Fog like a feather."

The half-unbuckled harness shifted, throwing us sideways, and our weight dropped onto the remaining straps.

We spun crazily in the air, and Perry started weeping, loud, gasping sobs.

"No! *Please*, Chess—don't!" He squeezed me as he pleaded. "Don't, no . . ."

I stretched for the straps on his other side. I couldn't reach the buckles, so I jerked at his harness and said, "You should've left us alone, Perry."

"Please," he begged. "Please, don't."

I wedged my hand into a slot on his harness, flung myself in a wild circle, and grabbed Perry's other side. He screamed in fear and frustration, and I wrapped my arm around his neck and reached over his head to grab his tether.

The hinge of his shoulder buckle felt like ice under my fingers. If I popped that one, the rest would tear and he'd fall—but I'd keep my grip on his tether.

Perry bucked wildly, but I clung tight and said, "This is for Loretta."

"Please," he wept, going limp. "Please don't kill me."

For Loretta. I half loosened the buckle . . . and wondered what Hazel would say. She'd say, "Good riddance, serves him right." Swedish would say, "Drop him and let *them* sort him out." Loretta would stab him a few times before ditching him.

And Bea? She wouldn't blame me for dropping Perry—but she'd never understand how the same guy who patched her overalls and told her bedtime stories had killed someone. And she'd never look at me the same again.

"I'll help you!" Perry babbled in his high-pitched voice. "I'll help you against Kodoc. I promise. I swear on my mother's life! Just don't drop me!"

"I'm not going to drop you," I told him, and in my mind, Bea's green eyes shone with relief.

"Thank you!" Perry said, weeping even more. "Thank you. You won't regret it, I promise. . . ."

As Perry sniffled, I pulled myself higher on the tether until I was standing on his shoulders. My knees felt stronger, swooping through the air. My vision cleared. The other tetherkid, the skinny boy who'd smashed through the window, swung on his tether in front of us, toward a dark fleet in the night sky. Fifty torchships and gunships, a handful of big Rooftop warships, and Kodoc's personal flagship, the *Predator.*

I looked behind me, toward Port Oro. Patches of smoke swallowed the moonlight where roof-trooper attack ships had been shot down. The rest of them, with torn balloons and burning sails, were retreating through the sky toward me.

They were damaged but successful. Mission accomplished. They'd provided a distraction while Perry had snatched me.

The tether trembled in my grip in time with the throbbing of the airship engine far above. I turned back and watched the *Predator* draw closer, a sweeping warship with a steel-banded balloon. Cannons and portholes dotted the hull, and huge propellers gleamed in the starlight. Underneath her, a massive scaffolding supported a dozen tethers and winches: a salvage rig so big that a dozen tetherkids could dive at once.

As the *Predator* grew larger, my blood ran colder. Without my goggles, I felt the wind bring tears to my eyes, and I blinked at the airsoldiers crowding the *Predator*'s main deck, armed with swords and steam-bows. On the upper deck, a man in a fancy uniform watched me through a spyglass.

Lord Kodoc.

Even from this far away, his gaze raised goose bumps on my arms. The stealth ship swept me downward. The wind whipped, and finally the skinny tetherkid's boot scraped the *Predator*'s deck. A moment later, Perry collapsed in front of the steps to the upper deck.

I landed a few feet away. I stumbled, my legs unsteady, then peered through my hair at the Roof-trooper soldiers flanking me. Nowhere to run. Good thing I'd already given the cogs the map. Maybe Jada and Mochi could find the Compass.

Except they couldn't. Only a fog-eyed diver could find the Compass, and now Kodoc had kidnapped the only one. What would Port Oro do? What would the crew do? Well, at least Kodoc didn't have the map. No matter what happened, I could never tell him about the map.

I chewed the inside of my cheek—and my neck jerked backward. Pain flared between my shoulders, and a punch knocked me to my hands and knees.

"You're going to pay for that," Perry snarled at me in his high voice. "First I'll break your thumbs."

I blinked tears from my eyes. So much for "I'll help you against Kodoc, I promise. I swear on my mother's life!"

"Then I'll break your knees." Perry booted me in the ribs, and I fell onto my side. "And you know what I'll do after that?"

"Rub my feet?" I gasped, curling into a tight ball.

He raised his boot to stomp my head. "Break your face."

"Enough," Kodoc's silky voice said.

Perry's boot hovered over me. "He almost killed me, m'lord."

"If you disobey me," Kodoc told Perry, strolling down the steps toward me, "it won't be *almost.*"

Perry shifted uneasily. "Yes, m'lord."

"Tetherboy." Kodoc looked down at me. "This time there is no escape."

I wanted to say something sharp and unafraid, but it's hard to sound sharp and unafraid when you're curled in a ball on the floor. And even harder when you're feeling dull and terrified.

"Stand up," Kodoc said.

"Go fog yourself," I mumbled.

"Watch your mouth, cockroach," Perry said, kicking my neck.

Pain slashed from my skull to my shoulders. I crossed my arms over my head, trying to lose myself in a dark cocoon before the beating started. Muffled voices sounded. The deck rolled, the rigging snapped . . . and nobody hit me. Seconds crawled past inside my fearful bubble until eventually, I lifted my head.

I heard Kodoc politely asking, "I said 'enough,' did I not?"

"Y-yes, m'lord," Perry said in a small voice. "I'm sorry."

"And when I say 'enough,' what do you think I mean?"

"You m-mean you don't w-want no more, m'lord."

"Yet you still kicked him." Kodoc turned to his soldiers. "Escort the young man to the railing."

"I'm sorry!" Perry squawked. "I'm so sorry, m'lord!"

Peering through my hair, I watched two soldiers grab Perry's arms and drag him toward the rail at the edge of the deck.

"I won't do it again!" Perry's boot heels scraped across the floorboards. "Please, *please*, my lord!"

"You'll never disobey me again?"

"Not ever!" Perry's yellow hair fell around his desperate, teary face. "I promise! Never!"

The soldiers shoved Perry against the railing. He flailed his arms, but they pinned him there.

Kodoc rubbed his chin thoughtfully. "Shall I help you keep that promise?"

"Yes! Please, whatever you want! Please, I'm begging you, please—"

"Very well." Kodoc looked to his soldiers. "Help the lad."

Perry's eyes widened in terror—then the soldiers shoved him over the railing, and he fell from sight.

His scream hung in the air a long time.

"There," Kodoc said, turning to me. "Now he'll never disobey me again."

24

BLOOD TRICKLED DOWN *my cheek and pooled under my chin. Glimmers of lamplight reflected in the spreading puddle, and I watched them for what felt like a long time.*

Then Bea knelt beside me, pale and trembling. "Hazy? Hazy!" Her green eyes filled with horror, and she shouted, "Help! We need a doctor!"

She brushed the braids from my face, and footsteps scuffed closer. Legs blocked my vision, doctors bandaged my head, then silence fell. A coldness spread to my fingers and toes. My dizziness smeared into darkness, and I lost consciousness . . . until a hand clamped my shoulder and shook me awake.

"Hazel?" Swedish's voice said from far away. "Hazel!"

"Leave her alone," a doctor said. "She needs rest."

"I don't care," Swedish growled.

"She's hurt."

"She's the captain," Bea said, and Swedish shook me harder.

The dizziness faded. The world snapped into place, and a sledgehammer pounded behind my forehead. When I saw Swede's frantic face through my tears, I whispered, "Tell me."

"Kodoc snatched Chess," he said. "Three hours ago. He's on the Predator."

Right. Of course. I knew that already. Kodoc had Chess. The thought punched a hole in my heart, but I didn't have time to waste being stupid, so I forced myself to think. "Is the battle still going?"

"No," Swede told me. "The Rooftop ran off after they got Chess."

"What do the mutineers say?"

"That they can't do anything."

Loretta slouched beside my bed. "Stupid muties. They can attack."

"Now you sound like Vidious," Swedish told her.

"Captain Vidious wants to blitz Kodoc," Bea

told me, and I saw from her eyes that she'd been crying. "Except he knows he can't beat the armada."

Loretta grunted. "The muties have been waiting for days to kick Kodoc's bony butt."

"Holding him off at the Port is one thing," Bea told her. "But out there, in open skies? They'd get slaughtered."

My head throbbed in time with my heartbeat. "We're going to sneak onto the Predator."

"We can't get close enough," Swedish told me. "Kodoc will spot any ships coming at him above the Fog." He glowered toward the window. "Even at night."

"He's got torchships in a big circle," Bea explained, "shining lights in every direction, so nothing can slip past. And the sound of approaching engines is a giveaway."

Loretta frowned. "They can't hear other engines above their own ships."

"Engines all sound different," Bea told her.

"If you're you."

"I am me!"

Loretta glared. "I mean, other people don't talk to engines."

"Any gearslinger can hear the difference," Bea said. "Well, unless a ship's using glide-wings or something, and flying silent. But they'd still see it."

The flicker of an idea sparked in my mind. Torchships? No. Spotting ships above the Fog? Engine noise? No. I scanned the room as I thought. The wheeze of infirmary machinery mixed with the ticking of the skyscraper. The lanterns flickered against the rows of bottles and flasks. Six beds lined the wall. Mine. Chess's, now empty. And—

"Where's Mrs. E?" I asked.

"Down the hall," Bea told me. "The doctors say she doesn't need—"

"Above the Fog!" I said as the spark caught fire in my imagination. "Above the Fog."

Swedish grunted in satisfaction. "There we go."

"Where we go?" Loretta asked.

"Wherever Hazel says," he told her.

"She's got a plan," Bea explained.

"A bad plan," I told her. "Maybe the worst ever."

"Well, Kodoc grabbed Chess," Loretta said, scratching the burn scar on her arm. "We need a bad plan."

"The badder the better," Swedish told her.

I shook my head. That didn't make a lick of sense. We need a bad plan? I turned toward Chess to share my amusement—then a hole opened in my chest, a sudden pang of loss.

"Kodoc can see anyone coming above the Fog, right?" I asked.

"Right," Swedish said.

"So we're going to need . . ." I frowned at Bea. "A tether strong enough to hold an entire raft."

She chewed her lower lip. "Like . . . like that crane at the fishing pier?"

"Exactly. And glide-wings like the ones in the workshop, and an engine we can start from a hundred feet away by yanking on a cord."

"Like a—a pull start?"

"At least a hundred feet," I said, then turned to Swedish. "Find Captain Osho. We need his navigation tools."

"Why?" Loretta asked. "What're we doing?"

"We're flying blind," I told her. "And getting Chess."

Two of Kodoc's airsoldiers dragged me down a corridor into the belly of the *Predator*. A third soldier unlocked a metal door, which opened with a squeal like a rusty cat. A rough hand shoved me, and I stumbled into the darkness of what felt like a cell.

Breathing sounded in the gloom as the door locked behind me.

"Perry got off easy, boy," a soldier called from outside. "Do what you're told, or you're next."

I heard sniffling, so I turned and blinked into the darkness. A few shapes huddled against one wall, and I thought I saw the gleam of watchful eyes.

"Who—" My voice cracked. "Who's there?"

"Nobody," a tiny whisper said.

"Just us," an even littler voice added.

A handful of skinny kids huddled together in the corner. Seven or eight years old. Definitely not tetherkids-in-training. Mrs. E once told me that tetherkids looked like feral cats after they'd caught the scent of a dog, but these kids looked like animals who lived in a cage.

I sat against the opposite wall and rubbed my bruises. Moving slowly, trying to calm my fears and give the kids a chance to look me over. The second part was easier than the first. Locked in a cell on the *Predator*, still hearing the echo of Perry's scream, didn't really calm my fears. And that was before I started to think about what Kodoc wanted from me. And what he'd do to get it.

At least my fingers trembled only a little as I tightened my bootlaces. I frowned at the floor. What would Hazel do? I tried to imagine what she'd tell me, but all I heard was the frightened whispers of the kids across the cell.

"I'm Chess," I told them.

The kids fell silent. With my eyes adjusted to the dark, I saw them more clearly. Skinny and flinch eyed, wearing rags and hairnets, with dark smudges on their faces.

Except those weren't smudges. They were indentations

from breathing masks.

"You work in a refinery," I said. A factory where stinking machines refined the Fog into foggium. The bosses bought kids from the junkyard, then made them wear masks when they worked so they'd survive the Fog for longer.

A kid with missing teeth—I couldn't tell if it was a boy or a girl—nodded.

"I'm a tetherboy," I said. "With a salvage crew."

The kid nodded again, and they all seemed to relax a little. They knew a tetherboy wasn't a threat.

"Kodoc snatched me," I told them.

"He bought us," the kid said. "From the 'finery."

"Why?"

The first kid rubbed his—her?—sniffling nose with a grimy hand. "Don't know. Soldiers took us and locked us in here is all."

"They didn't tell us a story or nothing," another kid scoffed.

"Is that right?" I rubbed my sore arm. "Do you want to hear one? A story, I mean."

The kid with missing teeth stared at me with hope and wariness. Something about the expression reminded me of Bea, so maybe she was a girl. And maybe I should wait to tell them a story until they got used to me.

"What's your name?" I asked.

"Quancita," she said.

"That's a nice name," I said, then shut up, afraid of pushing her.

The silence gave me time to think. Which was bad. If Kodoc got the Compass, he'd wipe out anyone who disobeyed him. Did he know I'd found the map? Was he going to force me to draw a copy? Or did he just plan to dangle me in the Fog until I stumbled across the Compass?

I needed to get away. I needed to stop Kodoc from burying Port Oro. From killing the mutineers, the fisherfolk, that guy who'd given us a cucumber. Families, children, old people, babies . . . Mrs. E and the crew.

When the refinery kids started chatting about home, I stretched out on the floor. The girl named Sally promised that she'd never make trouble again if they lived through this. The boy called Radiz pretended to think that they'd been sold to Kodoc for a job on his warship, while Perla kept talking about a "picnic," when they'd snuck a few handfuls of blueberries.

My eyes felt hot and swollen. Everything they said made me want to cry. I huddled in my jacket, and the weight of exhaustion pressed on me, but I was too scared to sleep.

After Perry's scream had faded, I'd snapped. I'd thrown myself at Kodoc, shouting and swearing. I didn't know why. I'd hated Perry, and I'd almost ditched him myself. A soldier had slammed me to the ground before

I got anywhere near Kodoc, though, and put her boot on my cheek.

"Where d'you want him, m'lord?" the soldier had asked.

"In the cell. We're in no rush. The only way my victory could be sweeter would be if the mutineers try to rescue him." Kodoc raised his voice. "We are prepared for an attack, Lieutenant?"

"More than prepared, my lord," a man's voice had called. "We are eager."

"Take him away," Kodoc had said, and that's when the two soldiers had dragged me to the bowels of the ship.

Giving up on sleep, I leaned against the cell wall and rummaged through my pockets. I found a chunk of smoked fish in my belt pouch and told Quancita that it made my tongue swell. She eyed me like she knew I was lying, but Perla sniffled that she was hungry, so Quancita snatched the fish from my palm and handed it around.

As they ate, she said, "What kind of story?"

It took me a second to realize what she was asking, then I said, "From the time before the Fog."

"There's always been Fog," Sally said. "Forever and ever."

"You know about before the Fog?" Quancita asked me.

"A little." I stifled a yawn. "I know that a long time ago, there was a tribe called the Amazons. They were fierce lady warriors who fought battles and sold books."

"Books?" Sally said. "Weird."

"Yeah, I'm not sure what the—" I stopped, and laughed at the thought of Loretta.

"What?" Quancita asked.

"I've got this friend," I explained. "A fierce girl warrior who's got a thing about books."

I told them about Wonder Woman, an Amazon princess with a stealth jet and a sparkly swimsuit. I knew she was just a story, like Batman and Fireman, but I told them the whole tale anyway: that she delivered books in her stealth jet, eating Wonder Bread and hanging with Alice in Wonderland.

When I finished, Radiz told a story about a superhero called Supreme Curt until Sally's snore interrupted him. We spoke in whispers for a while. Then the gentle sway of the floor and the far-off thrum of the engine rocked Radiz to sleep.

I snuggled under my jacket and smiled at how quickly little kids fell asl—

25

THE CLANG OF metal woke me. Stifling a yawn, I listened to footsteps in the hallway outside the cell. Soldiers on patrol, maybe. My back ached, and my arm itched. I wanted to scratch, but Quancita was sleeping with her head on my shoulder. Her hair smelled of burning plastic, the perfume of a refinery.

I drowsed there as memories drifted across my mind: escaping the Rooftop, exploring the Port, diving into the Station. My thoughts snagged on that moment in the Fog when everything seemed to click. *A lightning bolt. A thunderclap.*

It still didn't make any sense, so I thought about our plans to start a new life on the Port instead. I thought about finding the map, too, but my thoughts always ended in the same place: with me locked in a cell on Kodoc's warship.

I eased Quancita onto the floor, then used the latrine in the corner—enough said about that—and poked around the cell, looking for a weak spot.

"C'mon," I whispered to a bolted panel in the wall. "Pretend I'm Bea and tell me how to get out of here!"

The panel didn't say anything. Neither did the bars in the door or the rivets on the ceiling.

After the refinery kids woke, a soldier with pigtails slammed the door open. She stomped into the cell and dropped a bucket of mashed turnips and a jug of water on the floor.

"Eat up," the pigtailed sailor said. "This could be your last meal."

"What—" I gulped. "What does Kodoc want with—"

Pigtails backhanded me against the wall. My vision blurred, and my teeth cut the inside of my cheek.

"*Lord* Kodoc," Pigtails told me.

I wiped my mouth and tried to act like I wasn't scared. "What does *Lord* Kodoc want with a bunch of refinery kids?"

"You'll find out," she said, and left.

We ate the turnips and drank the water, and then the kids taught me a game called A Thousand Black White Cards, where you made up a new rule every turn. The first rule was: You can't give yourself points. That was Quancita.

The second rule was: You get five points if you decide not to make a rule that turn. That was Radiz. The third rule was: You have to call me Caterpillar Pants or you lose half your points. That was Perla. The fourth rule was: Every other turn, you can steal one point from the person who looks the most like your favorite animal. That was Sally.

The fifth rule was: I don't get it. That was me.

Quancita explained again, and I pretended I understood. We played the game until there were a hundred rules, none of which made any sense. Apparently the point wasn't to win; the point was to keep the game going. After an hour the score was:

Quancita—34

Radiz—51

Sally—froglegs

Perla—9 and 21

Me—*hoo-hoo-hooo*

"*Hoo-hoo-hooo* isn't too bad for your first time," Quancita told me, then shrank into the corner when Pigtails and another soldier slammed inside.

"You!" Pigtails snarled at me. "Come with us."

She dragged me upstairs to a hallway with evening light streaming through porthole windows—apparently I'd spent an entire day in that cell. She shoved me into a clammy room with vats of water and told me to wash up. I splashed with one hand while I checked the floor and walls for loose boards.

No luck.

Pigtails yelled for me to hurry, so I undressed and climbed into a vat and groped for the drain at my feet. It was too small to slip through. I scrubbed with soap powder that smelled like tar, then climbed out and opened a vent in the wall that blew hot engine air to dry me.

After I dressed, the soldiers marched me upstairs and into the brisk air under the evening sky. I glanced at the edge of the deck, my mind scrambling for a way to escape, but Pigtails shoved me toward an ornate door that opened into a small, fancy dining room.

Hooded lamps glimmered in the corners. A plush carpet covered the floor, squares of framed art called "giftwrap" lined the walls, and mesh chairs surrounded a table heaped with food.

Kodoc twirled a chopstick at the head of the table. His lips narrowed when he watched me stumble inside, and his monocle flashed.

Sweat sprang to the back of my neck.

"Sit him down," Kodoc told the soldiers. "There."

Pigtails shoved me into a chair beside Kodoc.

"Now leave us," he ordered.

The door closed behind them. I didn't move, studying the roasted pigeon legs on the table, heaped beside steamed buns and bowls of drippings and okra and spiced churros. And a plate of what I was pretty sure were oranges. They were orange anyway.

I'd never seen so much extravagant food in one place, not even in the Assembler skyscraper.

"Eat," Kodoc told me.

"Not hungry," I muttered.

"Are you sure," he asked politely, "that you want me to repeat myself?"

My hand shook a little as I grabbed a roasted pigeon leg. I ducked my head and nibbled at the meat. Tender and hot, with some kind of tangy crust. I took a bigger bite, and juice ran down my chin.

"You like the duck?" Kodoc asked when I finished. "Have another."

Duck? Huh. I grabbed another drumstick, then speared a steamed bun with a long fork-thing, and wondered if I was fast enough to get across the table and spear *Kodoc* with the fork-thing—

"What is the threat?" Kodoc asked.

I almost choked. Could he read my mind?

"Don't be afraid," he said with a terrifying calm. "I made you. You're my creation, my tool. A man does not break his own tool . . . unless he must. Now tell me—what is the greatest threat we face? The greatest threat to our survival?

Getting thrown overboard by loco Rooftop lords, I thought.

"The Fog," he told me. "Wouldn't you agree?"

"Y-yeah," I stammered. "Yes."

"If the Fog rises, we're finished. Not just the Rooftop, not just Port Oro. The entire human race, dead forever."

He paused, waiting for me to say something, but I didn't know what he wanted to hear.

A chill frosted his eyes. "Do you understand what I'm telling you, boy? Raise your head. I've seen your eye already. I *gave* you that eye. Can you hear the words I am saying? Do they mean anything to you?"

"Yes," I said.

"What happens if the Fog starts to rise? Next week, next month, next year. What happens?"

"We—we're finished." I tried to remember the words he'd used. "The entire human race is dead forever."

"And you think *I'm* the villain?"

I hunched my shoulders and glanced at Kodoc's neck. A sharp fork in my hand and desperation in my heart. Yeah, he was the villain, all right. I'd never been a fighter, but I was fast. Maybe fast enough to get over the table and stab him in the throat.

"You disappoint me." Kodoc lifted a napkin beside his plate to reveal a steam-bow. "Put the carving fork down."

Heat flared in my face, and I set the fork aside.

"I'm the only thing standing between the Fog and the moldering remains of humanity," he told me. "I'm the only thing standing between the Fog and all the snot-nosed children, all the huddled families, all your friends and family."

"You—" My voice cracked. "You killed my mother."

"I've killed more than your mother, boy. I *will* save the human race, whatever the cost. Ask me what the price is."

"Wh-what's the price?"

"Turning myself into a monster."

I bowed my head, my pulse pounding in my ears. Why was he telling me this? What was he saying? What did he want from me?

"You think I don't know what I am?" he asked in his slithery voice. "Of course I know. Only a monster can beat the Fog. Only a monster is willing to do *anything*. Kill your mother, kill your crew. I'll ditch the entire junkyard and bomb Port Oro into ashes. And for what?"

I watched grease thicken around the duck bones on my plate.

"To activate the Compass," he said, "which is our only defense against the Fog, our only hope. Do you imagine there is anything I will not do?"

"No," I said. "But—"

"But what?"

I kept my eyes on my plate. But Kodoc wanted to do more than just beat the Fog. I knew that. I knew *him*. Sure, the Fog was the greatest threat to the human race, but he wasn't about to lower the white and then disappear. He wasn't going to disband his army and stop ruling people. No, he had some other plan.

When I didn't answer, Kodoc touched his steam-bow.

196

"I will control the Compass, boy, and I will lower the Fog. But first I need the map you found."

Tendrils of fear squeezed my heart. "I—I don't know—"

Without warning, the *Predator* spun and tilted. The dining room jerked. The lanterns flickered, and the drippings in the bowl sloshed. An orange rolled from the plate and plopped to the ground.

Kodoc grabbed the table, glared toward the door . . . and the warship righted herself. The lanterns glowed steadily, and the orange stopped rolling in the middle of the carpet.

"You were saying?" Kodoc asked, his cold gaze shifting toward me.

"I d-don't know what you mean," I said. "I didn't find any m-map."

"Don't lie to me."

"No, really, I—"

Kodoc lifted the steam-bow and pointed it toward me. Panic stopped my heart. He fired and the *click-hiss* whispered death in my ear, but the steam-bow's dart flashed inches past my neck and embedded into a corkboard on the door.

Three bells dangled from the board, and they jingled at the impact. A moment later, the door opened. "My lord?" the soldier with pigtails asked.

"What happened, a moment ago? The *Predator* does not run so rough."

"The engineers think it's a snag in an intake valve, m'lord."

"That is not acceptable." He tapped his finger on the steam-bow. "Everything is prepared for the boy?"

Pigtails bowed her head. "Yes, my lord."

"Take him."

Kodoc dabbed at his mouth with a napkin, then sauntered outside. Pigtails dragged me along, across the deck toward the stern. A squad of soldiers drilling with grappling hooks sneered at me, and three gearslingers rushed past, muttering about "bird strike."

Pigtails brought me to a small quarterdeck where a few soldiers stood over four huddled kids.

"Quancita," I said.

Her teary gaze shifted toward me, then she looked away. Toward the Fog. *No.* Toward a diving plank ten feet from her and the other refinery kids.

"You dove into the Station," Kodoc told me, strolling toward the plank. "You found the map. Yes, I know everything. The mutineers aren't the only ones with spies."

I tried to answer, but horror choked me. He was going to make the refinery kids walk the plank. He was going to drop them into the Fog.

"One by one," he told me, seeing the realization on my face. "Until you draw me the map."

"You can't—" I struggled to get away from Pigtails, but she just clamped my arm harder. "They're just kids."

"Not anymore," Kodoc said. "Now they're kids you care about. Now they're *leverage.*"

At his nod, one of the soldiers shoved Rizal onto the plank, then prodded him forward with the tip of a sword. Rizal's legs trembled, and a keening came from his throat. The soldier jabbed Rizal's back, and he fell to his knees and clung to the plank.

A sudden grinding crackled above the rush of blood in my ears. The aft side of the *Predator* dipped, and Rizal shrieked and clung tighter. The soldiers grunted, and I stumbled. Pigtails grabbed my jacket, and Kodoc snatched at a railing for support, then crossed the tilted quarterdeck.

He put his mouth to a voicepipe. "Engineering! Report!"

A tinny reply came: "It's not an intake valve, m'lord. We're . . . tracking the malfunction down."

"Track faster," Kodoc snapped.

"Yes, m'lord."

Kodoc turned from the voicepipe and told me, "You're lucky that your little friend didn't fall already."

The grinding noise stopped, and the *Predator* straightened just as jerkily as it had dipped.

"Are you going to stand there," Kodoc asked me, "and watch him die?"

"No," I whispered.

"How about the next one? The girl called Sally?"

Nausea rose from my stomach to my throat. "No," I repeated.

None of the kids looked at me, none of them pleaded or begged. They were slumkids: pleading and begging had never helped them before.

"Well?! Will you draw me the map?" Kodoc grabbed my hair in his fist. "Or shall I start dropping—"

"I'll draw it," I told him. "I'll draw the map."

26

KODOC STARED AT my freak-eye for a long, trembling moment—then released my hair.

"Bring him," he snapped, and stalked across the deck.

The soldier with pigtails twisted my arm behind my back and pushed me along. Airsoldiers climbed ladders and adjusted valves, trying to track down the ship's malfunction. I stumbled past a stairwell leading into the depths of the *Predator*, toward a huge copper barrel called a "capstan."

Kodoc nodded to a clear patch of deck behind the capstan. "Put him there."

"Yessir," Pigtails said, and shoved me forward.

"My lord!" a roof-trooper called from the rigging. "The third aft rudder is . . . twitching."

"Twitching?" Kodoc snarled. "My flagship does not 'twitch.'"

"The drive system's acting up. Never seen anything like it."

"Put him to work," Kodoc said. He tossed a canvas pack to the soldier with pigtails, then strode away.

Pigtails pointed to the floor and told me, "Sit."

I sat, and she rummaged in the pack for a sheet of paper called "housewrap" and a waxy red pencil called a "crayon," then told me to get drawing. I spread the house-wrap on the deck. How much did Kodoc know about the world below the Fog? Would he recognize the roads and mountains and parks and city?

Probably. Which meant I needed to keep this map *almost* correct. After thinking for a minute, I drew a wavy line. I made a river, then sketched in a few parks, more or less in the right places. Next I drew a stick figure with a straw hat—but on the wrong side of the intersection.

I spun the paper around, started outlining the city, and the warship jerked again. The engine backfired with three loud *POP*s. Airsoldiers shouted, and the smell of melting bronze filled the air.

"Hoy!" Pigtails kicked my leg. "Keep drawing."

I shaded in the city, then started on the Compass. Except I put it far to the north of the city. Nowhere near the real Compass. The ship jerked a few more times, and the buzz of activity grew angrier each time, like a wasp's nest. I ignored the shouting and drew the lines of train tracks or pod-car paths—until Pigtails lifted me by the scruff of my neck.

I tried to break free, but she just shook me as Kodoc stepped closer and eyed the drawing on the ground.

"That's a tidy map, boy," he said.

Pigtails released me. "Say thanks."

"Thanks," I muttered.

"How closely does it match the map in the Station?"

I hunched my shoulders. "Pretty close."

"You're sure?"

"Yeah—yes, sir."

"Any changes you want to make?"

"No, I—" I shook my head. "It's good."

Kodoc crouched beside the map and traced one of the tracks with a fingertip. "If you're lying to me, I will find out. Sooner or later. You know I will. Then I'll draw a line right down the center of the junkyard, and I'll ditch one half of that festering slum. Do you know how many people will die?"

My stomach soured. He was right. He'd find out eventually. Of course he'd find out.

"Thousands," he said, answering his own question. "If you're lying, there will be a reckoning, Chess. The screams of the falling will ring out across the Fog."

My mouth opened, but no words came. At least— at least he was doing this in a crazed attempt to save humanity, right? That's what I told myself. Sure, he was a monster, but in the end, he'd lower the Fog, right? Right?

"Now, then," he purred. "Are you *certain* you don't want to make any changes?"

"Maybe a . . . a few. I—I'm trying to remember."

"No more games," he told me, and walked away.

My hand trembled as I started fixing the map. I'd show Lord Kodoc how to find the Compass. I'd give him the tool he needed to control the Fog's nanites. Then he'd lower the Fog—or bury Port Oro and rule us forever.

As I drew the map, the crayon left red marks on my fingers like blood.

Pigtails snorted. "Did you really think you could outsmart Lord Kodoc, slumrat?"

"No," I muttered.

"Well, you can't," she said. "No stupid kid can—"

SSSSHHRR! Dozens of vents slid open across the ship, and jets of superheated foggium hissed out. A soldier screamed, and Pigtails spun, turning away from me.

I didn't have a plan, I didn't have a clue, but the instant she looked away, I *moved*. I grabbed the map and vaulted onto the flat top of the capstan. Pigtails shouted behind me, and her hand gripped my boot. I kicked backward, clipped her arm, and heaved myself across the worn copper lid.

I slammed to the deck and rolled away, hearing Pigtails clambering after me. She screamed for help, and I rose into a crouch and launched myself toward the railing. I was beyond thought, beyond reason. I was going to hurl myself overboard and . . . see what happened.

But two airsoldiers stepped in front of me, blocking my path.

"Hey!" the bald one barked.

"Get him!" Pigtails screamed.

The bald guy grabbed my jacket, but I tore free in a desperate twirl. As I turned, Pigtails punched at my face. Instead of dodging, I tried a trick Loretta had showed me: I bowed. Pigtails's fist hit the dome of my skull, and she gasped at the pain.

My head rang like a bronze bowl, but I slipped past her—and a bearded soldier shoved me into a wall. The blow knocked the wind out of me, and the map was flung from my outstretched hand.

It floated back and forth, drifting to the deck. If I'd been in the Fog, I could've snatched the map from the air and landed twenty feet away. But I wasn't in the Fog.

I grabbed for map—too slowly. A dart fired by a steam-bow *thunk*ed into a coil of rope beside me. I jerked backward and rushed at the bald guy, then faked left and spun right. The only bootball move I knew. I scraped past him—but he caught my ankle with his foot, and I lost my balance.

I flailed and fell to the floor. Pigtails stomped the deck an inch from my face, and I rolled across the deck . . . right into a stairwell.

The first few steps slammed me; then I grabbed the railing and half slid, half tumbled the rest of the way down. I might've groaned, but I also kept moving. Boots thundered behind me, and I staggered through a brass door into a red-tinted room where three massive, gleaming, ticking machines lined either side of a narrow aisle.

Gears spun and pistons pumped and the heat hit me like a fist. The air stank of exhaust. I sprinted down the aisle, and a wall rose past the last machines.

A dead end. No way out.

The door slammed open behind me, and I spun to see Pigtails stepping into the engine room. The other roof-troopers crowded into the hallway behind her. She stalked closer, shaking the hand that she'd smacked on my skull.

"Kodoc wants you alive," she growled. "But he don't care if you're bleeding."

I backed away. Out of ideas, out of luck, out of time. Out of room.

Pigtails grabbed my throat. "I'm going stomp you into gravy."

"Wait!" I gasped.

She shoved me against the wall with her left hand and punched me in the stomach with her right. Pain spread through my gut, and she tightened her grip on my neck and cut off my breath. My lungs started to burn.

27

After I buttoned my jacket, I slumped against the infirmary doorframe with my head in my hands. Pain throbbed in my temples. Blinking back tears, I told myself that the throbs of pain were a drumbeat, urging me onward. Get Chess, get Chess, get Chess.

"Bea," I said between gritted teeth, "this all comes down to you."

"Y-yes, Cap'n," she said.

"Run to the gearslinger garage. Start on the crane and pull-start engine. You've got one day to rig a ship like nothing anyone's ever seen."

"What about us?" Swede asked as Bea scampered off.

"We're getting a scout ship," I said. "The fastest in the mutineer fleet."

"How?"

"Your first job," Loretta told him, "is keeping Hazy on her feet."

She'd never called me Hazy before—nobody did but Bea—and at any other time, she would've been embarrassed. But at any other time, Chess would've teased her. Right now, none of that mattered.

When Swede stepped beside me, I wrapped an arm around his shoulders. "We need the cogs," I said.

Four flights up, Assemblers packed the roof, peering nervously into the distance. Swedish shoved through the crowd like an aggravated bear, and I leaned more weight on him as we climbed the steps onto the heliograph platform.

The cogs flanked the heliograph—a polished bronze disk that caught the rays of the sun, then flashed codes to a distant target. The heliograph operator waited in her chair, but she wasn't sending any messages. She was looking through a telescope, just like the cogs.

"Bonita." Cog Isandra lowered her spyglass when she noticed me. "I'm so sorry about Chess."

"There's nothing to be sorry for," I told her.

"We're getting him back. I need a scout ship, the fastest you've got."

Cog Isander rubbed his glassy white eye. "We don't have one."

"All we have left is floating bathtubs," Isandra said. "The mutineers are using everything else."

Loretta gasped. "They're still there!" She pointed toward the horizon. "Kodoc's ships are still in sight."

"After he grabbed Chess," Isander said, "Kodoc started retreating from the Port . . . very slowly."

"He's taunting us," Isandra explained, her gray dreadlocks bobbing. "He's trying to draw the mutineers into a battle they can't win."

I scanned the sky with my spyglass. Three dozen mutineer ships trailed the armada, keeping their distance. Still outnumbered, still outgunned. Ignoring the conversation around me, I focused on Captain Nisha's Anvil Rose and then on Vidious's Night Tide. Airsailors climbed through the Tide's rigging, and the aft propellers flashed.

"Vidious is going to attack," I said.

"What?" Isandra lifted her telescope to her blue eye. "That's suicide."

"It's exactly what Kodoc wants!" Isander said. "None of them will survive."

"Maybe that's the point," I muttered, too softly for anyone to hear.

Vidious knew he couldn't win, so he must've been hoping to sink the Predator before he got shot down—with Chess and Kodoc still aboard. Without Chess and Kodoc, the Port was safe. Except there was no way he could take down the Predator with an entire armada around her. And there was no way I was going to let him sink Chess.

"Send a message," I told the heliograph operator.

"What? Pardon? Excuse me?"

"Do as the girl says!" Isander snapped, the first time I'd ever heard him lose his patience.

"Tell him we have a plan," I said.

The heliograph disk tilted and creaked, and a minute later, a reply flashed from the Night Tide: The Subassembly knows nothing about combat.

"Kodoc wants you to attack," Isandra said. "Tell him that."

We don't have time for fogheads, Vidious replied.

"Tell him it's Hazel," Swedish said. "Tell him Hazel has a plan."

The heliograph tilted and flashed once more. Nothing happened for what felt like a long time. Then the Night Tide spun in the sky, swooping *back toward the skyscraper, with Nisha following close behind.*

"Why do they care what some girl thinks?" the heliograph operator asked.

"'Cause they're not stupid," Loretta told her.

The minute Nisha and Vidious landed on the skyscraper roof, I asked them, "What's the fastest scout ship on Port Oro?"

"The Cloudfall," *Vidious told me.*

"Why do you need it?" Nisha asked.

"You know why," Vidious told his sister. "To rescue her tetherboy. The question is, how?"

"Get me the ship," I said, "and I'll tell you. Bea's already in the garage, putting the gear together."

Vidious told his lieutenant to commandeer the Cloudfall, *then took my arm and led me toward the elevator. "What happened to your face?" he asked.*

"Look who's talking," I said, glancing at the scar on his cheek.

Vidious showed me his lopsided smile. "I cut myself shaving."

"What were you shaving with?" Loretta asked. "A harpoon?"

"Perry whacked Hazel when he snatched Chess," Swedish told him.

Vidious's smile died, and his eyes turned cruel.

"Perry," he said, his voice as soft as a noose. "What does he look like?"

As we crowded into the elevator, I felt something I'd never expected: pity for Perry.

"He doesn't matter," I told Vidious, my heart beating fast.

The gears squeaked, the elevator basket swayed, and then Captain Nisha said, "Tell us your plan, Hazel. What's the scout ship for?"

I wiped a few braids off my face. "We can't approach the Predator above the Fog. So we only have one choice."

"We can't fly inside the Fog," she said.

"Right," I told her, "but we can glide."

"Turn the Cloudfall into a glider . . . ," Vidious muttered.

"Visibility is zero in the Fog," Nisha said. "It's impossible to navigate."

I shrugged. "Captain Osho's tools will help."

"You'd need a pilot who's good enough to fly blindfolded."

"That's the easy part," Loretta told her, putting a hand on Swede's arm.

"What about fogsickness?" Nisha asked.

"The Assemblers cured Mrs. E," Swedish told her, flushing at Loretta's touch. "They'll cure us, too."

"She's in a wheeled chair."

"She spent an entire night in the Fog," I said. "We'll glide for an hour or two at the most."

When we reached the garage, we found Bea slicing the frame of the glide-wing as other gearslingers assembled a "crane-and-sling" to attach to the top of the Cloudfall, along with a disposable, one-shot engine with a long pull cord.

"You're not gliding for an hour or two," Vidious told me.

"Depends how far Kodoc's torchships can see," I said.

"We're *gliding for an hour or two*." He tucked a braid behind my ear, his touch softer than I could've imagined. "My sister and I and a hand-picked crew. This is a daring, brilliant, reckless plan. If you go—"

"You'd die," Nisha cut in. "But we've got a chance . . . a small chance."

"No," I said.

"We're not asking," Vidious said. "This is how it's going to be."

So I started screaming at them. I cursed and raged. I threw a gearbox at Vidious, and even managed to cry a little. Still, Chess would've known that I was faking. I needed to make a scene so they wouldn't suspect what I'd already planned. I was *going to steal the glider.*

The gearslingers worked through the night, and Swedish and I spent the next morning practicing tapping signals until Bea finished the Cloudfall.

It looked like a chickadee with an eagle's wings. A chickadee wearing a backpack full of cables and tubes: the "skyhook" crane. Two fans squatted beside the engine, and straps and loops for the crew were riveted to the frame, with a saddle in front for the pilot.

"She's a little goofy," Bea said. "But she's raring to go."

"What will you call her?" Cog Isander asked.

"The Peanut*!" Bea announced.*

"Or," Isandra said, "we can still call her the Cloudfall.*"*

Bea wrinkled her nose. "I guess."

"Captains Nisha and Vidious are on the way," Cog Isandra announced.

For the fifth time that day, I glanced aside to catch Chess's eye—looking for support, for strength, for feedback—and for the fifth time, loneliness chimed in my chest.

"We'll greet them on the roof," Isander said, "and give them a proper send-off."

Once they'd left, the gearslingers trickled from the garage. When we were alone, Loretta jammed the doors with wrenches. We opened the flight panels on the wall, then Swedish widened them with an ax, chopping a hole big enough for the Cloudfall.

Shouts of alarm sounded in the distance. Fists pounded the locked door of the workshop. I swung into place behind Swedish, and Loretta strapped herself to the hull.

Then the engine roared to life, and Bea called, "On your mark, Cap'n!"

"Hit the sky," I said. "Chess is waiting."

Swedish jerked a lever, and we launched from the skyscraper.

Captain's Log: Supplemental

I'm scrawling this on the Cloudfall minutes before we dive down to glide in the Fog. I'm light-headed with fear. Still, the ship is strong, and Swedish responds to my taps with such speed that I almost feel like I'm the pilot.

I've also learned that Loretta sings when she gets nervous enough. She's been belting out songs for twenty minutes now. We are going to fly in the Fog.

I'm afraid we're trying the impossible. I've fixed the location and speed of the Predator, which is still barely visible through my spyglass. Now I have to *approach her from within the Fog, resurfacing at exactly the right moment to intercept her from beneath. Without being spotted. Without crashing. Without missing. There is no room for error.*

I don't know if I can do this.

28

IN THE ENGINE room of the *Predator*, the soldier with pigtails squeezed my throat. My breath came in pained gasps. Dots of light swam in my vision.

Her fist cocked to punch me again when a voice said, "Hey, roof rat."

She glanced aside, and through my tear-blurred eyes, I caught a glimpse of Swedish. He sprang forward and head butted Pigtails in the face. Hard. Skull against bone. A nasty *crack* sounded. It was ugly; it was bloody. It was the best thing I'd ever seen.

Pigtails dropped like a sack of rust, and I gulped air. "S-Swedish?"

"I got you," he said, and wrapped his arm around me, keeping me on my feet.

Kind of hugging me, too—and I almost burst into tears. Instead, I caught motion near the door and gasped, "L-look out. . . ."

The bald roof-trooper stalked into the room, aiming his steam-bow at Swedish. "Drop the kid," he growled. "Hands by your side or I'll put a dart in you."

"Sure thing," Swedish told him, shoving me aside.

With a growl like an angry bobcat, Loretta sprang from above, landing on the bald soldier's neck. She brought him to the ground on the other side of the aisle, and his boots drummed against the floor.

The bearded soldier burst inside, pulled a hatchet, and sidled toward Swedish.

"*Yaee!*" Loretta howled.

As the soldier spun at the noise, Swedish took two loping steps and body-slammed him into a wooden post.

I stumbled behind the last machine, caught myself on a lever box—and saw Bea sitting cross-legged at a tangle of cables, snipping and splicing, and apologizing under her breath.

My heart grew seventeen sizes, and my eyes swam with tears.

Then I heard Hazel's voice. "Chess."

My blurry gaze shifted. Her braids fell around her face, and a bandage slanted across her forehead. For a moment, neither of us spoke. For the first time since Perry had grabbed me, I knew that everything would be okay.

I wanted to tell her that. I wanted to tell her a thousand things. I wanted to fall into her arms and cry.

Instead, I said, "Kodoc was going to make them walk the plank."

"What?" Hazel's brow knit in confusion. "Who?"

"Refinery kids. So I drew him the map."

Her lips narrowed. She stepped closer, her eyes glinting. She looked angry—until she gave me a fierce hug. Her skin smelled like home.

"Soldiers!" Loretta said, trotting around the machine.

Bea squealed when she noticed me. "Chess!"

"A whole squad," Swedish said from behind Loretta.

"Bea first, then Chess." Hazel pushed me toward a hole in the wall where they'd removed a grate. "Now! Go!"

Bea squirmed through the opening, and I followed her into a square tunnel. "What is this?" I asked.

"Engineering crawl space," Bea whispered over her shoulder.

"Whoa." I'd never heard of anything like that. "Big ship."

"Which way now?" Bea asked.

I frowned at her backside. "How would I know?"

"I'm not talking to *you*," she scoffed, crawling deeper into the ship.

Oh. Of course. She was talking to the *Predator*.

"Not the bays." She tapped the ground with a mallet from her tool belt and listened to the *thook*s. "What? No, we want to head down, under the hull. . . . Yes, of course! To your diving platforms."

A fist jabbed my butt, and Loretta's voice said, "Keep moving!"

"Bea's arguing with the floor."

A roof-trooper bellowed, "They're in the walls!"

"Faster, Bea," Hazel said, her voice tight.

"This way!" Bea said, and scurried around a corner.

My hands and knees scuffed on the rough wood floor. Gears the size of camel wagons crowded the crawl space, narrowing the passage. Swedish grumbled that he couldn't get through, but he somehow managed, and we squeezed down a slanted passage. Waves of heat wafted around us, and a *rattle-creak* sounded, along with the urgent murmur of soldiers' voices.

"Gearslingers," Hazel said, low and controlled.

"Trying to fix the ship," Swedish said.

The *rattle-creak* sounded again. "Those are wheels," Hazel said. "They're on carts. Coming fast."

Bea opened a hatch on the floor and dropped into a narrow room full of gauges. At the far end of the room, she tugged at a porthole with a window of woven wires.

"Locked," she said, rummaging in her tool belt.

Rattle-creak. "They're still coming . . . ," Hazel said.

"Good." Loretta cracked her neck. "Let 'em come."

"Close the hatch," Hazel snapped at her.

"Or that," Loretta said with a sigh.

The voices sounded louder, angrier, rougher. The *rattle-creak-creak-creak* scraped closer, then paused directly above us. "—find those crudknuckles and shred them into fetti."

Not gearslingers. Airsoldiers.

"Unlocked!" Bea whispered, and pulled the porthole open.

She squirmed through, and the rest of us jostled behind her. Swedish closed the porthole an instant before a skinny roof-trooper fell from the ceiling hatch—and spotted us beyond the woven wire.

"Here!" he bellowed, and Swedish slammed the lock closed.

With the airsoldiers pounding behind us, we dashed through a hallway crisscrossed with pipes. My mind whirled with questions, but I kept my mouth shut and my feet moving until Bea removed a panel that opened into a vertical shaft.

"C'mon, down the ladder!" She squeezed through, and her voice sounded from the gloom. "We're almost there!"

"What ladder?" Loretta scowled at the opening. "There's no ladder. I don't see a ladder."

"The same one we climbed up," Hazel said, nudging her forward.

"That's not a ladder," Loretta grumbled, putting one leg into the hole. "It's a death trap."

"Wait," I said. "You climbed *up*? Up from where?"

"The Fog," Swede told me.

"No, you— What?" I turned to Hazel. "What did you *do*?"

"You'll see," she said with a hint of a smile. "After you get your tetherbutt in gear."

Shouts and hammering echoed around us. Hazel nudged me at the opening, and I groped inside, then clambered into the shaft. The "rungs" of the ladder were two inches long and studded with rubber grommets. Bea's headlamp glowed feebly below me. My fingers cramped as I climbed down, and I followed the sound of Loretta's cursing.

"You flew in the Fog?!" I asked, my voice hollow. "You can't—engines don't work in the Fog."

"We glid!" Bea exclaimed from the darkness below me.

"Glided," Hazel called out from above me.

"That's what I just said," Bea told her.

"We didn't use an engine," Hazel said. "We glided to the scaffolding under the *Predator*."

"You landed on a diving platform?" My mind spun. "How did you see? How did you glide? What if you get sick?"

"Bea built a skyhook," Hazel said, like that made sense. "A modified crane, on top of the glider, to hook their diving platform from underneath. From inside the Fog. We climbed up that."

"Hazel used Captain Osho's gear to find the *Predator*," Swedish said from lower down.

"And we got lucky," Loretta said.

The shaft ended in a big chamber with a domed sheet-metal ceiling. Dozens of winches lined the floor, each with a tether coiled on the ground. Doors were evenly spaced in the walls, and Swedish jogged to one with an airlock-type wheel keeping it closed.

"These are for Kodoc's tetherkids?" I asked, looking at the winches and tethers.

"Yup," Bea said. "We're directly above the diving platforms."

"We hooked onto the *Predator* from down below," Hazel told me. "Swedish—hurry with the lock!"

"What do you think I'm doing?" Swede said, grunting over the wheel in the door.

"So our ship's inside the Fog?" I asked.

"Yeah, dangling down," Hazel said. "That way the air-sailors couldn't spot her while we were looking for you."

"How're we going to take off?"

"I built a remote engine with a long chain!" Bea said from farther in the chamber. "It'll power the fans from high above, so we can launch the glider over the Fog—"

"We hope," Swedish grumbled, as the wheel squeaked.

"—where the real engine will kick in!"

"Forget that!" Loretta elbowed me. "Check *this* out."

She pointed to a big mesh cube in the corner, sprouting vents and a spool of nano-wire, squatting on top of a locked trapdoor.

"What is it?" I asked as Bea ran her fingers over the

nano-wire braid. "A foggium generator?"

"I think these wires are a fuse," Bea said.

"Look closer," Loretta told me. "Inside the box."

Shafts of light streamed through a vent on the wall and glinted inside the mesh. It wasn't a cube—it was a cage. A weird shape hung in the center, held in place by a web of wires. A raindrop shape. A *teardrop* shape. And as light touched it, the shape glimmered with a zillion colorful sparkles.

"Whoa." I blinked at the shimmering colors. "That's, that's . . ."

"Diamonds," Hazel told me. "Thousands of diamonds."

"No," I breathed.

"With a fuse." Swedish gritted his teeth as the wheel in the door slowly turned. "I told you they were collecting diamonds for a mountain-buster bomb. I *told* you!"

"C'mon, Swede," Hazel urged. "Open it!"

"Almost there," Swedish grunted as airsoldiers' voices sounded closer.

"Bea—" Hazel's eyes narrowed. "Figure that fuse out."

"He's some kind of cannon." Bea fiddled with the wires. "At least, I think so."

"He's not telling you?" I asked, only half teasing.

"I've never met anyone like him before." She chewed her lower lip and untwined a few wires. "Oh! I think he's a remote friction trigger, a super-purple version of the hand-brake bell on Chess's tether—"

The clang of metal echoed into the room. Footsteps scuffed and weapons jangled in the corridors outside.

"Done!" Swedish said, yanking the door open.

"Go, go!" Hazel barked. "They're almost here."

"No." Kodoc's slithery voice filled the room. "We *are* here."

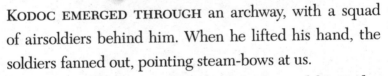

29

KODOC EMERGED THROUGH an archway, with a squad of airsoldiers behind him. When he lifted his hand, the soldiers fanned out, pointing steam-bows at us.

"You latched onto my ship from beneath?" Kodoc arched an eyebrow. "How ingenious."

"Smarter than your crusty camelface," Loretta muttered.

"Sadly," he said in his slithery voice, "I have no need for you, except as hostages to keep the tetherboy obedient. And you've been sabotaging my ship. For that, you will pay."

"Bea," Hazel said, low and urgent. "Tell me you know how that works."

Bea nodded, her green eyes wide with fear. "Ready

when you are, Cap'n."

"Ready for what?" Kodoc led his men closer, steam-bows raised. "Do you honestly think you can—"

"She'll trigger the bomb," Hazel interrupted. "She's got the fuse in her hand."

"That little girl?" Kodoc sneered at Bea. "She'll do no such thing."

"She'll do what I tell her," Hazel said, and the confidence in her voice made the airsoldiers glance at one another uneasily.

Kodoc frowned at Hazel. "You're hardly more than a little girl yourself."

"Unspool the fuse, Bea," Hazel said, still watching Kodoc. "We're leaving."

"If you cross me," Kodoc snarled, raising his own weapon, "I'll ditch you all into the Fog."

"Go on, Bea," Hazel said, ignoring him. "Through the door."

Bea edged toward the door that Swedish had unlocked, unwinding the nano-wire fuse behind her.

"Take aim!" Kodoc ordered, and his soldiers settled into firing position. "Fire on my mark!"

The steam-bows gleamed in the faint light, and the barrels looked like death. For a moment, the world stopped spinning, and even the Fog grew still.

Then Hazel said, "Look at me, Kodoc."

Something in her tone must've struck him, because he

gazed at her with his grim eyes.

Hazel didn't flinch. "If you pull that trigger, I swear by the Fog that I'll drop this ship from the sky. I swear by the silence and the white that we'll trigger that bomb." Her soft voice grew even softer. "I swear by all the high places that I will kill everything I love before I ever let you lay a hand on Chess again."

Goose bumps rose on my arms, and a few airsoldiers took involuntary steps backward. Clockworks ticked, steam-bows bristled from soldiers' fists, and the scent of sweat and engine grease wafted through the room.

"You won't," Kodoc said.

"You know I will," Hazel told him. "*You* would."

"The next time I see you, girl," he spat at Hazel, lowering his weapon, "I'll put you down myself."

Relief turned my legs to jelly as his airsoldiers lowered their steam-bows, and the rest of our escape seemed to happen in flashes. We shoved through the airlock door onto a deck that hung from the bottom of the *Predator*. Swedish slammed the door, and Bea wrapped the fuse around the handle to keep it closed.

"Maybe Chess has Fog in his eye," Loretta said, cracking her neck. "But Hazel's got loco in hers."

Dozens of ladders lowered toward the Fog like a crazy trellis, with loops and pulleys and planks. At the bottom of the scaffolding, a massive claw with grappling hooks like octopus arms clamped onto the ladders: the "skyhook" that Bea had built. A foggium engine sat beside the claw, and a chain dropped down beside a cord with evenly spaced knots, swaying into the Fog fifty yards below.

A hard, cold wind made the diving platform creak and sway. I grabbed the knotted cord and started down ahead of the others. When the world turned black with Fog, I loosened my grip and dropped until my boots scraped a huge glide-wing. The knotted cord ended at the fans of the airship.

The others followed, and I led them into place. After I strapped Hazel down behind Swede, she shouted, "Chess! Fire her up!"

I scrambled to the rear of the glider and tugged the chain. High above, the foggium engine must've roared. The chain blurred, and the fans started spinning. Then Hazel called my name, so I vaulted past Loretta—who was bellowing "The Stars-Tangled Panda," for some reason.

"Here!" I yelled to Hazel.

She shouted, "Cut us loose! Top of the wing!"

I grabbed a loop and swung to the top of the glide-wing. The ship zoomed forward, tilting upward like a pendulum, still connected to the *Predator* with the sky-hook. I groped in the dark Fog around the crane, then yanked a quick-release lever.

The airship rocketed upward through the inky black mist. Sheer terror filled me—and pure exhilaration. We rose higher until the sky opened. The whirr of the fans suddenly sounded louder, and so did Loretta bellowing, "—does that stars-tangled panda yet waaaaave, on the land of the Fog and the food that we crave!"

Then the engine kicked in, the pistons growled, and the Fog blurred beneath us.

"Stay low," Hazel told Swedish. "Kodoc's still close."

When I glanced over my shoulder, the Rooftop armada shone like a globe of fireflies in the night. Dozens of small, bright torchships orbited Kodoc's warships, illuminating the area to watch for attackers.

"Whoa," Swedish gasped.

"Yeah," Hazel said. "We're still in eyeshot."

"I'm not talking about Kodoc."

Hazel scanned the sky. "What, then?"

"We're alive!" Swedish told her. "I did not see that coming."

Bea giggled, and Hazel shushed her—then she started giggling, too.

A wave of relief rose in my heart, and I started grinning madly. A moment later, we were all laughing like lug nuts, skimming over the Fog in a freaky glider.

When we settled down, I said, "If you ever do that again, I'll kill you!"

"Eh," Swedish said. "It was nothing."

I'd been kidding, but a sudden chill shriveled my heart. They'd risked their lives on a loco long shot, trying to snatch me from inside the *Predator*. They could've died. Every single one of them. "You flew in the Fog," I said. "You *flew* in the Fog."

"You're not the only fog-monster around here!" Loretta crowed.

I glared at Hazel, my fear making me angry. "If you'd missed the *Predator*, you would've crashed."

"She didn't miss," Bea said.

"And you brought *Bea*!" I snapped.

Hazel looked so stricken that I almost wished I could take it back. But not totally, because we both knew the rules: Bea came first.

"I know," Hazel said in a soft voice. "I'm sorry."

"You—" I took a breath. "You saved my life. I know you did. But Bea isn't, she's not . . . You can't just—"

"There wasn't any other way," Hazel told me.

"Next time . . ."

"I'll leave Bea behind."

"I hate you two," Bea said.

Swedish scowled at me from the wheel. "Hey, Chess. There's a reason you're the diver."

"So?"

"So there's also a reason Hazel's the captain."

The glider banked leftward, and I swayed with the motion, grabbing a strap. Swedish meant that even though we all knew the rules, Hazel also knew when to break them.

"You're right." I took a slow breath. "I just— This is peanuts! I can't believe the mutineers let you glide through the Fog. This is *beyond* peanuts."

"Don't look at me." Loretta rubbed the tattoo on her face. "I voted to leave you there."

"You did not!" Bea called from the engine. "You asked me to build you a portable harpoon with an airtank-backpack."

Loretta pointed her forefingers like guns. "And a launcher strapped to each arm."

"See?" Bea told me.

"But not to rescue Chess!" Loretta insisted. "Just because they'd be cool." She aimed her imaginary arm-mounted harpoons at the armada. "*Pew. Pew-pew.*"

"What happened after Perry grabbed you?" Hazel asked me.

I told them about the flight to the *Predator*. I told them about Perry kicking me, and Kodoc ditching him off the side of the ship. "I hated him, but . . ."

"Not a good way to die," Loretta said with a nod. "I'll toss some rice into the Fog for him."

"I don't see how that'll help," Bea said, chewing her lower lip.

"It's how gangs remember their dead," Swedish told her, then looked at me. "Then what?"

My voice cracked when I told them about the refinery kids in the cell. I described my meal with Kodoc and the soldier prodding Rizal along the plank. I told them that now that I'd escaped, Kodoc wouldn't have any reason to make the kids walk the plank—and I prayed I was right. Then I took a breath and admitted that I'd first drawn a messed-up map for Kodoc . . . and then an accurate one.

"You didn't have a choice," Swedish said.

"Of course he did," Loretta said. "What does Chess owe the junkyard? He should've let Kodoc ditch the whole place."

"There are kids there," Bea said. "And—and people like Mrs. E."

"Ignore Retta," Swedish told Bca. "She's just talking."

Loretta aimed a finger at Swedish. *"Pew!"*

"You know I'm right."

"What do we do now?" I asked, looking to Hazel.

She scanned the sky behind us. "First we stay ahead of Kodoc's pursuit—"

"His *what*?" Loretta said as I spun toward the armada.

Sure enough, the round globe of glowing torchships now had a long point, aimed directly at us. We'd been spotted.

"How long before they reach us?" I asked.

"The glider's not built for speed," Hazel admitted. "Bea?"

"Depends on the wind." Bea chewed her lower lip. "And if they're mostly fixing the *Predator* or mostly chasing us."

"So what's the plan?" I asked.

"The plan ended with saving you from Kodoc," Hazel told me. "Uh. I guess we keep heading for Port Oro, and hope we run into mutineers."

"They're not going to be thrilled to see us," Swedish said.

"Why not?" I asked.

"We sort of stole the glider from them."

"And by 'sort of,'" Loretta told me, "he means 'totally.' Vidious and Nisha were supposed to fly it, but Hazel got there first."

I winced. "So nobody's waiting to pick us up?"

Hazel shook her head. "Nope. And it's a long glide home."

"We don't have to worry about gliding home," Bea told us, still watching the Rooftop armada. "Kodoc will reach us way before we get there."

The glide-wing creaked in an updraft, and the frame trembled. The air seemed to thrum with tension, and nobody spoke until Loretta said, "*Now* don't you wish I had a couple of armpoons?"

Swede gave a bark of laughter. "You call them 'arm-poons'?"

"*I* don't call them that!" Loretta said. "It's what they're called."

"*Pew!*" Bea aimed a finger at the gunships following us. "*Pew-pew!* I got one!"

When Hazel glanced at me, I saw fear in her eyes, and

strength, and the furious whirl of her thoughts. Her brain moved at the speed of sunlight. I watched her face as steam hissed from an exhaust vent and—

THUNK! THUNKTHUNK-THUNK!

Four spears jutted through the glide-wing from above, with wicked barbs like metal fangs.

The glider jerked upward, and Loretta sprawled to the deck. I staggered, and Swedish swore, struggling with the wheel. But he'd lost control. We'd been skewered by harpoons shot from a warship hovering above us.

30

I SCRAMBLED TOWARD Bea to protect her from Kodoc's airsoldiers—then stopped. Because with her head tilted upward and her green eyes wide and shining, she looked thrilled instead of afraid.

"*The* Night Tide*!*" she blurted. "I'd know that engine anywhere."

I exhaled in relief. We'd been fished out of the sky by mutineers. The *sssszzzzt* of a pulley on a zip line cut through the strain of our engine, then boots slammed down on the glide-wing.

"Captain Vidious." Hazel swept her braids behind her head. "You came."

His mouth twisted into a grin. "Of course I did, poppet."

"But I didn't even hear you!" Bea said.

"That's why she's called the *Night Tide*." Vidious raised his head and yelled to his sailors. "All secure! Bring us up!"

Swedish killed the engine. The harpoon lines twanged as the winches lifted the glider toward the *Tide*.

"You stole the glider—" Vidious told Hazel.

"We stole *our* glider."

"—but you got Chess."

"We got *our* Chess," she said.

"Hazel!" he snapped. "Enough!"

She glared at him but fell silent.

"What you did was reckless," he said, his tone sharp. "And dishonest."

Hazel chewed on a braid.

"Not to mention disrespectful." Vidious's cloak billowed as the harpoon lines lifted us toward his ship's hull. "Don't sneak around behind our backs. Without trust, we have nothing. Without trust, we have no chance against the Rooftop."

"Sorry," Hazel said, ducking her head like me.

"Running off was stupid," Vidious told her. "And—"

Hazel's gaze shifted past him, and she cocked her head. "You towed our ship." She stared at a raft with three balloons floating beside of the *Night Tide*, hooked to the hull with long cables. "You brought the *Bottom-Feeder*."

"Stupid and reckless," Vidious continued. "And nobody else could've done it."

For a moment, I didn't quite understand what he'd said. Neither did Hazel, I thought. Then a smile tugged at her lips. "Not even you?"

"Of course *me*," he said. "But that's it."

"You knew!" she blurted. "You knew we were going to steal it!"

"Slumkids." He scowled, but there was a glint of humor in his eyes. "You'll steal anything that's not nailed down."

"And you—you came here to wait for us." She went still. "But why did you bring the *Bottom-Feeder*?"

"As insurance, just in case . . ." Vidious turned his scarred face to me. "Did you give Kodoc the map?"

My cheeks burned, and I didn't answer.

"So he knows where the Compass is," Vidious said.

"I—" I gulped. "I guess so."

"I guessed, too." Vidious stood over me with his cloak billowing. "Kodoc is a persuasive man. Now fix it."

"How?" I croaked.

Rope ladders fell around us from the open cargo bay of the *Night Tide*.

"Ask your captain," Vidious told me, grabbing a ladder. "She knows."

"He *always* gets the last word," I muttered as I climbed toward the *Night Tide*'s cargo bay.

Hazel shifted the bandage on her forehead. "He brought the *Bottom-Feeder* because he wants Chess to dive."

"And it's got to happen now," Swedish said, "because Kodoc has the map?"

"Yeah, it's a race," Loretta said. "Us against Kodoc. Everyone's trying to reach the Compass first."

I rubbed my aching head. That *almost* made sense—but we couldn't outrun Kodoc in the *Bottom-Feeder*, not with his armada forty minutes behind. What was I missing?

"Almost everyone," Hazel said, then disappeared into the bay.

When I followed, Vidious was handing her a scroll. "The cogs compared Chess's drawing with a hundred old maps," he said. "They put this chart together."

Hazel unrolled the scroll. "It shows the way to the Compass?"

"As near as they can tell," Vidious told her.

"How near is that?" Swedish asked.

"Nobody knows *what* the Compass is," Vidious told him. "Forget about where."

"They know it self-assembles!" Bea said.

Vidious opened a hatch that led onto a narrow deck. "This way, my poppets."

After we filed through, a boarding plank slid from the deck and stretched to the *Bottom-Feeder*, floating ten feet away.

"When the nanites build a Compass," Vidious told us, "that means the Earth is clean and the Fog can leave. So the Compass is a timer, a trigger. The emergence—" He glanced at Bea. "The *self-assembly* of the Compass tells the Fog that its job is done. And it's the tool we use to lower the Fog."

"You think," Swedish said.

"The *cogs* think," Vidious said. "And if anyone would know, it's them."

"How's Chess supposed to find the Compass," Hazel asked, "without knowing what it looks like?"

"I don't care." Vidious escorted her onto the boarding plank. "As long as he does."

"Great," I muttered.

"Activate the Compass," Vidious told me. "Or bring it to the cogs. Or—"

A boom sounded in the night, the crash of a cannon. My heart jumped, Bea yelped, and Loretta groaned.

"That's my sister," Vidious said.

"Captain Nisha is here?" Bea asked.

"Flying high," Vidious told her. "That's a warning shot, telling us that Kodoc's getting closer. No time to waste."

Hazel eyed him from the boarding plank. "We have supplies?"

"Everything you need."

"Goggles?" I asked. "Tether and harness and hacksaw?"

"And a spare," he said.

"A bootball for good luck?" Swedish asked.

"Twisty wires?" Bea asked. "A full set of hex wrenches?"

"Of course."

"Armpoons?" Loretta asked.

Vidious cocked an eyebrow. "Everything you need. I loaded her personally."

"A boot-sheath and bracers?" I asked.

"*Everything*," he said.

I frowned at the *Bottom-Feeder*. "So we just follow the chart and find the Compass?"

"While you hold Kodoc off?" Hazel added.

"Don't just 'find' the Compass," Vidious told me. "Trigger it. So if Kodoc hits the Port, people can flee down the mountain onto clear land. Now, is there anything else?"

"No." Hazel bit her lower lip. "Except . . . stay safe."

"Where's the fun in that?" Vidious asked, and drew his cutlass.

He twirled the curved blade, then offered the hilt to Hazel. She seemed to hold her breath for a moment, then took the sword. Vidious turned and disappeared inside the cargo bay, and the hatch clanged closed behind him.

"Wait," Swedish said, looking at the cutlass. "What just happened?"

"We're racing Kodoc to the Compass," Hazel told him. "And we're going to win."

Twenty minutes after we sped away from the *Night Tide*, cannons crackled across the night behind us as the mutineers opened fire on Kodoc. That's what Hazel had meant by "almost everyone"—the mutineers were staying behind to give us a head start.

Loretta and I stared into the distance. We couldn't see ships in the dark, but the flashes of explosions danced across the Fog like matches flaring. A few seconds after every flash, we'd hear another boom. And as we flew through the night, the flare of cannon fire spread across the horizon.

"The mutineers aren't engaging in a full-on battle," Hazel said. "They're staying between us and Kodoc, hitting and running. Trying to slow him down. A quick shot, then a quick retreat, like a wasp tormenting a bear."

"You've seen a bear?" Loretta asked.

"I've seen Swedish," Hazel told her.

"Hey!" Swedish said.

I smiled weakly. "How long can they hold him off?"

"That depends," Hazel said, "on how much damage they're willing to take."

31

My hammock rocked with the swaying of the airship, and the balloons above me bobbed in the chilly morning breeze. The *Bottom-Feeder* looked a lot like our old salvage raft, except better. Reinforced mesh strengthened the gray balloons, and the sails unfurled beautifully in the wind. We even had a little harpoon overhanging the deck, with a barbed arrow peeking from the end of a copper tube.

I rolled over and peered toward the horizon. The orange rays of dawn brushed the peaks of the Fog. Two hawks rode an updraft in the distance, but I didn't see any airships.

I hoped Vidious and Nisha were okay after fighting Kodoc's armada. I hoped they weren't willing to take *too much* damage.

At the wheel, Loretta yawned and scratched her head. We'd piloted the ship in shifts through the night, keeping her flying straight as Swede dozed beside the cockpit, ready to wake at the first hint of trouble. Bea snored beside me, and Hazel stood in the crow's nest, her spyglass in one hand. The wind played with her braids and ruffled her skirt.

"What're you doing awake?" I asked, climbing beside her. "Didn't you have the shift before Swede?"

She nodded. "Just double-checking our route."

"For the millionth time."

"Yeah," she said.

"That's not *double*-checking."

She stuck out her tongue at me. So even with Vidious's cutlass at her hip, she was still Hazel.

"Why'd they put a city in the middle of nowhere?" I grumbled.

"It used to be the middle of everything," she said.

After lunch, Swedish pushed the ship hard, swooping and diving, to see how she handled. When he finally slowed, Loretta threatened to beat him to death with a wooden spoon, and Hazel dragged a box to the deck.

"You'll never guess what I found," she said.

"Cucumber juice," Loretta said. "Please let it be cucumber juice."

"Even better," Hazel said, and flipped open the lid.

Inside, I saw bottles of paint. Light yellow, brick red, dark green, and—

"Purple!" Bea squealed when she saw it. "Did Cap'n

Vidious leave that? He is such a cuddlebunny."

"Yeah," I said, "that's exactly how I'd describe him."

"He gave us paint to keep us busy," Hazel said, twining a braid around two fingers. "So we don't get nervous thinking about the dive."

"Good plan!" Bea said, grabbing a brush.

She climbed the spars and painted smiley faces on the balloons. Loretta added blood splatters until Swedish convinced her to draw racing flames instead.

The next morning, Hazel spent an hour frowning at the scroll and her new navigational devices. She told Swedish a little ahead, a little to the left, past that ridge. Then she said, "Full stop. We're here. The city is directly beneath us."

I peered at the misty white waves. "Can you imagine the time before the Fog? There were entire fields of skyscrapers, and forests and farms and amber waves of green."

"Think of all that *room*," Swedish said. "Instead of living squeezed together."

"Yeah." Bea paused. "I bet everyone had their own personal mountaintop."

"They didn't only live on mountains, Bea," Hazel said. "They lived everywhere."

"That's just weird." Bea tilted her leather cap back on her head. "Living on the ground."

"Better than flitting around in airships," Loretta said.

Hazel turned to me. "You know what to do?"

"Wander around," I said. "Until I spot a self-assembled whangdoodle from the Foggy depths."

"The Compass should be on the shore of a lake or ocean," she told me. "Find the shore and follow it until you see . . ."

"A whangdoodle?" I asked.

"Yeah. The cogs figure you'll know it when you see it."

"What if I don't?"

"Then keep looking."

"In that case, I'm totally ready," I said, and we crossed to the diving plank.

Hazel exhaled and said, "The city's big. You've never dived anywhere like this. There's going to be broken glass, sinkholes, toxic sludge. Poison snakes—"

"Mickey mice," I said. "Haze rays."

"It's a city, Chess," she said, not smiling. "Driftsharks like cities."

I nodded. "I'll be careful."

"If you start feeling iffy—"

"I know, I know. I'll run."

"No," she told me, her voice soft. "Stay."

I swallowed. She'd never said that before, but this was one dive I needed to complete. This time, there was no turning back.

"We're out of time." She looked northward. "Kodoc's on the horizon, and we can't let him get that Compass."

32

I DOVE OFF the airship. Wind numbed my cheeks and roared in my ears until the whiteness swallowed me. My tether whizzed through the reel on my harness. I fell and fell, then a wall whipped past—a tower of steel and glass, with half the windows shattered.

My breath caught. I'd never seen anything so grand.

When I felt the ground approaching, I slowed, dangling three feet over a smooth black street. Except it wasn't asphalt beneath me. Ripples spread through the green-black surface, and ferns bent in the swamp-smelling breeze.

What had once been a four-lane street was now a slow-moving river at the base of a skyscraper in the center of a city. Water bugs skated on the current, and mosquitoes buzzed in my ear. A lumpy frog stared at me. Looked like good eating, but I was too amazed to be hungry.

With a steady hand, I squeezed out a message. *I'm okay.*

The brake twitched in response. *Okay okay okay.*

I smiled at the relief in all those *okay*s from Hazel, then I sent: *Raise me. Slowly.*

The tether jerked, and I rose from the river, past mud and rusted pipes to a concrete bank studded with metal posts that Mrs. E called "parking greeters."

Stop, I told Hazel.

I swung toward the nearest parking greeter and pulled myself onto a cracked sidewalk. Fifteen feet below, blurred in the white, the sluggish, swampy river flowed along the sunken remains of a city street.

I checked my map. A coastline wiggled across the edge of the city, and a few lakes dotted the interior; but the map didn't have a "You Are Here" label, so I'd mostly use it to keep from walking in circles while I looked for a shoreline.

High above me, Hazel started to fly in a spiral of expanding circles. I trotted along the sidewalk . . . then froze. Something looked wrong. Something *felt* wrong. I checked for driftsharks—and ticktocks—but nothing moved other than the Fog. Except it seemed thinner, somehow. More transparent.

I was seeing farther than ever before. Not ten feet

through the white, not fifteen. Twenty feet—maybe even thirty.

"Whoa!" I said.

A spark of excitement rose in my chest—I could *see*! All the way to the second floors of the buildings and straight through a shattered window into a Walmart, though I couldn't see any walls for sale. Plus, the buzz of mosquitoes and the croak of frogs sounded clear and loud.

Then a wave of anxiety dowsed the spark. What was happening? Had the Fog changed? Had *I*?

I rubbed my normal eye, wondering if the mist was drifting in it again. I couldn't tell. I looked toward the airship, out of sight hundreds of yards above, and touched my hand brake nervously. I wanted to signal Hazel to pull me up, but there was no time. Kodoc was flying closer every minute.

"Stop thinking," I told myself, lowering my hand. "And find this thing."

I swallowed my nervousness and trotted along the cracked street, scanning the mist for a beach or lake. The city rose around me like a glassteel canyon. Ivy climbed traffic lights, and birds nested in spy-cam housings. Prairie dogs chirped in a "software" store—I poked my head inside but didn't see anything soft to wear.

Then I heard the chuff-grunt of a boar or a bear and scrambled away.

A few blocks later, my tether jammed on one of the

skyscrapers. I worked my hand brake, and Hazel raised me to the ninth or tenth story, where I unwound the cable from a jutting beam. Through a broken window, I saw weeds growing in a layer of windblown dirt beside a collapsed desk.

No Compass, though.

I climbed the outside of the building like a fly on a wall. Birds flapped away, and I almost crushed a sunbathing lizard that was enjoying the warmth that the nanites reflected to the ground. The Fog somehow transferred the sun's light and heat to the plants and animals that thrived in the mist—it didn't kill anything except humans.

When I reached the roof, I sniffed for the scent of water. Instead, I smelled epoxy and mildew. Standing there, I suddenly felt exposed, imagining driftsharks gathering at the fringes of my vision. I told Hazel to start circling faster, then hopped and swung from rooftop to rooftop, balancing on narrow edges, hoping to find a shoreline.

After pausing to gaze at the map, I leaped to a roof and landed in the middle of a troop of monkeys—they screamed at me, and a big male showed his teeth. I sprang up in the air, dodged a satellite catcher, and swerved away.

I searched for hours but didn't find anything resembling a Compass—or a whangdoodle, for that matter. And time kept ticking away.

Finally, the skyscrapers flattened into a plain of lower

buildings. Bushes and trees rose from the crumbling pavement, and the streets were lined with the husks of drone-tanks from the wars that had started when the Fog rose. I stopped at a puddle for a drink and saw tracks surrounding it—mostly raccoon, but also what looked like a big cat, probably a mountain lion or jaguar.

Maybe I wasn't so thirsty. I marked my map and kept moving. A few blocks away, as I was untangling my tether from an ad board selling some kind of space money called "Star Bucks," the hand brake on my tether jerked.

Hazel sent, *Okay*?

Okay, I told her.

Okay, she said.

Then I looked at my hand brake and kept walking.

A beaver slapped its tail in a river beside a sparse forest of bamboo. I rushed closer, hoping to find a bigger body of water, but instead the current disappeared into a massive sinkhole. So I followed a collapsed walkway along bullet-pocked walls, chewing a rice biscuit and fretting about the time.

"C'mon," I told myself. "How hard can it be to find a shore in a city? Ought to be as easy as finding an eagle in a haystack."

I vaulted a wall, passed a bunch of ruined trucks with trees growing through them, then trotted into a shipyard littered with cargo containers. Heavy chains swaying in a breeze went *creak-creak-creak*—and I felt a sudden drop in the pressure, like the heaviness in the air before a storm.

Except the pressure was coming *toward* me. I spun, and a driftshark thickened from the Fog twenty feet away. Ropes of mist formed a bulky head, and feathery tails lashed and writhed.

Panic almost froze me—but I'd *felt* that shark before I'd seen it. I knew driftsharks now. I changed them; I blunted them. I groped in my mind for the link between the Fog and my freak-eye . . . and I felt the *click*.

Swirls of mist froze in the air. The breeze died; my heartbeat slowed to a dull thud. The driftshark flashed toward me, and with a flick of my attention, I nudged the Fog. I felt my mind catch on the nanites, like pushing a fingertip through a spiderweb . . . and the shark veered sideways.

Its misty tails streamed past my face, then vanished into the white. The breeze kicked back in, my heart pounded, and I laughed.

"Hey, Loretta!" I shouted at the sky. "Even driftsharks don't mess with the fog-monster!"

Still grinning, I crossed the shipyard. I'd chased off a driftshark! I'd actually turned it *away*. Well, either that or driftsharks now thought I belonged in the Fog, because they didn't see me as human anymore.

My grin faded. "Well, that's a little creepy."

I reached for my hand brake to tell Hazel to raise

me, because I wanted to talk this through—and to have her check my eyes. Something told me that the Fog was unfurling inside both of them again.

Except Hazel's words echoed in my brain: *If you start feeling iffy . . . stay.* And how near was Kodoc? Could she see him through her spyglass? Was he a distant speck, or was she staring down his cannons?

I decided to check my eyes myself. I jangled over a chain-link fence and poked around until I found a pile of broken glass. I grabbed a shard and held it to my face, checking my reflection.

Yeah. Even my normal eye was swirling with Fog. White clouds shifted and flowed across my pupils. That was bad enough, but it also looked like the nanites were swirling *between* my eyes, like billows of mist drifting inside my head.

"Guh!" I said, flinging the shard of glass away.

That was all I needed, a whole new level of freakishness. I stomped across a weedy field and angrily vaulted a concrete wall, and my boots landed in something soft.

Sand? A beach!

"Ha!" I said, forgetting my eye.

I headed down the sloping shore, sniffing for the scent of water. Instead, I smelled heaps of molding sludge and corroding iPhones. I wrinkled my nose and noticed a black, crunchy film coating the ground. That wasn't sand, and this wasn't a beach. It was a whole valley of garbage.

I sighed. If I couldn't even find a lake, how was I supposed to find the Compass?

"There's no way," I grumbled.

I crouched and ran my fingers across the film. It felt brittle and sharp, like the dried crust left by every liquid that had oozed from the city in centuries. Coughing syrup and Pep-C and nano-ink—the oozing remains of a million households.

Gross.

Then a cloud of shiny blue flies bumped against my face. I shuddered and leaped upward, pulling myself higher on my tether. I dangled in midair as trash rolled past in the Fog below. Shredded mattresses, slabs of flooring.

To my right, a herd of deer grazed on a hill covered in strange bushes. To my left, dozens of rotting "car seats" scattered a low mound. Mrs. E once told me that they were portable restraints for little kids, which made me wonder how much rowdier children had been back then. Like knee-high gangsters.

A wall of trash loomed from the Fog in front of me, one side of an immense hill. I kicked off a weird pod-car printed with the word *canoe*, rising higher on my tether. Slime cascaded downward like a filthy waterfall, and I kicked again and again, breathing through my mouth until I reached the top of the hill.

"Biggest outhouse in the world," I grumbled, crossing a

mound of rotting couches, and *tick tock*.

Tick tock, tick tock.

My breath stopped. I spun toward the sound—

Bladed pinchers slashed at my stomach through the Fog. Cables groaned and squealed, writhing around the misshapen body of a ticktock that was grinding closer. Repulsive flashes of the monster appeared through the mist. Orange fluid spat from puckered vents, and a gasp wheezed from the hoses that snaked through the air at me.

With a horrified shriek, I jumped straight upward, pulling my knees to my chest. The pinchers missed me by inches. *Tick tock.* I twisted in the air and landed on a heap of half-melted roofing shingles, panting with terror.

The wheeze of the ticktock sounded faint in the white. Too far to reach me. I needed to—

Another ticktock erupted beneath me, wreathed in a cloak of Fog. Rusty tentacles vacuumed at the air, and a gout of flame erupted from a gearwork valve.

I squeezed my hand brake without thought, just an animal reflex. *Up. Up. Up.*

The ticktock squealed toward me through the whiteness, and a lumpy chain lashed out. Pain burst in my temple. My vision blurred, blood dripped down my cheek—and my tether yanked me upward.

As I lofted higher, the ticktock shot more feelers into the Fog, like chain-link harpoons. One whipped my calf, and I yelped and jerked away. The others fell harmlessly around me, and a moment later I'd risen too far for the ticktocks to reach.

Safely slumped in my harness, I shuddered in horror.

Instead of the Compass, I'd found *ticktocks*. They were real. Murderous junkpiles with serrated blades and rusty shells, wrapped in coils of Fog. But why did they want to kill me? Who'd made them?

Well, they'd probably just grown from all that trash, from every substance ever created by human civilization. They built themselves, and—

"Built themselves," I breathed. "*Assembled* themselves."

In a flash of insight, I knew that I'd done it. Forget the shore—I'd found the *Compass.*

WHEN THE FOG dropped away, I spun at the end of my tether and shouted, "I found it! It's *ticktocks*! The Compass is ticktocks. They're assembling in a mountain of junk!"

"Got him!" Hazel's voice was faint above me, muffled by the engine noise. "Go, Swede, *go!*"

The winch jerked, and my harness dug into me. "Ow!"

"He's bleeding," Loretta called out, peering down from the winch. "He's hurt."

"Now!" Hazel yelled.

The *Bottom-Feeder* shot faster through the air, and I trailed behind, spinning wildly as the winch pulled me upward. Fog, sky, Fog, sky. Every time I twirled, I scanned the horizon, but I didn't see Kodoc's armada anywhere.

What were we running from this time?

When I reached the hull, Loretta squeezed her eyes tight and reached for me, afraid of seeing the long drop below. "Grab hold," she said. "J-just don't pull me over."

I ignored her outstretched hand and grabbed the boarding ladder. "What're we doing?"

"Kodoc," she said, warily opening one eye.

"He's nowhere!"

She pointed almost straight upward. "There."

"No way," I said, feeling a stab of fear.

I clambered on deck and shoved my goggles to the top of my head for a better look. Wispy gray clouds stretched across the sky. For a moment, I didn't see anything. Then I noticed a dot through the clouds. A speck. A grain of sand.

The *Predator*, insanely high above us.

"What's he doing?" I asked.

"Getting into position," Bea told me, furiously splicing cables together.

"Retta!" Hazel shouted. "Stop the bleeding! Swede, open the throttle! Move, *move!*"

"She can't go faster!" Swedish told her.

"Then we'll die!" Hazel yelled, her voice rough with fear.

Swedish hammered on the organ keyboard. The deck shuddered, and the props hummed a shrill note. The *Bottom-Feeder* zoomed forward. When I stumbled, Loretta grabbed my arm and shoved a cloth against my slashed temple. I howled and swiped at her, but she crammed the cloth in place.

"It hurts," I gasped.

"I can tell," she said, "by the blood."

My head pounded in time with the throbbing of the engines as she twined a bandage around my head. Then at the same time, we both said, "What happened?"

The *Bottom-Feeder* veered sideways, and Loretta grabbed a rail. "You first. You found the Compass?"

"Yeah."

"Did you get it? What's it look like?"

"It's a junk heap the size of a mountain. There's chemicals in there, smart alloys, quantum chips, *everything*. Rotting, sparking, mixing together. I think the Fog assembles ticktocks from all that trash."

"Ticktocks?"

"They're real." I touched the bandage. "They did this."

"So . . . a junk heap?" Loretta asked. "The Compass is a junk heap?"

"One that makes ticktocks. Or—or maybe the ticktocks *are* the Compass, I don't know."

"What part of this lowers the Fog?"

"I-I don't know."

"Your other eye's foggy again," she said, squinting at my left eye.

"Yeah," I said, and didn't bother trying to hide it. "Maybe the ticktocks defend the Compass? Maybe that's why they attacked me."

"Like they're guards?"

"Well, maybe."

"Did you trigger anything?"

"No." I shook my head. "I don't know how."

"Chess!" Hazel called from the crow's nest. "I need you in the rigging!"

Loretta frowned. "He's bleeding!"

"He can bleed in the rigging!" Hazel yelled, her skirts snapping around her like even *they* were angry. "We need the hurricane sails in place, now!"

"The what?" I peered at the calm skies. "There's no storm in sight, why—"

Hazel shot me a look that singed the air. *Yikes.* Forget about my pounding head and aching leg—a second later, I was climbing into the rigging to unfurl the hurricane sails.

"We waited as long as we could," Hazel told me.

"For what?" I asked sharply. We used hurricane sails only when typhoon winds threatened to shake our raft into splinters. "What's going on?"

"We spotted Kodoc a couple of hours ago, climbing higher and higher."

"Why didn't you tell me?"

"Didn't want to distract you," she said, then screamed at Swedish: "Keep her steady! Three wisps to the left!"

Swede's angry reply was lost in the lashing wind, but somewhere below our ship, the rudders shifted.

"He's not trying to catch you, Chess. He knows the Compass is in that city, right?"

"Yeah, but he can't find it without me."

"He's not trying to find it." Her jaw tightened. "He's flying super high so the *Predator* won't get caught in the blast."

"The blast? What blast?"

"Remember the trapdoor under that diamond teardrop in the *Predator*?" Hazel braced herself as the prop whined and the *Bottom-Feeder* strained forward. "He's bombing the city. He's blasting the Compass into ash."

"No way. It doesn't make sense. Then he'll never control the Fog."

"He's not trying to *use* the Compass, Chess," she said. "He's trying to destroy it."

Her words chilled me. *Trying to destroy it.* Trying to destroy the Compass, humanity's only hope. My mind blanked with dread, and my stomach burned. I stared at Hazel . . . and saw a flash of horror on her face.

When I followed her gaze, I caught a glimpse of a tiny gem falling from the dark smudge of the *Predator*. Diamond sunbursts winked, and a glimmering, colorful trail tumbled into the pure white Fog.

"Cut the engine!" Hazel screamed. "Drop the fans, reef those sails!"

Swedish jerked a lever, and the clockworks fell silent. The fans folded against the deck, and Bea lashed them into place. I scrambled across the rigging, raised the hurricane sails, then shaded my eyes and looked behind the raft.

At first nothing happened in the Fog over the city. Nothing, nothing . . . until a massive circle of Fog dipped downward like a whirlpool, miles across and spreading.

The teardrop bomb had exploded in the middle of the city.

"Strap in," Hazel shouted.

My gaze flicked to Bea—safe inside a hatch—then I ran to Loretta. I checked her straps as Fog exploded from the "whirlpool" behind us. I snapped a repair tether to my harness and watched the shock wave roll toward us. Fog rippled and spat. Bits of charred brick and plasteel exploded into sight, then vanished behind the onrushing wave of Fog. The blast kept spreading toward us, from the trash hill—the Compass—across the plain of low houses to the skyscrapers and beyond.

A "mountain buster," like Swedish had said. Leveling an entire city.

Then the shock wave hit. An invisible hammerblow batted the *Bottom-Feeder* across the sky, faster than any airship should move. The deck heaved and the balloons shrieked and Loretta bellowed, "Twinkle twinkle." In the middle of the maelstrom, I caught a glimpse of Hazel shouting at me and pointing. I struggled across the deck to restrap a torn sail—and then the main blast hit.

The *Bottom-Feeder* tumbled across the sky. The impact

slapped me off the deck into a hurricane, flinging me like a rag doll at the end of my repair tether.

A pulse tore through the whiteness below me. For a handful of seconds, in the wake of that ripple, the mist cleared. I caught a glimpse of the endless sprawl of the ruined city.

Just ahead of the blast, seagulls hopped and soared over a landscape of mounds and ditches, a pack of dogs chewed on a carcass, and ticktocks lurched and crept. I saw them clearly for the first time. They looked like rusty armadillos the size of minivans, with dozens of insectoid feelers and tentacles. In a meadow, five of the gearwork monsters joined together, hoses linked, antennae braided. On a curving black surface, another ticktock slashed at an orange barrel, sucking shreds of plastic into a vent—

The pulse passed, and the Fog billowed back into place. The explosion tossed me like a twig in a waterfall. My vision spun and blurred. The repair tether strained, my harness dug into my chest, and I trailed behind the *Bottom-Feeder* as she shot madly forward above me.

Swedish surfed the edge of the shock wave. He balanced on the brink of destruction, playing tag with the blast and rocketing away from Kodoc. Nobody else could've ridden a hurricane. Nobody else could've even stayed in the air.

"And that," I said, before the howl of the wind stole my breath, "is why he's called Swedish."

34

A SOFT PURR surrounded me. Gentle arms rocked me, and a warm blanket snuggled me tight.

I opened one eye and saw a million pinpricks of light. Stars. A cool draft tickled my nose, and the hammock swayed beneath me. Oh. Not arms, then. And the purr didn't come from a cat but from the raft's engine. The blanket was a blanket, though.

So, yay. I snuggled underneath and fell back asleep.

The next time I woke, the stars looked dimmer in the glow of dawn—and ticktocks rushed at me from the fragments of a nightmare.

"No!" I gasped, and twisted away.

I got tangled in my hammock and flopped to the deck. A barbed antenna grabbed at my wrist, and I lashed out and heard an *ooof*.

"It's *me!*" Hazel said, her grip tightening on my wrist. "It's me, sweetie. You're safe—you passed out in your harness."

The last flickers of nightmare faded when I heard her voice, and I lay back on the deck and watched the balloons sway overhead, past the now-tattered rigging. The freshly painted designs glowed in the early light—smudged by the storm but still cheerful.

I looked at Hazel and saw her exhausted eyes and unkempt hair. She probably hadn't slept all night. "Did you just call me 'sweetie'?" I asked.

She shoved my shoulder. "No."

"Well, the bad news," Swedish said from the wheel, "is that Chess still thinks he's funny."

"What's the good news?" Loretta asked, leaning on our little copper-tubed harpoon. "That Kodoc dropped a bomb on the city?"

I frowned as memory returned. *The Compass, the ticktocks, the bomb . . .*

"What did he *do*?" I asked, sick with a sudden horror. "He blew up the Compass. He—he lied to me. He never wanted to lower the Fog."

"Yeah," Hazel said. "He likes the world exactly how it is."

I gulped from a canteen that Bea handed me. "But . . . but if he lowered the Fog, he'd expand his turf! He'd control all the new land."

"Except what if the Fog lowered too much?" Hazel rubbed her tired eyes. "Then people could leave the

265

Rooftop. Imagine if everyone in the junkyard just walked away from Kodoc, into the woods."

"Sounds like a dream," Bea said. "Walking away from the slum."

"The only reason Kodoc is strong," I said as understanding dawned, "is because there's so little land."

"That's what *they* do," Swedish grumbled. "Keep people hungry, keep 'em weak."

"Kodoc needs the Fog," Hazel told me. "If there are only ten servings of food at a table, the guy who owns nine is king. But if a hundred more tables show up? Suddenly he's just a guy sitting alone."

With my mind still hazy, I wasn't sure I completely understood, but I knew one thing: giving Kodoc the map had been even worse than I'd thought.

"What do we do now?" I asked.

Hazel wiped my hair off my forehead and checked my eyes. "We go home."

"To Port Oro?"

She nodded. "Yeah."

"What about the Compass? What about Kodoc?"

"Your eyes look okay," she said, patting my hair into place. "The Fog's only in one again."

"I don't care about my eyes!" I said. "What're we going to *do*?"

For once, Hazel didn't have an answer . . . which was the worst answer of all.

I'd led Kodoc to the Compass, and he'd blown up an entire city. Forget the human race, forget lowering the Fog. Mrs. E once told me that I could change the future . . . and maybe I had.

I'd made it worse.

Rain clouds followed us northward, wetting the balloons with drizzle. Trickles dripped down the gutters and filled the water barrel. Hazel spotted a rainbow, but even that didn't raise our mood.

Kodoc had won.

On the second afternoon, I removed the bandages on my calf and washed in the drizzle. A red line snaked around my leg from the ticktock "antenna," like I'd been whipped with barbed wire. And I kept seeing flashes of the city, flattened by that diamond bomb. I'd blown my only chance to lower the Fog. I'd failed the crew. I'd failed everyone on Port Oro . . . and on the Rooftop, too. The kids in the Noza Home and the shipbuilders in the docks, the friendly bootball players and the grumpy trolley rider.

Loretta cooked dinner that evening, which looked like fried caterpillars in a potato peel sauce. The night air smelled stormy and electric, so Bea fed the lightning rods into the foggium converter while Swede stared at me.

Probably in disappointment, because I'd doomed the world to eternal misery. I ignored him until he turned away to set the autopilot that Bea had rigged; then we tucked into our hammocks and listened to the patter of rain on the balloons.

In the darkness, Bea said, "Tell the story, Chess."

"Nah," I said.

"C'mon, please?"

"The story's no good anymore."

"'Before the Fog rose . . . ,'" she prompted.

"You've heard it a million times."

"I've only heard it a thousand," Loretta said.

"Pretty please?" Bea said. "With caterpillar on top?"

"Fine." I rubbed my face. "Before the Fog rose, the Smog covered the Earth and made everything sick. People, plants, animals. The Smog was killing every single living thing."

"So the nanotech gearslingers . . . ," Bea said.

"The *engineers*," I corrected, "created the nanites to scrub the air and water and ground. But the Fog spread, out of control, and buried everything until only a few survivors remained, clinging to life on the Rooftop and Port Oro."

From her hammock, Hazel softly said, "There are more mountains out there."

"But *they* don't want us know that," Swedish added.

"The ancient engineers studied the Fog," I said, changing the usual story, "and predicted that one day a 'Compass' would self-assemble. A special machine that could lower the Fog when the time was right. Then the entire human race would get a second chance."

When I stopped talking, the whirring of the *Bottom-Feeder*'s engine sounded loud in the quiet. The cool air smelled fresh, and I pulled my blanket closer.

"The cogs predicted that a kid with a Fog-eye would find the Compass," I continued. "And finally, after hundreds of years, one did. Then he led Lord Kodoc straight to it."

"That's not fair," Hazel said. "You did your—"

"Kodoc destroyed the Compass," I said, speaking over her. "In order to stay in power. And we lost our chance to lower the Fog."

"That's not how the story goes," Bea said in a small voice.

"It is now." I closed my eyes. "The end."

35

THE NIGHT PASSED, and a gray morning light spread across the sky. Drizzle pocked the deck while Hazel scoped the Fog and I sewed a patch on Bea's backup shirt. Nobody said much until a few hours later, when the storm clouds feathered away and we sailed through a sudden brightness.

"Four wisps to the left, Swedish," Hazel called. "Then the Port's dead ahead."

"Where?" Loretta asked.

"Just over the horizon," Hazel told her.

"I still don't know how you can tell." Loretta peered into the distance. "It all looks the same to me."

Swede clattered on the organ keyboard and said, "That's what *they* want you to think."

"Would you stop with that?" I grumbled. "It's getting old."

"*They* want us to think what?" Bea wrinkled her nose. "That the Fog all looks the same?"

"You," Loretta told Swedish, "are the chuzzlest of wits."

"I didn't mean that," he said, shaking his shaggy head. "I've been thinking about the Compass."

"You mean the one Kodoc blew into a million pieces?" Loretta asked.

"Yeah," he said. "Except I don't think he did."

"We saw the bomb."

"Yeah."

"We saw the *explosion*."

"Yeah."

"Chess says the city got all flattened and destroyed."

"Yeah," Swedish said, tapping the wheel thoughtfully.

"Swedish!" Hazel called from the crow's nest. "What are you talking about?"

He shrugged a meaty shoulder. "Maybe that wasn't the Compass."

"I saw it," I told him. "It's the place where ticktocks self-assembled."

"You saw it," he said, his eyes narrowing. "Because *you* were there."

"Riiiiight," I said. "Because if I hadn't been there, I wouldn't have seen it."

"But what if the Compass isn't a trash heap or a ticktock?"

Swede looked toward Hazel. "What if it's Chess?"

Loretta smacked his arm. "*Chess* is Chess."

"Think about it!" Swedish turned to me. "Every time you saw ticktocks, *you've* been there! That's the one thing every sighting has in common!"

"Well, but—if *I* wasn't there, how would I have seen them?"

"Exactly! Because you trigger them!"

"That doesn't make sense."

"The Compass is a sign, right?" he asked. "A signal that the Earth is clean and the Fog can go away?"

"Probably," Hazel said, swinging down to the deck.

"Well, Chess's eye is the sign," Swedish told her. "A baby was born in the Fog and *lived*, with nanites in his head, and he—" He turned to me. "You learned how to handle the driftsharks, right?"

"A little."

"That's the Compass. That's the trigger. You."

A lump formed in my throat. "That's loco, Swedish. I found the map to the Compass. It didn't lead to me."

"You found *a* map with a compass on it. I guess the cogs think it's *the* compass." He glanced at Loretta. "But . . ."

"Sometimes old stories get garbled," Loretta said, scratching the burn scar on her arm.

"And you felt a *click* in the Fog, right?" Swedish asked me. "When you dove down to the Station? And that was

272

the first time anyone saw a ticktock in forever. The Fog's been waiting for a . . ."

"A fog-monster," Loretta said.

"Yeah," Swedish said. "To activate the nanites. What did Mrs. E say?"

"That the Fog doesn't change Chess," Hazel said. "He changes the Fog."

"Maybe she was righter than she knew. Maybe this is how the Fog ends."

"Look around!" I gestured angrily. "The Fog's still here."

Swedish glowered into the distance and didn't say anything.

"And people *have* seen ticktocks before," I told him. "That's how we know about them. I'm not the first kid born like this. If they were Compasses, how come they didn't lower the Fog?"

"Because they failed."

"So did I."

"Maybe not," Swedish told me. "Not yet."

"That's stupid," I said, and turned to Hazel. "Would you tell him?"

She started to speak, then stopped. She furrowed her brow and didn't say anything.

"Some of that sounds right." Bea squinched her face at me. "You felt that click, and you saw ticktocks, and you control the Fog. And the cogs don't think the Compass itself lowers the Fog."

Hazel brushed a braid off her face. "Yeah, they think it's a signal. Like a real compass, it just points the way."

"Now you're listening to *Swedish*?" I asked her. "He thinks I'm the Compass because every time I see ticktocks, *I* happen to be there!"

"Maybe the Compass is a fail-safe, a backup plan." Bea twisted her leather cap in her hands. "You know, a device that stops the damage if a machine breaks."

"So they knew the Fog might go crazy," Hazel asked her, "and programmed the nanites to include an off switch?"

"Pretty much," Bea said, rubbing her nose. "Except after hundreds of years, everything got cattywampus."

"If Chess is the switch," Loretta said, "how does he turn the Fog off?"

Bea bit her lower lip. "I don't know—ask Chess."

"How would *I* know?" I said. "You try being a switch."

Hazel tapped her spyglass against her leg. "So Kodoc wanted a Fog-eyed kid to help him find the Compass and didn't realize he'd *made* the Compass himself?"

Worry wormed in my heart. "Do you really think I'm the Compass?"

"I don't know," she admitted. "You kind of emerged from the Fog with your eye, didn't you? And ever since you felt that *click*, your other eye's been turning white. Ticktocks swarm when you dive, and you stop driftsharks with your mind. Do *you* think you're the Compass?"

"No!" I said, but she kept looking at me. "Maybe . . . I don't know."

"We'll ask the cogs if—" She stopped suddenly, staring southward. *"Kodoc."*

The fear in her voice chilled me. I peered across the sky and saw a dark cloud swirling toward us . . . with metal glinting and propellers spinning. It was the Rooftop armada, moving fast.

"He's coming for us," Loretta said. "Maybe he *does* think Chess is the Compass."

"He's not after Chess," Hazel told her, her voice strained. "Not anymore. Now he's hitting Port Oro."

The chill seeped into my heart. "What?"

"He thinks he destroyed the Compass," she said, "and he wants to end this, once and forever."

"But—" Bea's green eyes widened. "But he never beat the Port before."

"He never tried."

"Why not? Why *now*?"

I rubbed my face. "Because he figured the Subassembly would lead him to the Compass eventually. He needed to keep them alive. Until now."

Hazel looked at me for a moment, then said, "Fast to the Port, Swede! We need to warn the mutineers."

Hazel kept an eye on the armada, Bea goosed the engines, and I stayed busy in the rigging, trying to convince myself that Vidious and Nisha would beat Kodoc.

Except what if they didn't? If I really was the Compass, maybe I hadn't lost our last chance. Maybe I still had a shot at lowering the Fog and giving the Port an escape route. But if I was the Compass, I wasn't *me*; I was a fail-safe device predicted by ancient engineers.

And I still didn't know how to lower the Fog.

"There she is!" Hazel called from the crow's nest when Port Oro appeared on the horizon, a tiny green-black splinter rising from the Fog.

"I wonder how Mrs. E is doing," I said, partly to myself.

Swedish turned from the keyboard organ. "She's probably pulling wheelies in the hallway."

"I'm going to make her the purplest wheeled chair," Bea announced. "With foggium boosters and everything!"

"You'll probably fire her into the sky like a cannonball," Loretta said.

"I will not!"

"We have ships incoming!" Hazel called, peering through her spyglass toward the Port. "Well, rafts." She paused for a second. "Uh, Chess, come check the raft in front with the yellow sails."

I swung beside her and scoped the ships bobbing toward us. There were a dozen Assembler airships, most of them even smaller than the *Bottom-Feeder*.

When I spotted the raft with yellow sails, I frowned in surprise. "What're they doing here?"

"Who?" Loretta asked from below.

"Mochi and Jada," I told her.

"The tethergirls?"

"No," I said, "the *other* Mochi and Jada. Of course the tethergirls!"

Thirty minutes later, the *Bottom-Feeder* swept to a halt beside the yellow-sailed raft, which flew in the front of the raggedy band of Subassembly airships.

"What're you doing out here?" Hazel shouted.

"Looking for you!" Mochi yelled back. "In case you need help with—y'know."

"The Compass," Jada said.

"And we're passing messages to the cogs," Mochi told us. "From ship to ship to ship, so they're ready when you get in, in case you need anything. To trigger the Compass!"

Jada leaned in toward us. "Do you have it?"

"We're not sure!" I said.

"We're pretty sure," Swedish called.

"Stop messing around!" Jada yelled at us.

"Fine," I told her. "They think *I'm* the Compass."

Mochi gasped, but Jada just said, "Then start triggering."

"So far, all I managed to trigger is ticktocks, and they're trying to kill me."

"Wait, wait, hold on," Mochi babbled. "You? You're the Compass? You can't be the—"

"Let's get you to the cogs," Jada called.

"Yeah, before Kodoc gets back," Mochi said. "The mutineer navy is crushed and we're defenseless and—"

277

"Mochi!" Hazel gestured behind us. "He's already here!"

Shouts of alarm sounded as Mochi and Jada spread the news. Then the ragtag Assembler fleet wheeled in the air, retreating toward Port Oro. Mochi filled us in as we flew beside the yellow-sailed raft. After the crew had rescued me from the *Predator*, Vidious and Nisha had battled Kodoc's armada through the night. By dawn, the *Anvil Rose* had been hanging limply in the sky, and the *Night Tide*'s primary igniter had been blasted into scrap. The rest of the mutineer warships had fared no better, and with the Port navy in tatters, Kodoc had turned his armada to chase the *Bottom-Feeder*.

Every sailmaker, carpenter, and gearslinger on Port Oro had spent the last few days furiously repairing the damage—but the navy's strength had been broken.

"The mutineers can't beat him," Jada called from the deck of her raft. "They can't even hold him back."

"Open her up, Swede!" Hazel ordered. "Let's move!"

When Swedish tapped the organ keyboard, we shot ahead of the tethergirls, speeding toward the Port. Toward a fight we knew we couldn't win.

36

WHEN SWEDISH LOWERED the *Bottom-Feeder* toward the skyscraper roof, I watched Assemblers priming their cannons. They were preparing for the invasion, but all that firepower wouldn't even dent the *Predator*.

I caught Hazel's eye. "What do we do now?"

"Fight," she said.

"What about—y'know—the whole Compass thing?"

"You can't trigger the Fog if you don't know how," she said.

Our ship clanged onto the skyscraper's landing pad. The rigging sagged, the deck shuddered, and the fans spun down. Bea popped up from a hatch and squealed, "Mrs. E, you're outside!"

She scrambled off the airship and peeled through the

crowd toward Mrs. E, with the rest of us following close behind. Mrs. E was sitting in her wheeled chair beside Isander and Isandra, and her wrinkled face cracked into a smile at the sight of us.

Isandra turned from the heliograph operator and told Hazel, "*Bonita*, the mutineers have a question for you."

"Oh!" Hazel said. "Yes?"

"As you can imagine," Isander told her, "the Port is arming every airworthy craft. Cargo ships, fishing trawlers, all working to—"

"—form a shield between the mountain and the armada," Isandra finished.

"Will that stop Kodoc?" Mrs. E asked.

Hazel shook her head. "Not for long."

"Which brings us to Captain Vidious's question," Isandra said, her blue eye intent on Hazel. "He's wondering if you have a plan."

"Oh!" Hazel fiddled with her braids. "Um, no. Not yet."

"And is there"—Isandra's blue gaze shifted to me— "anything we should know about the Compass?"

Isander put his hand on my shoulder. "The heliograph messages said that the Compass is *you*."

"We need you, Chess." Isandra leaned on her cane. "If you can lower the Fog, if you truly are the Compass—"

"—then this is not the end of Port Oro," Isander said, "but the beginning of a new era."

"I can't lower the Fog!" I said, my cheeks flushing. "I

don't know how! Stop waiting for me to fix things. I'm not special. I just got lucky and *survived*. I never asked for any of this."

"You're right," Mrs. E told me. "You didn't ask for this. The only things you ever ask for are—"

"A full belly and a warm bed," Hazel said, elbowing me softly.

"And a tether," Bea added. "And a harness and goggles. And a hacksaw."

"And a needle and thread," Swedish said. "And your scrapbook."

Loretta scratched her tattoo. "That kind of adds up, when you think about it."

"And to keep the crew safe," Mrs. E told me. "And together."

"Yeah," Hazel told me. "You're a *friendly* fog-monster. "

"Even *they* know that," Swedish told me.

Isandra clunked her cane against the floor. "Perhaps it's not fair, Chess, but the entire Port is depending on you. The entire Subassembly, and all of—"

"I don't care about that," I said. "The entire Port can get fogged for all I care, and the whole Subassembly too. All I care about is my crew."

A gasp sounded, and I saw Mochi standing beside Bea.

"And Mochi," I added lamely. "And I guess Jada."

"Not my brother and sister?" Mochi asked in a small voice.

"Well, them, too, if they're your family . . ."

Mrs. E smiled faintly. "And the children in the Noza Home?"

"Sure. I mean, they're just kids."

"How about the guy who gave us the cucumber?" Loretta said. "And those nice bootball girls you almost stabbed?"

"You almost *what*?" Isander asked, blinking at me.

"In the junkyard," Loretta told him, flashing a gap-toothed smile, "stabbing's just another way of saying hello."

"But we're not in the junkyard anymore," Hazel said.

Bea didn't say anything. She just stood there with her big green eyes, holding Mochi's hand.

And Hazel was right. We weren't in the junkyard anymore—and I was tired of carrying it around with me. We were part of the Port now. *I* was part of the Port now. Live or die, win or lose, we'd become part of something bigger than ourselves.

"Well, I'll do what I can," I said. "But only because that was a really tasty cucumber."

Isander clapped me on the shoulder. "Good lad. The only question is, how can you trigger the—"

A steam whistle interrupted him, and the clamor of engines filled the sky.

"That's the final alarm," Mrs. E said, her knuckles whitening on the arms of her wheeled chair. "Calling all ships to the defensive line."

"What now?" Loretta asked Hazel.

"We don't have time to do this right," Hazel said, her dark gaze on me. "So we'll stick with Plan B."

"What's Plan B?" Isander asked.

"Fight with the mutineers," Swedish told him. "And go down in a blaze of glory."

Loretta laughed a little wildly. "Our favorite kind of blaze."

But I knew what Hazel really meant. We didn't have time to coordinate; we didn't have time to think. Instead, we needed to scrape through by the skin of our teeth, like always. Plan B was me.

37

THE PORT ORO fleet drifted past the skyscraper, a scruffy collection of fishing ships and personal craft with a handful of fighting ships. Grim pilots flew toward Kodoc's oncoming armada, while fisherkids nervously fingered chain slingers converted from net trawlers.

"Look at *them*," Loretta muttered, squinting at an old, fancy-dressed couple in an antique thopper.

The fancy couple smiled bravely at us as they flew past, and I wondered if they'd left any children at home. I wondered if they'd last ten seconds against Kodoc's warships.

"C'mon, Bea," Hazel urged from the crow's nest of the *Bottom-Feeder*. "Now?"

"Not yet," Bea said, elbow-deep in the engine.

Hazel lifted her spyglass to watch the Port Oro airships

form a defensive line, while Kodoc's armada—ten times bigger—swept closer like a dark cloud. "C'mon, c'mon!"

"Not yet," Bea said, then told a valve, "Don't be silly— you're all gummed up."

"I see Vidious!" Hazel frowned. "He . . . he's flying the burned skeleton of the *Night Tide*."

"How burned?" I asked.

"Her balloon's okay, I guess. She should be in the repair bay."

"How's the *Rose*?" I asked.

Hazel swiveled her spyglass. "Not good. There's five, six . . . eight mutineer gunships. Four warships. And two hundred civilian craft—scraps of floating driftwood for Kodoc's target practice."

"She's ready, Cap'n!" Bea sang out.

"Go!" Hazel barked at Swedish. "Swing starboard!"

The foggium cylinders roared to life. Hoses whooshed and valves clattered—and a clanging of bells sounded from Port Oro. *Tong tong-rong*. A happy chiming, like for a wedding or a feast. *Tong rong tong rong*.

"Weird," I muttered, looking behind us as we lifted off the skyscraper.

Across Port Oro, people gathered on roofs with swords and pipes and a few steam-bows, preparing for the invasion. Motion caught my eye in a metalworking yard lower on the mountain, where two tiny figures slammed sticks onto a big copper disk. *Tong rong-rong-rong*. That wasn't a bell—it was a gong.

"What're they doing?" Loretta asked.

"Encouraging us?" I guessed.

"They're pointing at the Fog," she said.

Below the metalworking yard, rows of crops covered the mountain slope and disappeared into the steamy ocean of the Fog. A few rusty husks of farm machinery stood among the crops, and one bulky tractor poked from the shallow Fog, left there until the mist ebbed slightly.

Two other tractors chugged uphill from the Fog, heaving over hillocks and hauling loads of scraps or—

"Full stop!" Hazel shouted, her voice shrill. "Swede, turn, *turn*! Back toward the Port, now!"

"Cap'n!" Bea yelped. "What? What's wrong?"

"The ticktocks." Hazel lowered her spyglass with a trembling hand. "They're attacking Port Oro."

38

JETS OF FOG seeped from nozzles on the "tractors."
They were *ticktocks*, rusty gearwork monstrosities heaving across the farmland. Alumina panels shuddered and flaked as they crept uphill, crushing crops beneath heavy, misshapen treads.

"*T-tick!*" Loretta stammered, pointing. "*Tick! Tick!*"

My bones turned to mud. That gong wasn't chiming encouragement; it was signaling an alarm. Another alarm. Even closer than Kodoc—and even deadlier. Ticktocks would sweep through the neighborhoods like a wildfire, destroying everything in their path.

"There's more over there . . . ," Hazel whimpered in horror. "Five of them."

"Ticktocks." Bea covered her mouth with her hand.

"They're not . . . possible. They're not *human*."

"What're they doing?" Loretta paled. "Are they working for Kodoc?"

"They're following Chess," Swedish said, turning the *Bottom-Feeder* in a tight circle toward the skyscraper.

A rush of blood in my ears muffled the gonging. "They're not," I whispered.

"They showed up right after we did," he said. "How else would—"

"Over there!" Hazel pointed with her spyglass. "They're tearing through buildings; they're ripping homes apart. Stop them, Chess. Make them stop!"

"How?" I almost wept. *"How?"*

"I don't care!" she yelled. "Just do it!"

I reached a hand toward the ticktocks and shouted, "Stop!"

On the mountain near the Fog, a ticktock's barbed antennae jabbed the ground, then it pulled itself higher on the slope. *Stop. Stop, stop.* I closed my eyes. *Retreat! Go back.*

"Stop!" I shouted again. Except when I opened my eyes, the ticktocks were still grinding toward the neighborhoods. "I can't, Hazel! I'm too far or I'm not the Compass or . . . I *can't.*"

"Bring her down, Swede!" Hazel yelled. "Onto the skyscraper. Fast."

With a spin of the wheel, we slammed onto the landing

pad. The balloons swayed, a few Assemblers shouted in surprise, and I told Hazel, "I'm sorry, I tried, I—"

"Grab your wrenches, Bea," Hazel snapped, talking over me. "We're taking a cannon from the roof."

"Which one?" Bea asked.

"The six-pounder." Hazel pointed. "Chess, Swede, roll it on board. Loretta—"

"Yeah?" Loretta asked.

"Don't let anyone stop them."

"Yes, ma'am!" Loretta said.

Horrified cries rose from the mountain at the sight of the ticktocks. I swung from the *Bottom-Feeder* to the skyscraper roof, then helped Loretta down. Hazel stayed in the crow's nest, but the rest of us raced toward the cannon as Assemblers shoved to the edge of the roof, gasping and pointing.

"Why would they follow me?" I asked Swedish. "It doesn't make sense."

"They're made of trash and Fog," he said. "You think they make *sense*?"

"Hey!" Loretta called to the Assemblers at the cannon. "We're taking this for Captain Hazel."

One of them started to object but froze when explosions boomed in the distance: the sound of Kodoc's ships meeting the farthest fringe of the mutineer navy. Bea unbolted the cannon, then Swedish strained against the wheeled stand, while Loretta and I pushed the sides.

"Maybe that's what . . . you do," Swedish grunted to me. "Lead ticktocks around. A compass gives directions."

"If they're following me," I said, shoving the cannon with my shoulder, "why can't I control them?"

Swedish's face flushed as the cannon rumbled across the roof. "Good question."

The wheels turned faster after Bea whispered encouragement, and a minute later we reached the *Bottom-Feeder*. The airship bucked when the cannon *thunk*ed onto the deck from the boarding plank, and Hazel said, "Harpoons don't hurt them."

"What?" I asked.

"On the Port, they're firing harpoons at ticktocks."

Loretta scowled. "They don't work?"

"One looks like a pincushion, and it's not even slowing down." She looked at me. "What are their shells made of?"

"*Everything*, I think," I told her. "Under a layer of rust."

"What do they use for fuel?"

"Uh, foggium?"

"Foggium doesn't work in Fog," Bea reminded me. "But ticktocks do."

"Oh, right," I said. "Just Fog, then?"

"Driftsharks are made of Fog," Hazel said slowly, "and you can control *them*."

"If I'm close enough," I told her. "Maybe. A little."

Hazel eyed me, then told Bea to fix the cannon to the

290

deck and scanned the mountain through her spyglass. "People are running," she said, her voice flat. "Grabbing kids, screaming. Ticktocks are smashing into houses, grinding them down."

"Why?" Swedish asked in a gruff voice.

"I don't think they're *trying* to hurt anyone." Bea bit her lip as she tugged her wrench. "They're just flailing around like, like an airship without a rudder."

"They're doing worse than flailing," I said, shading my eyes.

Families fled along narrow streets, and clouds of dust drifted over smashed homes. One ticktock shuddered in an intersection, spouting fire like a flamethrower. Farther on, another lashed its blades wildly, shattering cement and fiberglass.

"They're shooting cables at a roof, like harpoon lines," Hazel said. "They can reach thirty feet in the air with grappling hooks. Oh, sweet soda can, it's tearing the roof down. It's—"

A boom echoed from the southern tip of Port Oro as something exploded.

"Hurry with that cannon!" Hazel's voice shook. "People are fighting ticktocks in the streets."

"It's going to be a massacre," Loretta said.

As Bea and Swede finished bolting the cannon to the deck, Hazel called, "Wait, they *got* one! They dropped a pod-car on it with a crane. With a hard enough impact, those things die. One down and—"

"How many are there?" Swedish asked, wiping sweat from his face as he stepped to the organ keyboard.

"Nine, by my count. Eight now."

"Done!" Bea shouted. "Cannon's in place, Cap'n."

"Swede," Hazel said, "loop around to the west."

"Um," I said, strapping an ammo chest beside the cannon. "Does anyone know how to shoot this thing?"

"I'm a quick study," Loretta told me.

"We're not a warship," Hazel said. "The gun's a last resort. Chess, get into your harness. Bea, hook the heavy netting to the cargo tether."

"What are we doing?" Loretta asked her.

"We can't stop those things," Hazel told her, "so we're not going to try. We'll airlift people to safety."

"There *is* no safety. Kodoc's coming!"

"Yeah," Hazel said. "And he'll make everyone slaves. But they'll live."

"Most of them," Swedish muttered, and opened the throttle.

Bea dove into a hatch, and I grabbed my goggles and crossed toward my harness. A rescue mission. Trying to save the Port from ticktocks . . . so Kodoc could conquer it.

Still, Hazel was right. We needed to save lives.

I shrugged into my harness, working the buckles until a dark wriggle caught my eye on the mountain. The writhe of a ticktock above the Fog, not far from the marketplace we'd visited.

No—*two* ticktocks. Big ones, the size of pickup trucks. They looked like mounds of trash crossed with nightmare insects. One rolled forward on mismatched wheels and a bulldozer tread, with a few spidery legs for traction. Overlapping scales shifted under the layer of rust that covered the ticktock's back, and shuddering pipes spat sludge and vapor. Cables and blades sliced through the air like a deadly cloud.

"Hazel!" I squeaked. "Look—down—there!"

"Two of them," Hazel said, scanning with her spyglass. "No, *three* of them."

"That's the home for kids," Loretta said, pointing higher on the mountain. "The Noza Home—over that bridge. They're heading for those kids!"

39

"SWEDE, GET LORETTA a shot at that thing!" Hazel shouted. "We've got to knock it off course!"

The *Bottom-Feeder* swooped toward the hillside, and the ticktocks clattered higher. The two big ones rolled forward on treads, while the smaller one swiveled on a jerking tripod with whipping chains.

Then a bone-rattling *boom* sounded. The raft shook, and a buzzing filled my ears. What *was* that? Was Kodoc already here? Were we hit?

When my hearing returned, Hazel was shouting, "—next time, *warn* us first!"

"Sorry," Loretta yelled, her face black with soot.

She'd fired the cannon. She'd missed the ticktocks, but at least she'd alerted the neighborhood. People poured from doorways, shouting and confused. Except in the Home for Kids, nobody noticed: the factory machines were too loud.

"Okay," Loretta yelled. "Here goes! Three, two—"

I covered my ears, and the cannon fired again. A direct hit into the flank of the biggest ticktock. Its antennae writhed, and its rusty shell shuddered. A thrill of hope rose in my chest—then the ticktock continued grinding uphill, still on course.

"It's not working!" Loretta yelled. "The cannonball's not heavy enough."

"Chess," Hazel called, "get ready to dive. Clear that bridge the ticktocks are heading for. Don't let anyone set foot on it."

"What?" I asked. "Why?"

"Because when the ticktocks reach the middle," she said, "Loretta's going to blow it out from under them."

"They'll fall and smash," Loretta said in wonderment. "Hazel, you are a *thug*."

"Swedish," Hazel called, "take us in."

As the raft swooped closer, the small ticktock swiveled on its tripod, following the big one toward the bridge, but the medium-sized one veered off and climbed a ledge toward the next hill. Taking a shortcut toward the Noza Home.

"Got a bad feeling," Swedish muttered.

"We've got to warn the kids," Loretta shouted.

Hazel shook her head. "After we take down the bridge."

"That won't stop the ticktock on that ledge! It's gonna chew through the factory."

Cannon fire sounded in the distance from Kodoc's armada, and Hazel swung from the crow's nest to the deck. "I'll drop with Chess," she told Loretta. "And run to warn the kids while he clears the bridge."

"There's only one tether," Swedish said.

"Chess will hold me."

"Unless he drops you."

"He won't drop me."

"We need you here," I told her.

Hazel clamped her jaw. "I'm not about to send Bea down."

"*I'll* drop with him," Loretta said, nervously finger-combing her spiky hair. "I'm smaller than you, and better at running away."

Hazel turned to me, a question in her eyes. I nodded—that ticktock was crawling closer to the Noza Home every second.

"Okay," Hazel said. "Loretta dives; I'll take the cannon."

I adjusted the winch, then led Loretta to the end of the plank. She groaned and wrapped her arms around me, trembling in fear.

"You sure about this?" I asked. "I know you hate heights."

"I d-do not," she said, her teeth chattering. "I'm f-f-f-fine."

Swedish brought the raft into position, Hazel gave the okay, and I said, "Hang on—this won't take a second."

Loretta started belting out a song: "Row, row, row your boat, sitting in a tree! *K-I-S-S-I-N-G!*"

I jumped, and we landed at a crossroads not far from the bridge. I staggered on impact because of Loretta's extra weight, but even after I caught my balance, she didn't stop squeezing me. Or singing in my ear. "—then comes marriage, then comes baby in a railway carriage."

"We're down," I yelled.

She took a breath. "I know that."

"You can let go of me."

"That's what *you* think." She took another breath and released me. "Where's the Noza Home?"

I pointed. "Three blocks."

"Okay—pick me up before I get chomped."

She started running, and I turned toward the bridge. The ticktocks were close, judging by the sound of screaming and crunching. People stampeded past me, carrying bawling babies and armloads of gear, blocking my path. The upward tug of the tether made me feel light, so I jumped experimentally. I rose seven or eight feet in the air, bending my knees so I didn't kick anyone in the head.

Jumping again, I swung across the street and landed on

an awning. I scrambled to the roof and spotted the smallest ticktock lurching toward the bridge, while the big one rampaged through houses.

C'mon, c'mon. I jumped closer. *Head for the bridge.*

For once, I got lucky. The big ticktock's vents clattered, tendrils of Fog seeped from its nozzles, then it chugged right toward the bridge.

I raced across the roofs, swung down to the street—and almost got flattened by the crowd fleeing from the ticktocks.

The bridge was packed, so I shoved and shouted, trying to keep anyone else from pushing onto it. A skinny lady leading a camel cart elbowed me in the head, right on my wound. Pain flared, and I gasped and leaped high. Then I fell ten feet, straight down onto a corner of her cart.

My boot stomped hard enough to overturn the cart, which slewed to a halt, blocking the path onto the bridge. The skinny lady screamed curses I'd never heard before, but the crowd stopped shoving onto the bridge.

The *tick tock tick-tock-tick-tock* sounded louder—closer. The lady cut her camels free from their reins, and they clip-clopped away seconds before the gearwork monster smashed through the cart.

Wood and plastic exploded at me. I yelped and scrambled backward onto the bridge. The last trickle of traffic disappeared off the far side of the bridge, and a clubbed chain smashed the planks behind me. I shouted and sprinted away. The smaller ticktock followed on swiveling tripods while the larger one crawled steadily after, carving furrows in the wood.

A bladed claw bit into the bridge beside my foot, and when I glanced over my shoulder, I saw a frayed cable lashing toward my back.

Stop, I screamed inside my mind. *Stop—stop!*

The frayed cable fell short, and with a spurt of speed I reached the highest point of the bridge and vaulted over the side. My tether tugged me upward, and a roar of cannon fire from the *Bottom-Feeder* split the world.

The blast swatted me through the air. My ears rung and my eyes watered, and I barely saw the bridge collapse. Just a single glimpse of one ticktock's antennae groping wildly before they both plunged into the ravine and disappeared in the Fog.

I slumped in the harness as the winch dragged me higher. Columns of black smoke twined in the air, and after what felt like a long time, I climbed the boarding ladder and collapsed on deck.

"You okay?" Swedish asked.

"That," I panted, "is easier . . . in the Fog."

A hatch popped open. "Hey!" Bea said, her leather cap askew. "Did you see that?"

"You mean the bit where I blew a bridge out of the sky?" Hazel asked, her eyes sparkling. "Or the bit where I blew a *bridge* out of the *sky*?"

"I mean when that ticktock was about to whack Chess, then stopped."

"I—uh." I swallowed, suddenly nervous. "I didn't see that."

Except I had. That frayed cable had suddenly fallen short when I'd thought *Stop!* Had I done that? Could I affect ticktocks like I affected driftsharks—by the skin of my teeth, in a desperate panic—even if I wasn't in the Fog?

"Where's the other one?" Swedish asked, spinning the wheel. "Where's Loretta?"

He swung the raft toward the Noza Home, and more cannon fire boomed behind us: Kodoc's armada battling toward Port Oro. They sounded close. Too close.

Hazel pointed at the mountain and said, "There."

The third ticktock hunched outside the dirt patch where the Noza kids had played the pebble game. Tentacles swayed from its armored slats, spiked chains rattled, and malformed humps shifted inside its flaking carapace. Farther along, Loretta ushered kids from the factory compound. Actually, she *chased* them from the compound with a metal pipe in each hand and a scowl on her face.

Still, I couldn't argue with the results: kids streamed through the gate and bolted away from the ticktock.

"Swing in, Swedish," Hazel said. "We'll grab Loretta and warn everyone in that ticktock's path."

But when our ship swooped toward Noza House, the

ticktock suddenly spurted toward Loretta, spiked tentacles slashing the air.

"Loretta!" Swedish opened the throttle. *"Run!"*

The *Bottom-Feeder* jerked forward, and Loretta spun toward the factory gates. One last group of stragglers rushed toward her, skinny kids covered in dust and grime. Too late. They'd never get away before the ticktock cut them off.

40

"Run," Swedish breathed. "Run, run, run."

Loretta didn't run. Instead, she turned to face the tick-tock and raised the pipes in her hands.

Flame spat from the ticktock and singed a clump of weeds. Tentacles scraped at the plaster-and-Styrofoam fence, and three bladed tubes slid from the ticktock's head, jerking and chopping. Loretta stepped forward, putting herself between the gearwork monster and the kids scrambling away behind her.

The ticktock slashed at Loretta, and she knocked the blade away with her pipe. Another tube slashed, and she knocked that away, too.

I raced to the plank. "I'll get her!"

"Bea, unbolt the cannon!" Hazel screamed, ignoring me. *"Go!"*

I didn't know what she was talking about: the cannon couldn't stop a ticktock. It couldn't even fire if it was unbolted.

"Let me get her!" I shouted again.

"You stay!" Hazel snapped at me.

So I just stood there and stared at the Noza kids running to safety behind Loretta. But she couldn't follow; she couldn't turn her back on the ticktock. She dodged the bladed tubes slashing at her; she ducked and backpedaled—and stumbled when a razor tip slashed her leg.

She deflected two slices, then a third slashed her forearm. She parried a fourth, then a chain coiled around her ankles and dragged her to the ground.

Swedish made an anguished sound. He spun the prow toward the ticktock and opened the throttle. The *Bottom-Feeder* dove, wind screaming through the rigging, the engine howling, and the deck cutting downward.

"Two wisps higher!" Hazel shouted, grabbing her strap. "Stay on target!"

Swedish grunted, gritting his teeth.

Hazel spun to Bea, who was crouched beside the cannon, tugging with her wrench. "Faster, Bea! How long?"

"Five seconds." She rammed a bolt free. "Four . . ."

Except we didn't have four seconds. Loretta didn't have four seconds.

In the street below, the ticktock shuddered, its blades rising above Loretta. She looked so small. An undersized gang girl with tattoos and burn-scarred arms, facing down a ticktock to save a bunch of kids she didn't even know. Armed with two pipes and a gap-toothed smile.

A blade stabbed toward her stomach—

"Chess!" Hazel screamed, raw and terrified. *"Please!"*

I knew what she wanted, because I always knew what Hazel wanted—and her desperation sparked a firestorm in my mind. I gathered my terror and despair and launched them at the ticktock like a harpoon: *Stop. Freeze. Not another inch.*

The blade paused a foot from Loretta. The jagged tip jerked and twitched.

"Three seconds!" Bea counted, ratcheting another bolt free. "Two!"

The world shrank into a wavering tunnel between me and the ticktock. My heart stopped beating, my blood stopped flowing. *Freeze. No more.* The raft plummeted toward the street. *Do not move.*

Bea popped the last bolt free. "Done!" she yelled.

My focus slipped, the blade sliced at Loretta, and Hazel screamed, "Now-now-*now*!"

Swedish slammed a lever, and the raft turned sideways.

The deck jerked under me, and I slid into the forward mast and grabbed tight. The cannon, the half-ton cannon that Bea had just unbolted, thundered off the deck—plummeted downward—tumbled through the air—and smashed into the ticktock.

Gears and scales exploded across the street. The

ticktock's carapace crumpled like an empty alumina can, and a cloud of Fog belched from its broken slats.

With a heave, the airship straightened above the rooftops, the fans groaning and the vent hissing.

"Retta!" Swedish bellowed. "Retta!?"

I staggered to the railing and stared at the street. A haze of Fog faded from over a mound of ticktock rubble . . . and a hand emerged from the wreckage and weakly waved a pipe.

"She's okay," I called to Swedish. "She's alive!"

He brushed away tears of relief. "I'm going to kill her."

"Oh, thank fog." Hazel slumped in the crow's nest. "Take us down, Swede."

"Stupid bravery," he muttered, tapping the organ keyboard.

The airship swept lower, and Bea grabbed my arm. "They're full of Fog. The ticktocks are full of Fog."

"Yeah."

"You—you stopped it."

I rubbed my face. "For a second."

"*Outside* the Fog." She chewed her lower lip. "Maybe they really are following you."

"Maybe you can *make* them follow you," Hazel said from the crow's nest. "Swedish! Belay that—stay in the air."

"No way," he growled. "I'm getting Loretta."

"People are trapped," Hazel said, gesturing with her

spyglass toward the Port. "They're dying. We need to lead these things away before—"

"She's *crew.*"

Hazel pointed past him. "They'll get her."

A rickety salvage raft flew toward us from the south, with a guy I didn't recognize at the wheel. But Jada and Mochi stood behind him, in harnesses and goggles, looking toward Hazel like they were waiting for orders.

Hazel cupped her mouth. "Bring Loretta to the medics!"

Jada gave a quick salute.

"Ticktocks! Ticktocks!" Mochi shouted, her eyes wide and her frizzy hair bobbing. "Can you believe it? They're ticking and tocking and— *Look!* Look at them!"

Jada nudged her, and she quieted down.

"They've got her," Hazel told Swedish. "We need Chess to—"

An explosion roared behind us, and I turned to find Kodoc's armada looming just past the skyscraper, with the Port Oro defenders broken and fleeing before it.

Flames flickered on a fishing trawler with a tattered balloon. A gawky boy threw sand on the fire . . . until the trawler spiraled down into the Fog. I stared in horror, watching the Rooftop armada driving forward, cannons flashing and battle chains whipping into balloons and masts.

The *Night Tide* and *Anvil Rose* and two other mutineer warships fought bravely—and didn't stand a chance.

I glanced at the *Rose* before the sight of limp bodies on deck made me turn away, just in time to see a cannonball shoot the old, fancy-dressed couple in the antique thopper from the sky.

Then the *Bottom-Feeder* veered off, and I realized that Hazel had been calling my name. "Chess. Chess!"

I wiped tears from eyes. "Yeah?"

"Call the ticktocks. Make them follow us." She turned to the wheel. "Swedish, sweep past every ticktock, and once Chess grabs them all, head for the Fog."

"What about Kodoc?" Swedish asked.

"He won," she said. "He'll take the Port; he'll rule us forever. But we can still save lives."

We swooped toward the center of Port Oro, with Kodoc and the mutineers burning up the sky behind us. I scanned the hills and bridges but couldn't make sense of what I saw. Too much smoke and noise, too much fear and rubble.

"You can do this," Hazel said, swinging down beside me.

"Um," I said. "How?"

She brushed my hair behind my ear. "Bring the Fog into both your eyes."

"Will that work?"

"When you're out of ideas," she said, "all that's left is trying."

So I closed my eyes and imagined Fog blooming behind my eyelids. Nothing felt different, though. How did you force nanites to swirl through your brain? How did you attract trash-monsters from the Fog? How did you make them follow you like a pack of dogs following a trail?

A story from my dad's scrapbook sprang to mind. The tale of the Pie Diaper, who lured children with the scent of delicious pies . . . though I'd never understood the "diaper" part. As the ship swerved and the battle raged, I focused on wafting a delicious mental scent toward the ticktocks. *So sweet, so tasty. Follow me.* I imagined the ticktocks swiveling toward me, rumbling lower on the mountain, disappearing into the—

"No!" Hazel gasped.

My eyes flicked open. "What?"

"They boarded the *Night Tide*. . . ."

I thought "they" meant Kodoc's airsoldiers until I saw Vidious's warship hanging low over a smoldering building, caught by a handful of ticktock cables. One of the gearwork monsters strained at the warship, tugging the hull lower, while another lashed and shuddered on the quarterdeck. Through the smoke, I caught a glimpse of a mad-eyed Vidious attacking the ticktock on a deck slippery with blood and oil.

The *Bottom-Feeder* angled toward the *Anvil Rose*, where Nisha shouted orders, her blond hair whirling in the wind. Her gunners fired volley after volley toward Kodoc's armada, while the broken husk of a ticktock smoked and sparked below her.

Kodoc ignored the ticktocks and focused on the mutineers. He blasted through the Port navy, his armada closing around them like a pincer. Damaged ships spun from the sky, crashing into factories and gardens.

"We lost the Port," Hazel whispered. "And we can't stop the ticktocks."

A cold fist squeezed my heart. "This is my fault. All that destruction, all that death." I took a shuddering breath. "Get closer."

Hazel inhaled sharply, and I saw in her face that the Fog now swirled across both my eyes. "Swede!" she called. "Take us down, just outside ticktock range."

"What're we doing?" Bea asked.

"Going fishing," Hazel told her. "And Chess is the bait."

41

SWEDISH FLEW THE *Bottom-Feeder* like a racing ship, swooping through the air battle. Thirty feet below the deck, I swung wildly on my tether. Explosions burst around me. A cannonball clipped our carburetor, and harpoons speared our sails. While Bea patched the carb, the ship spun and swerved—bringing me closer to the ticktocks.

And they answered my call. *Come, come, follow me, this way.* One dropped from the *Night Tide*, two crawled from the husks of ruined buildings, and more clattered after us from marketplaces and neighborhoods.

"It's working!" Hazel called, far above me. "Keep going, Chess! Swedish, head for the Fog."

Swedish mumbled a question I didn't hear.

"Then Chess tells them to get lost," Hazel told him. "But first we have to get away from the Port—"

"There's one more!" Bea cried from the engine. "Past that factory."

Rudders swiveled and props spun. The raft banked into the wind, and my tether swirled over a handful of old people stumbling from a gutted house. The last ticktock, a stubby one with jagged antlers, clambered along a concrete pipe behind a smokestack.

Swedish brought me lower, and I swung past, thinking, *Come, follow, this way* . . . and the ticktock aimed a turret at me.

No! I thought at it. *Don't shoot!*

It didn't listen. Instead, it fired. A cable flashed past me and wrapped a cargo bracket, a metal hook jutting from the underside of the *Bottom-Feeder*. The airship jolted as she took the ticktock's weight. The rudders shifted and the propellers strained, but after a precarious moment, the *Bottom-Feeder* steadied.

Then she rose, lifting the ticktock up into the air. A moment later, we were flying toward the Fog with me dangling below the hull . . . and the ticktock dangling below me.

I glanced to Bea, who was poking upside down through a hatch in the deck.

"Can it board us?" I asked as she winched me upward. She eyed the ticktock. "Nah, its cable won't retract."

She wiped her face. "You did it, Chess. They're leaving the Port."

I grabbed the boarding ladder and looked behind us. Sure enough, a nightmare squad of ticktocks rumbled after the *Bottom-Feeder*, while the one with antlers hung below. We'd saved Port Oro from the ticktocks—for now. But beyond the smokestack, Kodoc's armada surrounded the defeated mutineer fleet. White flags of surrender rose on the mutineer warships. First on the *Night Tide* and *Anvil Rose*, then on all the others—and on dozens of buildings across Port Oro.

Kodoc had conquered the Port.

I clung to the ladder, my eyes stinging from smoke and tears. The *Bottom-Feeder* swooped away, and I rubbed my face before climbing on deck.

"Stay close to the Fog," Hazel was telling Swedish. "We need to keep the ticktocks following Chess."

"How far are we going?" I asked her, with part of my mind still saying, *Follow me, keep coming, you can't resist the Pie Diaper.*

"We'll see. We can't go back now."

"Loretta's still there."

"And Mrs. E," Bea said, her voice trembling.

"You think I don't know that?" Hazel snapped.

A breeze strained through the rigging. I ignored the jerks of the ticktock dangling below the ship and watched the last mutineer ships being forced to land on Port Oro

312

as Kodoc's armada formed a circle around them.

Nobody came after us except ticktocks. Nobody spotted us amid the smoke and the chaos. After a long, hopeless silence, Hazel swung down from the crow's nest and stood with Swedish at the wheel. Bea and I joined them, and we looked toward the silver-gray smoke hanging over the distant Port, with a red halo from the sun.

"From this far away," Bea said, "it looks almost purple."

"Something's not right," Hazel said.

"Nothing's right," Swedish said.

"What are we missing?" Hazel asked.

"Loretta," I said. "And Mrs. E."

"We got the Compass. So how do we lower the Fog?"

"Nobody knows," I told her. "The cogs don't know; Kodoc doesn't know. The next step is lost, like a story in the scrapbook without an ending."

"Why did the ticktocks attack?"

"They're oriented to me, I guess," I said. "The way a compass is oriented to the north. They're like driftsharks. Strong and mindless."

"Maybe they're trying to protect you," Hazel suggested, "and doing it wrong."

"Or they're the anti-Compass," Swedish said, "and they're trying to stop him."

I rubbed my eyes again. "Maybe they're programmed to swarm toward any fogless mountaintop and tear things apart."

"They're probably cattywampus." Bea started crying. "N-none of this nanotech stuff w-works right."

"We saved a lot of lives, honeybee," Hazel said, putting her arm around Bea. "Whatever happens, remember that."

I nodded and said something stupid about rescuing Mrs. E and Loretta. But even if we rescued them, where would we go? Kodoc controlled every inch of clear land now. There was no way to be free of him, not anymore.

Hazel returned to the crow's nest and Bea to the engine. Swedish stayed ten feet above the Fog. The engine thrummed, and the balloons bobbed. What happened next? Should we head for the Rooftop and try to hide in the junkyard? Surrender to Kodoc—

The raft jolted to a halt.

The prow slammed downward, and the gears howled.

I slid five feet, and Swedish pounded the organ keyboard, ignoring the blood dripping from a cut on his chin. The deck straightened halfway, then started lowering toward the Fog.

A hatch slammed opened, and Bea's voice sounded above the howl of the engine. "That dangling ticktock grabbed something in the Fog! A tree or a tower or— We're anchored; we're stuck. It's pulling us into the white!"

"Unstick us!" Hazel yelled. "Release the cargo bracket!"

"It's jammed!" A pounding sounded through the hatch. "The ticktock's dragging us down!"

"Swedish!" Hazel called. "Get us higher!"

"I can't." He slammed the keyboard. "Our compression's shot."

The raft shuddered and jerked lower. Five feet, six feet. If the engine touched Fog, it'd stop working, and we'd crash.

"Bea, drop that ticktock!" Hazel shouted. "Find a way. *Now!*"

The vents howled; the propellers strained. The ticktock dragged the raft closer to the Fog, and I stared over the edge, sick with horror.

Bea popped onto the other side of the deck, a rope looped around one shoulder, and scampered to the copper-tubed harpoon, babbling rapid-fire: "I can't unbend the cargo bracket, so I attached a rope to the crooked part, and when I fire, the harpoon rope will yank the bracket straight and the ticktock will fall."

By the time she finished explaining, she'd already knotted the rope to the harpoon, aimed high, and fired.

The harpoon flashed away from the raft, dragging the rope in a deep curve. The curve became a straight line, and the rope yanked at the crooked bracket under the deck. The ticktock must've fallen, because the straining fans suddenly launched the *Bottom-Feeder* into the sky.

We shot upward like we'd been fired from a cannon. The balloons squeaked, the rigging whipped, and the deck jolted.

"Way to go, Bea!" I yelled. "Nice jo—"

Hazel screamed, and I spun and saw Bea tumbling overboard, tossed backward by the sudden motion.

With a desperate sweep of her arm, she grabbed the harpoon barrel that swung over the edge of the deck. She dangled hundreds of feet above the Fog, her fingers slipping on the smooth copper. The raft was rising too fast for Swedish to control, and Bea was too far across the deck for me to reach.

Hazel swung toward her, shouting, "Chess, *Chess!*"

I was already moving, racing away from Bea. I snagged my harness without slowing and hit the diving plank at a sprint. I leaped overboard, shoved one arm into my harness, and pivoted in midair, facing the ship, falling fast.

Bea dropped into sight under the *Bottom-Feeder.* She was in free fall, hundreds of feet above the ground, four or five seconds to impact.

There, I told myself, tracking her fall. *Right there.*

Then the Fog swallowed me.

42

WHITENESS SURROUNDED ME, but in my mind I still saw Bea tumbling through the air, plunging toward the ground. *Not Bea, not Bea, not Bea.* Every slumkid knew pain and loss and grief—but *not Bea.*

At a tug of intuition, I clamped my tether, veering under the ship like the weight at the end of a pendulum.

My curving swing needed to intersect Bea's straight plunge, but I couldn't see her despite my sharper senses, couldn't hear her. Still, I *pushed* myself through the Fog, lashing desperately forward. Seconds ticked off, and I stared at the fringes of my vision for the slightest blur of motion.

Then I heard something.

A thin scream.

My heart clenched. Where was she? I spun and stared and—

There! A shadow plummeted through the air fifteen feet from me. Too far away. No way. *Not Bea.* I shifted the Fog with my mind, and the mist thickened and curled and swept me closer. The scream wavered, and I slammed into Bea. Her face was white with terror, and I squeezed her tight and tugged my tether to slow our fall.

The harness yanked my arm. Buckles twisted, and two straps tore free. I grunted and rolled in the air, condensing the Fog beneath us—

I slammed to the ground on my back. I lay there, aching and breathless, with Bea sprawled across my chest. She clung to me, shuddering.

"Well," I said. "Let's not do *that* again."

"I can't hear you!" she yelled, her teary eyes wide. "I can't see you."

I saw her, though. I saw the freckles on her nose, the stitches on her leather cap. I saw the torn harness, now connected to the tether by only a single strap. I saw a lichen-covered boulder fifteen feet away.

And I saw the ticktocks grinding closer through the billowing white. Swarming toward us. Barbed antennae probed the Fog, and bushes crunched under jagged treads.

I lifted my hand toward them. *Stop. Stop!* "Stop!"

They kept rolling closer. My mind stuttered, blanked

in panic . . . and then I knew exactly what to do. I shoved Bea's arms into my ripped harness, which was strong enough to hold one diver's weight, though not two. I fastened a buckle, then tugged the tether three times.

"Chess! Don't you da—" Bea blurred upward toward the ship, vanishing into the Fog.

Whoa. Even the ticktocks paused like they were impressed. Not for long, though. A second later, they heaved closer to me.

I stood and rolled my shoulders. Trapped in the Fog without a tether, surrounded by killer machines. I'd lost Port Oro. I'd lost Loretta and Mrs. E. I'd lost Nisha and Vidious, Mochi and Jada, and all the Subassemblers.

But I'd saved Bea. And maybe because of that, I didn't freeze when the ticktocks wheezed closer. I didn't scream or tremble.

I waited.

43

A DAY HAS passed since Kodoc defeated the mutineer fleet and seized Port Oro; the longest day of my life. Rooftop soldiers gathered every mutineer on the Port and forced us into a field of rubble where the ticktocks had flattened a neighborhood. Kodoc's armada surrounds us, hovering in a low circle, weapons aimed to ensure our obedience and—

No. That's not what I want to say.

I am avoiding writing about Chess. Can even he survive a night in the whiteness? Can even he find his way back above the Fog?

After we lost him, we crisscrossed the area

320

until evening, trailing tethers, praying for a tug on the line. Instead, Kodoc's patrol ships discovered us. They took the Bottom-Feeder and tossed us among the defeated and the injured in this destroyed neighborhood.

The tear-streaked crowd gasped when a sudden red glow shone across the field. The skyscraper was burning. Flames rose like a pillar into the darkening sky. Mrs. E was in there; Loretta was in there. Hundreds of Assemblers and—

"Beazy!" Mochi called through the crowd. "Over here!"

"Where's Mrs. E?" Bea shouted. "Where's Loretta? Is everyone—"

"They're fine!" Mochi interrupted. "Well, not fine. But they're here. Everyone ran across the bridge before Kodoc's soldiers started the fire."

She escorted us down earthen stairs into a root cellar, where we found Loretta sleeping in a makeshift infirmary and Mrs. E speaking with the cogs. Mrs. E's face glowed with relief when she spotted us—until she saw my tears. Her gaze shifted from me to Swedish to Bea . . . and grief dug furrows into her face when she realized that I'd lost Chess.

She opened her arms, and I fell into them.

The night passed slowly, bristling with dread. This morning, Bea woke in tears, and I woke from *a nightmare of sending Chess into the Fog for the last time. The others are looking to me for a plan, for a glimmer of hope. But how can I feel hope with Chess lost? How can I—*

Wait. Something's happening outside. I'd better see wha—

44

MY BREATH SOUNDED harsh as I jogged uphill, louder than the splash of my feet in the stream. My *numb* feet in the *freezing* stream, which I'd been following since dusk, trying to reach fogless air. Trying to reach the crew.

Drawing on all my new tricks—all my new powers—I'd stayed one step ahead of the ticktocks for hours. But with the sun setting, the Fog was darkening around me. Branches loomed from the mist, and a slippery rock twisted my ankle. I tripped, caught myself, then staggered onward.

I needed to reach the mountaintop. Being the Compass didn't protect me from mountain lions or hyenas—or from slashing myself on a jagged metal post.

A mossy log caught my shin, and I fell to my hands and

knees in the icy current. The cold stung my arms, and I wanted to cry—then I heard the crash of the ticktocks grinding closer.

They never stopped—they never slowed. They just kept coming.

I pushed to my feet and stumbled onward until I reached a meadow where the dark Fog glinted with moonlight. And halfway across, I dropped to my knees, shivering and dizzy—barely strong enough to turn at the rumble of approaching ticktocks.

A black shape clattered into sight, and I saw the ticktock with the stubby plaststeel horn, the one I called Snout. He'd followed me closest and fastest, and almost caught me a few times. I reached for the Fog inside his shell with my mind, trying to control him.

A moment later, Snout paused, grinding his gears and waving his antennae.

Two more ticktocks lurched from behind Snout, and I stopped them as well. But dozens more heaved from the woods—too many. My focus dimmed, the meadow tilted, and I swayed, on the verge of fainting.

My hold on the ticktocks snapped. They clanked toward me, and a spray of warm liquid spewed at me from a vent on Snout's side.

I shuddered and gagged.

My revulsion kept me from fainting, and I groped for the ticktocks with frantic bursts of thought. But the harder

I tried, the dizzier I felt. Snout's treads crunched closer, and wiry antennae shot from his flanks and knocked me onto my back. The other ticktocks hissed and fired. Pain flared in my chest and legs as a spiderweb of cables strapped me to the ground.

My teeth chattered, and I wanted to close my eyes and just . . . stop. Stop running, stop hurting, stop trying. But the crew needed me. Port Oro needed me. And like Mrs. E said about Hazel, Fall down seven times, stand up eight.

"Stop!" I mumbled. *No more! Stay away!* My mind poked feebly at the ticktocks surrounding me. *Stop! I have to save the crew. I have to lower the Fog and get to the Port!* "And I'm f-f-freezing. . . ."

Snout shuddered above me, straining to get closer. Vents covered his side like fish scales, opening and closing, shedding rust. Antennae whipped and gears turned, and a hose wrapped tightly around my arm.

I shut my eyes, summoning every tattered scrap of willpower. I needed to join the crew and stop Kodoc and lower the Fog. The nanites in my brain whispered to the ticktocks, screamed at them, pleaded with them. . . .

And a sudden roar answered.

The roar of fire, of the ticktocks' flamethrowers. My eyes sprang open, and the meadow was bright with flickering light. Streams of flame rose from the ticktocks like torches. Heat touched my skin, and I jerked upright—and realized that the cables weren't wrapping me any longer, and Snout was burning my feet.

Except . . . the flames weren't hurting me. No, Snout was *warming* me with a low flame and looming over me almost protectively.

The other ticktocks flailed at the Fog around me, and in the torchlight I saw them clearly. *Completely* clearly. Because I was sitting in a bubble of Fog-free air. A dome of perfect clarity, a hundred yards below the fogline.

"No way," I whispered.

All around me, ticktocks inhaled the Fog. Short hoses and crooked vents sucked nanites from the mist—and crusty nozzles shot out jets of clean, pure air.

45

WHEN BEA AND I climbed from the cellar, the Rooftop warships were hovering low over the field of rubble, and the mutineer crowd was eyeing the flat roof of a tannery that stood over us like a stage.

"Hazel," Swedish said, stepping beside me. "What do you think?"

"Let's see what's going on," I told him.

He shoved forward for a better view, and I grabbed Bea's hand and followed him onto a fallen irrigation tank.

"They got Nisha," Swede said, anger darkening his face.

"Oh, no," Bea whispered, and squeezed my hand. "Oh, Hazy . . ."

On the tannery roof, Captain Nisha knelt in front of a dozen airsoldiers. Heavy manacles clamped her wrists, and dirt streaked her blond hair. Vidious knelt beside her, also chained and filthy after a night in Kodoc's cells. Despite the blood on his face, his restless gaze roamed the crowd and—

The Predator fell from the sky and hovered over the roof. Dust rose in swirling clouds, and my braids whipped my face.

"What's happening?" Bea asked. "What's going on?"

Kodoc climbed down from a hatch in his flagship. He stepped behind Nisha and Vidious and raised a sword. The crowd gasped, and the Rooftop soldiers shouted for silence.

"No," I heard myself say. "No, no . . ."

Kodoc lowered his blade to Vidious's shoulder. "I am not a patient man," he said, his voice carrying across the rubble. "So I will say this only once. There is a tetherboy hiding among you named Chess. And a girl named Hazel."

Bea started trembling and squeezed my hand tighter.

"Bring them to me," Kodoc said. "Or I execute

328

your captains. One by one by one."

My skin prickled, and I swayed, suddenly light-headed.

"Where are they?" Kodoc asked, lifting his blade to chop at Vidious's neck.

A stillness fell over the crowd. Kodoc's blade flashed in the sunlight. His eyes narrowed, his shoulders tensed—

"Here," I shouted, my voice breaking. "I'm here."

"No," Vidious growled, and Nisha strained in her bonds.

When Kodoc pointed his sword at me, a squad of soldiers clubbed through the packed field. They shoved closer and closer toward the irrigation tank . . . until a roar sounded from the Fog.

A clattering, grinding, rattling howl.

Ticktocks.

The crowd surged in terror, and wild-eyed roof-troopers drew blades and steam-bows. Gears shrieked inside a dust cloud that wafted from the Fog. Concrete shattered. Valves gasped. Then a breeze rose, revealing a line of ticktocks heaving into the destroyed neighborhood.

Twenty ticktocks, grinding and shuddering and seeping Fog—until they stopped.

Motionless. Waiting.

A dozen barbed cables swept aside, opening a pathway between the ticktocks . . . and a kid slipped through. A wiry kid in a ripped jacket and filthy boots, with twigs in his hair.

A thousand people stared at him—yet Chess looked only at me.

The shouting faded into a faint hum. The distance shrank. There was a link between Chess and me, stronger than any tether. No matter how far apart we were, no matter how lost, no matter how alone, we were always connected.

"Took you long enough," I mouthed.

46

Took you long enough.

The spark in Hazel's eyes burned away my fear. With a twist of thought, I told Snout to scoop me onto his rusty shell and sent the entire row charging uphill.

The Rooftop warships hovering in a circle around the rubbled field spun toward me. Cannonballs flew, war chains whirred, and darts dinged off my ticktocks. I reached out with my mind to the ticktocks hiding in the Fog on either side of the field. *Fire,* I told them. *Now! Fire-high-now-fire-shoot-up-fire!*

Nothing happened, and I withered inside. What if the ticktocks didn't listen? What if they didn't understand? The Fog had built them—they'd built themselves—for one task. Not for this, not for battle.

Luckily, they'd also built themselves to follow the Compass. To follow *me*.

Before my heart beat twice, a hundred cables shot from the flanking ticktocks and pierced the hulls of Kodoc's low-flying ships. Airsoldiers screamed and gunfire roared and ticktocks answered with flames and blades.

The crowd scattered as my ticktock army rumbled across the flattened neighborhood. A squad of Kodoc's soldiers prowled toward me, encased in armor and hatred. They fired steam-bows; but Snout raised his jagged flaps to shield me, and the darts pinged off them.

A spiky ticktock swept the soldiers away, then I rode Snout over debris as my mind flickered across the battlefield, keeping the ticktocks focused on the roof-troopers and not bystanders.

"Bring down the ships!" Hazel's voice rang across the chaos. "If you destroy Kodoc's ships, the Rooftop falls! His whole fleet is here!"

"Yeah, I know," I muttered. "That's the idea."

But she hadn't been talking to me. She'd been talking to *everyone*. Every angry gearslinger and injured mutineer in this rubbled field seemed to pause. Maybe hearing the command in her voice, maybe struck by her courage, maybe surprised by her beauty, with the red glow of fire against her black skin.

"Do as the girl says!" Vidious roared in the shadow of the *Predator* on the tannery roof. "Take them down!"

332

The crowd burst into action. While my ticktocks battered soldiers and pulled airships lower with cables, the defeated mutineers started hurling rocks and swinging fists, swarming toward the boarding ladders of the Rooftop ships.

"Ready cannons!" Kodoc screamed on the tannery roof, raising his sword. "Kill that boy! Fire at my—"

Nisha sprang to her feet and clubbed him with her manacled arms. Blood spurted from his nose, and he staggered backward. A soldier slashed at her, but Nisha kicked him in the gut, then caught another airsoldier's sword with the chain of her manacle and twisted. The sword twirled away, and Nisha head butted the soldier savagely. Rocks slammed into the airsoldiers around Kodoc, and injured mutineers climbed the sides of the tannery.

"That's my little sister," Vidious bragged, before throwing himself into the brawl.

With a silent order, I urged Snout forward—but he veered away, charging toward Hazel instead. *No, Snout!* I thought. *Toward the roof!*

He ignored me. That was the problem with a machine that obeyed your thoughts. Instead of doing what you *said*, it did what you *wanted*.

"The *Predator!*" Hazel shouted at me as I heaved toward the irrigation tower. "Stop the *Predator!*"

"I'm trying!" I yelled back. "I can't!"

"Why not?"

"'Cause this stupid thing brought me to you instead."

"*Why?*" Then she looked at my face again and said, "Aw, that's sweet."

I flushed. "Oh, shut up."

"Hi!" Bea told Snout from the edge of the irrigation tower. "I'm Bea! What's your name?"

"Get back!" Hazel snapped at her. "No talking to strange ticktocks!"

One of Snout's knotted antennae snaked around Bea's stomach and hoisted her in the air. She yelped in fear—then surprise—then pleasure when it set her gently beside me. Another antenna grabbed Hazel and swung her to a rusty hump behind me, the closest thing to a crow's nest.

A segmented pole unfolded toward Swedish, and he grumbled something I didn't hear before the pole closed around his chest. Snout squealed and brought Swedish toward us—then shot a braided cable fifty yards in the other direction.

"What's it doing?" Hazel asked, grabbing a melted iSlate for balance.

I watched the braided cable disappear in the rubble. "No idea."

"Take Kodoc down," Hazel told me. "We can't let him get back to the Rooftop."

"He can't even get into his ship," I said.

The *Predator* dwarfed the flat-roofed tannery, massive propellers spinning beneath an endless sweep of hull—but dozens of ticktock cables coiled around the diving platform. They weren't heavy enough to keep the *Predator* from flying away . . . so instead, they'd spun a web between Kodoc and the hatch leading inside.

He couldn't retreat into his warship.

Kodoc's guards fired a barrage of darts at Nisha and Vidious, until mutineers swarmed the roof and attacked with a bloodcurdling cry.

Snout chugged toward them, dragging the braided cable behind us like a skinny tail.

"Not that way!" Hazel grabbed my shoulder. "Up that hill. Ten wisps to the left."

I didn't know what she was planning, but I told Snout to change course toward the hill. That time, he listened. The *Predator* started tearing free from the surrounding ticktocks, and Kodoc grabbed the lowest rungs of the diving platform.

Enraged screams sounded from the crowd, and Kodoc was lofted above the roof an instant before Nisha and Vidious reached him.

47

THE *PREDATOR* TURNED toward the distant Rooftop. And toward us, on our little hill. *Oh.* That's what Hazel was planning. She'd known the *Predator* would retreat directly above us. I exhaled and—

"Wahooooooo!" Loretta whooped, swooping through the air toward us, clasped by that braided cable. She was filthy, bandaged, and beaming. "Let me at him, fogface!"

It took me a second to realize that *she* was what Snout had been reaching for in the rubble, and another second to realize that she was calling *me* "fogface," and telling me to send her whipping toward Kodoc. Which actually sounded like a good idea.

But Hazel said, "Bea—the diving platform! Show Chess the weak spots."

"There!" Bea pointed toward the *Predator*. "There, there, and all over that part!"

I shot cables from Snout as she spoke, hitting each of the spots as she pointed to them.

The *Predator* swooped above the hilltop, blocking the sun and casting us into shadow. The diving scaffolding swept past, forty feet away, jerking Snout's cables tight— and Kodoc fired a steam-bow at me with cold precision.

I froze at the hatred in his face, and a dart whizzed past my left ear. Then Swedish tackled me and Bea, shielding us with his body. And as I crashed down onto Snout's rusty shell, I blasted every cable at the diving platform.

Still, the *Predator* didn't slow. And now the cables were fully extended. Snout's mismatched gears spun, Fog spewed from his hoses, and the warship lofted him—and us—up into the air, like his cables were tethers.

We dangled beneath the warship, with the ground slipping away below us. Swedish rolled off me and clapped his shoulder. The braided cable dropped Loretta beside him, and Hazel kept shouting, *Stop him, Chess, stop him.*

The damaged *Predator* headed for the Fog. Harpoons and grappling hooks rained around us, and Loretta said, "Swede, you're hit!"

He touched the dart sticking from his shoulder. "It's just a scratch."

"It's totally a scratch," Loretta said, her voice gentler than I'd ever heard. "I'm still a way bigger hero than you."

"Tear the diving platform off the *Predator*," Hazel told me as we rode the dangling ticktock toward the edge of Port Oro. "Before Kodoc gets inside."

I pushed to my feet and said, "Goggles down."

Then, with a twist of thought, I jerked all of Snout's cables at once—and the diving platform ripped free from the *Predator*'s hull.

We fell from the sky.

The impact slammed me to my knees and smashed a circuit block against my cheek. A fuel tank exploded inside Snout, and tendrils of Fog wafted around us. For a stunned minute, I lost track of myself. Then I heard Loretta say, "I didn't even feel that," and watched her faint.

Snout shuddered and died beneath me. His vents and hoses and gears fell silent. After a long, hollow moment, I stood and saw that we'd fallen onto farmland, scattering ticktock parts across the rows of crops that marched into the mist ten feet away. A tangle of beams and catwalks rose from the shallow Fog: the crushed remains of the diving platform I'd ripped from the bottom of the *Predator*.

But I couldn't see Kodoc anywhere.

I dropped to the ground beside the lifeless ticktock, and a lump of grief clogged my throat. I touched his scaly plasteel horn and said thanks. A second later, Hazel stumbled beside me, and together we headed toward the wreckage.

"The *Predator*," she said, looking upward.

The great warship spun in a slow circle like a stunned animal. Smoke seeped from vents, and gouges scarred her hull.

Then shouts sounded from the Rooftop gunships that were swooping closer—captured by the mutineers—and the *Predator* lumbered away over the Fog.

"They'll catch her," Hazel told me. "That's Vidious and Nisha in the pursuit craft."

As I watched the gunships shift into formation, a sunshine warmth touched my face. "Wait a second," I said. "Did we just *win*?"

"No, boy," a slithery voice said.

The warmth turned to ice. I turned and saw Kodoc standing up from the wreckage of the diving platform, waist-deep in the Fog.

"I lost," he said, pointing his steam-bow at us, "but you won't win. You'll never win."

"Wait!" Hazel said. "Wait, please—"

"I know how to lower the Fog!" I told him.

"We *all* know now," Kodoc said. "The Compass controls the ticktocks, and you're the Compass. The ticktocks lower the Fog, don't they?"

"Y-yeah. Yes. I triggered them without even knowing it. They'll lower the Fog! We won't need to crowd onto mountaintops! There's enough room for everyone to live without—"

"Without *me*," he snarled. "So you must die."

"No, wait!" Hazel said desperately. "What if I—"

"Will you swear by the Fog?" Kodoc aimed at her chest, his finger tightening on the trigger. "By the silence and the white? Will you do *anything* to save your friend?"

"Yes," I said, and reached into the Fog with my mind.

A driftshark erupted beside Kodoc. Terror flashed in his eyes, and he opened his mouth to scream. Too late. Misty jaws clamped his chest and slammed him into the deeper Fog. He disappeared without a sound, without a trace. Without a ripple.

48

THE STARS GLIMMERED overhead. The *Predator*'s deck swayed beneath me. Loretta played a tune on her flute, while Mochi and Bea swung in a hammock, making twistys together. Swedish bounced a bootball against a gearbox one-handed, his shoulder still bandaged, and Jada knotted ribbons in Hazel's hair.

Me? I sewed loops onto Bea's new overalls. She'd outgrown her old pair.

When Loretta finished her song, Bea said, "Tell us the story, Chess."

"Again?"

"Last time, I promise!" Bea considered. "Until tomorrow. The refinery kids haven't heard it!"

"We heard it twice," Quancita said from where she was

sitting with the others. "But we'd like to hear it again."

I tugged on a stitch. "A long time ago—"

"Skip that part," Hazel told me. "The Smog, the Fog, skip all that."

"So where do I start?"

"A short time ago," Bea prompted.

"A short time ago," I repeated, "a baby was born with Fog in his eye. But he got lucky. He survived. Then he got luckier. He fell in with a crew of cutthroats and chuzzle-wits."

"I know which one I am," Loretta said.

"We all know which one you are," Swedish told her.

She grinned—then eyed him suspiciously.

"When the kid learned to control the nanites in his eye," I continued, "he triggered the machines that lower the Fog. The ticktocks. But he didn't know that's what they were, not until he fell off an airship and—"

"You *dove* off," Loretta said. "After Bea."

"Yeah," Bea said. "If I hadn't fallen, none of us would be here!"

"Anyway," I said, "the kid was lost in the Fog, surrounded by ticktocks. Scared out of his boots. But then he saw it. He saw them clearing the mist. They could inhale Fog and exhale pure air. They just needed instructions." I paused. "And, uh, that's that. . . ."

"Your ending needs work," Bea told me. "You've got to say that now the ticktocks roam the fogline of Port Oro, chugging away day and night, lowering the Fog."

"And mention the fleet." Swedish gestured to the airships behind us, following Vidious and Nisha in the *Predator*. "Bringing ticktocks to the Rooftop to lower the Fog there, too."

"And to move the entire junkyard onto the upper slopes," Hazel said.

"Anything else I should add?" I asked.

"More about me," Loretta told me.

Swedish laughed. "More about the diamond."

Loretta patted her belt. "Not too late to start a gang."

"Sure," I said. "And is *that* all?"

"Not even close," Hazel said, gazing toward the dark horizon. "There are more mountains out there, across the Fog. There are more people out there, trapped and desperate, and praying for help."

I looked into the distance and wondered what she saw. Sure, the Fog swirled in my eyes—but the *future* swirled in hers. I sewed another stitch and listened to the propellers spin. Maybe our story wasn't over. Maybe the world was bigger than I'd ever imagined.

Acknowledgments

Many thanks to Caitlin Blasdell, Alyson Day, Renée Cafiero, Jenna Lisanti, Lindsey Karl, Matt Rockefeller, and Joel Tippie.